I0670762

WHO KILLED GREEN HOPE

R. K. SYRUS

Table of Content

Global Warming just became Cold-Blooded Murder in the Ellie Sato mystery: Who Killed Green Hope?

When her parents discover a grisly crime scene along a deserted road in rural England, investigative reporter Ellie Sato must unravel diabolical plots festering inside the innermost sanctums of London's powerful elites and is hurled into the midst of her most shocking and personal mystery yet as she races against time to discover: Who savagely murdered the environmental activist known as Green Hope?

Reader Suitability:
A few scenes of violence, moderate profanity.
Recommended for 16+

Prologue

Kore Energy Research Lab
Hereford, UK
Soon

I can't be caught!

That frantic thought races through her mind as she sits at her desk in the accounting department. It's well past business hours at the geothermal energy conglomerate, but her presence isn't unusual. Even though she's only twenty-five and she's worked here for less than a year, she's on several committees reporting directly to the president, Dr. Kore.

Just another boring twelve-hour day as a nerdy bean counter.

Like hell.

I won't be. I won't get caught, she reassures herself. A small, covert disk drive on her desktop, hidden by her handbag, loads a USB device one ingeniously disguised as a pendant earring. Surveillance is everywhere in the building. She's pretty certain everyone's computer monitor camera never shuts off, feeding live video from everyone's desk directly to Security in the basement.

Hurry! She flips through a sheaf of irrelevant spreadsheet pages, trying to look casual and boring, channelling her inner actuary, trying not to sweat. That would look odd; it's the middle of bloody winter.

She glances at the window. Snow continues to drift down from unseen clouds into the halo of lights illuminating the parking lot. She relaxes, just a little. Another light dot appears on the copying device. Almost there. Only one more...

And it's not like I'm stealing. Really, only borrowing. There was no way she could even attempt this very uncharacteristic bit of sneaky subterfuge without the help of Oppie.

She's been calling him that for so long she often blanks on his real name, the one he had before he joined the madcap London eco-collective. It *had* been mad, hadn't it? Wild. Camping out, spraying the PM's car with orange paint, hanging from bridges while all of London's traffic backed up, drivers honking their horns and staring up in astonishment. Mad, yes, but it had been wonderful sometimes... until against her own pigheadedness and, she finally admitted, worse judgement she listened to her mother and moved on before she ended up with a prison term of years, rather than just an overnight sleepover at Acton Police Station, and before she ended up throwing away all the benefits of the education she'd worked so hard for—one her mum had sacrificed so much to give her.

But what about this? Coolly as she could, she pressed her bag closer to the fuzzy felt-covered side of her cubicle as the USB device sucked bits and bytes out of the mainframe.

Compared to those protest pranks we did, is this an even bigger crime? Her heart beats faster. Kore was a defense contractor; could she be charged with espionage? Treason?

Oppie made it sound so easy—just a bulk file download twinning the normal daily data backup. These weren't even financial files. They were from the technical side: from the boreholes the company was drilling deep into the earth's crust to tap endless green energy.

I'm so sorry, she would say to the judge sentencing her, *but I was only borrowing—*

The last light silently blinks on. *Done.*

She disassembles the copy device, disconnecting the wireless connector and popping on the innocuous-looking plastic top. Oppie had camouflaged it to look like a tube of ChapStick. Classic Cherry. Totally normal thing to carry about during winter, right? On second thought, she'd better leave it in her desk in case they did a detailed search on her way out. As for the USB device which now held the data—that would be even more incriminating. Well, they'd never even thought to look at it the past week when she'd worn it along with the matching plain earring, to test if some type of hidden security scanner would pick up on it as they checked for weapons and explosives. Nothing— not even a longer-than-usual glance at the turnstile entry gates.

Bah. They'll never catch on this one last time. Casually as she can, she flicks her long blond hair back, snaps the pendant back onto its earring base, and rubs her earlobes, as though they were getting sore from the weight of the silver jewelry.

She locks up her desk. Is she coming back tomorrow? Wouldn't missing work or taking sick be a terrible giveaway? What if the data dangling from her left earlobe really is incriminating? Did Parliamentary committees have witness protection programs? If not, could she face the searching eyes of the security thugs who were always lurking about Kore Energy?

It might take Oppie days to decode the data. Maybe there was nothing in it, just the paranoid meanderings of the kookiest of her kooky eco-squad mates. *So, I'm risking an indeterminate stay at Château HM Prison Belmarsh for potentially cannabis-induced delusions? Mom will not be impressed, considering I promised her I'd utterly reformed. But…*

I won't get caught. She empties her wastebasket into the shredding sack. So close now.

Before she knows it she is strolling down the long silent corridor between desks. Overhead lights flick on as she passes, then off again.

Finally, she approaches the exit. Her body heat activates sensors and she can almost feel the invisible scan of the facial recognition system that unlocks the twin metal doors to the lift.

Her sigh of relief echoes the whisper-quiet slide of the brushed steel door of the lift as it closes behind her. Should she pop in to the 24-hour cafeteria and get the robots to make her a coffee? No, that'd be taking the 'act casual' act a bit too far. Best to focus on giving any security thugs a frosty half smile and a quick nod—nothing flirtatious. They must know how repulsive she finds them, since she always stiffens up whenever they come poking around the staff lounge or visit the fitness center, looking like flipping idiots in their dark suits, their beady eyes behind dark eyeglasses, ogling women in their Sweaty Betty yoga leggings.

Silence.

The light for the G button had come on when she pressed it. There should have been a "ding" as each floor passed. Did she miss it lost in her guilty, stressing thoughts?

Silence. And the LED location panel no longer showed "5". It didn't show anything. Blank.

A power failure? At the world's leading energy company? The papers would ridicule Dr. Kore, whom they'd already pegged as an eccentric member of the billionaire class. But then why would the overhead light still be on?

With her next breath she blows a soft stream of frost into the lift's interior. Was the heating down as well? Her hand hovers over the emergency button. Then, remembering the million photonic eyes about the place, she slowly lifts her gaze toward the nearest of the four visible surveillance cams. *Someone's got to see me.*

The muscles in her throat tighten as she fights off panic. It's a losing battle. She tries to slow her breaths; they come faster. Puff, puff, puff. Is it even this cold outside?

Screw it!

She jabs the red EMERGENCY CALL panel.

"Hellooo!" She waves to one camera, then the other, the next, and the last. Four unblinking eyes stare down at her. Spasms start deep in her abdominal muscles. She's shivering uncontrollably. *Where's my coat?*

Her thoughts seem to stick and run sluggishly through her head as an ache starts at the top of her skull and moves down the nape of her neck. *Car, ye, coat in… car. Never need it in the building, temperature's controlled by, ah, what is it, the building's artificial.. umm thing.*

The shivering is so bad now that she hunches over and can't right herself. She feels like completely on the polished lift floor and curling up. *So sleepy...*

No! must stay awake. *How...how is this happening?* She remembers something: hot air rises, right? There must be a warmer layer above.

Uncurling herself feels wrong. It exposes what must be protected at all costs: her middle, her vital core temperature. She shudders as tendrils of cold penetrate under her rib cage, threatening to freeze her lungs, her heart. Whatever she's going to try, she's got to be quick. She reaches up.

There must be some heat coming through the vent. Her hand gets close; she will never know whether or not she actually touched it.

A stream of *something* flows in through the air vent, but it's not warm. Just the opposite. Her whole hand goes instantly numb, like it's been turned to stone.

"Ahh!" She tries to yell. But her lips barely come apart, Shuddering convulsions lock her jaw shut. She touches her numb fingers with her other hand.

The fingertips, smartly manicured nails and all, break off. There's no blood—just a gentle plopping sound as the four small parts of her body drop to the lift floor.

Did that happen?

She starts to cry, but when she blinks the tears turn to slushy ice on her cheeks. Her vision is blurring. One last convulsion seizes her. Then she can't see anything, though she's certain her eyelids are open—frozen open.

The shivering stops. A weird and terrible warmth spreads through her. She feels as though she's falling, falling…

Chapter 01

Near the River Wye,
Hereford, UK

When the comfortable middle-aged couple had set out to their friends' house to watch *Great British Bake Off: Celebrity Edition*, only a light dusting of snow had affronted them during the initial leg of their drive, with lazy snowflakes descending from a blandly overcast and rapidly darkening December sky.

Barely halfway along to their destination, the rather narrow windshield of Mr. and Mrs. Sato's small three-wheeled electric car was bedeviled by an increasing swarm of enormously puffy, positively threatening snowflakes; these uncouth cotton ball puffs sped toward them, starkly lit by the harsh glare of their single headlamp, and dashed themselves to pieces against the foggy windshield. Directly ahead of them, the dimly lit road had, at some point during the early afternoon, received the curt attentions of the local snow plowing services department, but was fast refilling with wet slush.

Just then, a red icon began flashing on the dashboard. Mr. Sato's lips compressed while his wife glared daggers at the animated battery icon glowing crimson; its cartoon face wore a look of computerized disappointment pointedly aimed at their manifestly pathetic recharging skills.

"Oh my," Mrs. Sato said, trying hard not to let her teeth chatter audibly. "We've hardly any battery left. When we set out, it said we had more than enough to get to the Jacobs'."

"Aye, that's n'good at all," Mr. Sato said as casually as he could. "No matter, we're still en route, and we'll just be a little late."

"Late is what we'll be. The late Mr. and Mrs. Sato." His wife poked the stick-armed battery cartoon with her woolen-gloved forefinger. "It says we've got to choose between keeping the engine going or keeping the heater on. I don't fancy arriving at the Jacobs' as a frozen statuette."

Mr. Sato exhaled thoughtfully and immediately regretted it— his warm, moist breath not only fogged up the small area of window not covered by frozen snow but also frosted the thick lenses of his glasses, turning them nearly opaque.

"We mustn't miss the start of *Celebrity Bake Off*," his wife continued with noticeable urgency and personal angst. "It's 'sudden death,' and contestants can be sent off after any round: the signature, or the technical, or the showstopper. And you remember how Boris Johnson's team struggled so during Biscuit Week. How he'll manage reaching the finals with a single baker remaining on his squad I can't fathom. Really, I can't."

Mr. Sato made a noncommittal noise; he had quietly placed a hundred-pound bet on Team Greta Thunberg to win but had to keep his sentiments secret because his wife viscerally detested the perennially annoying Swedish activist and reality show contestant. He decidedly steered the convo to their immediate objective of not freezing to death on a deserted road in the middle of cow country.

"All right, let's assess," he said in a serious and analytical tone he reserved for occasions such as considering whether to sack an employee at their pub-restaurant. He checked the GPS route map. "As it stands, from what I gather from the dashboard uptakes of data, none of the charging stations on our route have any power. They're skint of electrons. Karput! As our Teutonic friends might say."

"You heard the weather report," Mrs. Sato said in a manner which was becoming undeniably accusatory, probably due to the intimate closeness of the interior of their vehicle. She expressed her frustration by jiggling her head. The motion sent the mounds of her freshly curled blonde hair quivering. "Cloudy with low winds. Always, always that pretty combo augurs disaster. Always. We should have topped up the car days ago."

"Our monthly energy 'llotment don't roll over until New Year. It's not even Christmas. We've got the business to keep goin' till then." Mr. Sato pressed the dash icon and turned the heater off. That added one solitary and slim green bar to their motor-function charge. "Gotta keep on forward at all costs. If we stop the engine, we'll just run the battery down and thenceforth be immobile."

"Oh! It's already nearly as cold inside as out." She mouthed the word "thenceforth," exercising that mild form of matrimonial mockery which had, over the past three decades and some months, turned Mr. Sato's husbandly hide thick as a rhino's.

"Exactly." His voice had a mild note of triumph as he took advantage of a straight section of road, took a hand off the gyrating steering wheel, and rubbed at the foggy windshield. "T'won't matter s'much, will it? Heater's quite superfluous wot, an' we'll be able ter keep on forward at all costs."

Perhaps it was their exigent circumstances, but Mrs. Sato became more rankled than usual by her husband's forced Northumberland accent. "And just speak normally, dear. We're not at the pub, and there are no locals for you to pander to."

"I thought my ability to blend in was what first attracted you? Y'know, in the romantical way, when I was a student come over from Japan."

"Genji, dear, you blend in with the locals like a rickshaw blends with black cabs on High Street."

"That's it," Mr. Sato said with mock outrage. "No more racist GB News for you. It's plum pollutin' yer mind. Soon you'll be wearin' a button supportin' Nigel Farage."

"Says the founding member of the Reform Party."

"Shhhh! Not even in the car. If our Labour friends ever knew…"

"Gahh! Look out!" His wife's gloved hand gesticulated at something careening at them out of the misty dark—a brightly lit, snowy blur caught in their headlight.

Mr. Sato braked, and their three-wheeled Reliant Sparrow curled into a skid. He just had a brief moment to wonder whether turning into a skid only worked for regular cars with four wheels as opposed to their eco-friendly but wobbly tripedal model when there was a wet *thump* as something hit them broadside.

They came to a stop, and all he could say was "Oh, oh, oh," his exclamations essentially keeping time with the thrashing of the single windshield wiper as it flicked back and forth like an enormous metronome. Something was caught on the wiper blade.

"Wassat?" Mrs. Sato said, aghast. "Is that some bit of clothing? Genji! What have you done to us now?"

They pushed open their respective doors, the missus having a harder time, as she was very near the snowbank lining that portion of the narrow roadway.

"Don't mind me. Go out and look—hmph!—then help me get out on my side."

"Me? How is it... Who would jump out onto the middle of an icy road well after dark? I swear they just jumped. Hang on..." A new icy terror gripped Mr. Sato's insides to match the creeping physical exterior chill. Had they hit someone? How badly were they hurt? The car was in the name of their business. What would happen if the injured party sued? Would they be ruined? Was it better if they were deceased or merely crippled, legally speaking? Terrible to think that way, and besides, how could they be injured? The failing batteries on the car were barely making twenty miles per hour, and whoever jumped out in front of them probably just got pushed along the ice.

Just bruised is all they could be, at worst, he thought. *We'll just put them in the back.* Assuming they were the size of a large sheepdog because that was all the room the Reliant had in its posterior cavity. *Right, right, we'll rescue them, pick 'em up, squeeze them in, and... and...*

"W-what is it?" Mrs. Sato blubbered as she peered out to see her husband pick up a wobbly broken object. "If that's a part of a-a-a body... oh! Where's my phone? We've got to call 999."

She saw Mr. Sato drop his hands and look toward the roadway; tracks of dirty slush were being filled in by the relentless fall of fat fluffy white blobs of new snow. Then he laughed.

"Haar-heeee."

"Look, Gen, if you've gone mental... Do I have to call for the armed police as well?"

Mr. Sato caught his breath. "Maybe you should better call a greengrocer. Could be they're the only ones who could fix this fellow's nose."

He tossed the accident victim's loose appendage toward his wife's booted feet. It rolled to a stop. Despite being crusted with icy flakes and having suffered compound fractures, it was unmistakably a carrot.

"The wankers!" Mr. Sato said, giving his lone front tire a short kick, an expression of blended relief and annoyance, which sent shudders through the Reliant's front end. "Look here, they even dressed it up with a tatty old scarf."

The low-speed impact had made a fatality out of the accident's sole casualty: three piles of mush were all that remained of a medium-sized snowman. Mr. Sato speculated that some idle country youth, dissuaded from waiting to throw eggs or snowballs at passing cars by the plunging temperatures and the scarcity of traffic, had assembled the frozen figure to prank the very next car to come along around the blind corner.

"That could've caused a serious accident," Mrs. Sato complained as she fingered the scarf which had decorated the rotund figure and wondered if it really wasn't bad quality, worth saving.

"If they've not been very long gone," he said, clambering up the roadside snowbank, "we could trace the little hooligans back to their homes."

"Oh, stop that," Mrs. Sato said, pulling him back by his sleeve. "They are long gone, and my nose feels as frozen as that ruddy carrot."

They were on their way again only a few minutes later, but somehow leaving the car switched on while stationary had caused an even more severe drain on the Reliant's increasingly unreliable battery than driving the thin-hulled eco-friendly contraption. The navigation screen showed their maximum range ending some six hundred yards short of their desired destination.

"How could that be?" Mrs. Sato shook her head, which was now covered by the humongous hood of her coat. "I told you we shouldn't have stopped."

"We had na choice. It could have been one of the delightful cherubs who put up the prank who we'd run down."

They decided it was best to be ready to call ahead for rescue, if necessary. However, the mere act of plugging their phone into the rickety dashboard's plug labeled "USB" instantly shortened their maximum range by half a mile.

"What now? Harley Jacobs won't drive that far to get us, not to save our lives, cheap bugger that he is. I bet he's only got his e-bike charged up."

Mr. Sato's lips compressed with gritty determination to get to their destination. "There are only two options: lighten our load by one hundred pounds, which would mean sacrificing you, dear, into the nearest snowbank, and that option I am wholeheartedly against."

"Thanks, love."

"Alternately… we can"—he squinted as a crossroads came into view—"take this shortcut."

"It's not on the computer map."

"They just cut and leveled it a week ago. No time to put it on the map. See, luv? It still pays for a man to know his own domain."

A large sign, bearded with icicles and topped with a dome of powdery snow, loomed over them:

KORE ENERGY LABS & ENGINEERING, LTD.

Dream Deep, Dream Green

Private Property – No Public Right of Way

Beside this less-than-encouraging greeting, there were gate posts but no gate between.

"How do you know it's a through road?" Mrs. Sato said, annoyed her husband had turned off and taken the detour without her getting any say at all. "If we get stuck in there—"

Mr. Sato hadn't thought of that possibility. But surely, if one end of the newly leveled road through the industrial park was open, it must come out somewhere. He had to pretend he'd thought of that.

"Of course I considered that alleged possibility, extraordinarily remote though it might be. What's the use of having an idle spinster for a daughter if she can't be relied upon to rescue us?"

"She's in London, three hours away when the weather's fine. What would we do until then? I'd better pre-dial emergency just in case. We may only have a minute of talk time."

"Spring'll come before any official help. Did you see the story in the *Juggernaut* about that poor old codger in Manchester? Broke his hip and had to wait eighteen hours fer an ambulance. An' during those eighteen long, chilly, utterly agonizing hours, they couldn't move him, so his family built a tent to shelter him as he lay in his own backyard shivering in pain all night long."

Mr. Sato steered the Reliant around a sharp turn. His wife braced herself against the door and recalled something else that irked her.

"Ellie isn't a spinster. She's barely thirty, is a famous author.

14

She even owns the *Juggernaut*, the most venerable newspaper in Britain. Spinster… What a chauvinistic— Oooh! I knew it! Blockade! Blockade! *Watch out!*'

More wary this time after being ambushed by the snowman, Mr. Sato pressed the brake steadily, letting off when he felt the car slide over the mixed gravel and snow. A series of bumps loomed straight ahead. Were they some kind of barrier or speed humps that had accumulated snow? The path they were on was narrow, and the shoulders on either side had a plenty steep drop; if they went over, they'd wreck for sure.

Nothing for it, then, he thought, gritting his teeth and bracing himself on the steering wheel as though that would help slow their forward momentum.

Mrs. Sato gave out a small, anticlimactic chirp of distress as a small thump echoed through the small car's cabin. Their forward skidding motion was finally arrested with a rattle and squeaking of suspension springs coming from underneath the small conveyance.

"I'm sure it's just some bushes or light rubbish," Mr. Sato said, getting out of the car to examine the obstruction that had most inconveniently popped up, impeding their way, and also, at the same time, not coincidentally, to remove himself from his better half's accusing stare. "I'll just shove whatever it is aside, and we'll be on our way."

The Reliant started emitting an annoying alarm sound.

"Look! All that braking! You've run the batteries near empty," his wife said as she studied the console, which was filled with LED icons; icons that, without her being able to refer to the vehicle's hundred-page manual, a manual so large it would not fit in the minuscule glove box and had been left in their garage, looked like hieroglyphs to her.

Mr. Sato had reached the middle lump of five, which lay still and motionless in the road; like the others, it was about seven inches across, roundish and festooned with powdery snow. Before kicking or tossing them aside, he first ascertained it would probably be prudent to see if these objects were indeed rubbish or something more solid like cement or steel, which would injure his foot and later, when that foot was eventually thawed out and relieved of its near-frostbitten condition, cause him an amount of pain proportionate to the vigor of his kicking. He touched the object with the tips of his gloved hand, causing a façade of frosty flakes to fall away.

"Agnes! Agnes, look…" He gasped as he recoiled in horror. "Uh, no, no, don't look! Under no circumstances are you to… What is going on?"

"For the sake of St. Jude, must I do everything?" Mrs. Sato got out as her husband continued to stare and blubber. Behind her, she dragged the phone-charging cable, which was still connected to the car's console, receiving the last dribbles of electrons remaining in their car's power cells. "That's it, I'm calling 999. A little drive through Hereford is clearly beyond our capabilities to manage without emergency assistance."

She fumbled with the touchscreen, her gloved fingers smearing condensation along its fogged-up glass. Instead of selecting the keypad, she accidentally dialed "Ellie-London" on video call in livestream mode. A small glaring LED flashlight lit up the ground in front of Mrs. Sato's feet.

"Hello?" Ellie Sato's voice said over the speakerphone. "Er, Mum, Dad? Why are you showing me a snowy road?"

Unable to hit whatever button turned the camera round to face her, Mrs. Sato merely shouted at the tiny inset image of her daughter. "We've just had a spot of trouble with the car—oop!"

Mrs. Sato skidded painfully to her knees right in the space between the Reliant's headlamps and the five lumpy objects blocking their path; the phone's camera autofocused directly on the nearest one. "How do you change this to... I just wanted to phone you. Not at all pleased with all this dashed video nonsense."

"Mum, what is that—"

Just then the long-suffering, overtaxed batteries of the car failed, and the lonely access road was plunged into complete darkness save for the cellphone's light, which illuminated a ghastly oval shape, frost-covered, open mouthed, and sightlessly staring back at the astonished Mr. and Mrs. Sato.

Chapter 02

Mayfair House
Mayfair, London

Just before the frantic call from her parents, Ellie Sato had been absorbed in the very less than frantic but still menacingly urgent search for the huge mansion's universal remote. Without the Wi-Fi, Bluetooth, and Far Link satellite-enabled gizmo, sending commands to a gazillion automated devices lurking in every room and hallway and staircase was next to impossible.

One supposition as to the remote's whereabouts—and not a very outlandish speculation at that—that came to her mind was that Magellan, the large and wicked macaw in residence, had, in a fit of vindictive spite, grabbed it in his hooked black beak and hidden it. In that case, she had considered she might need a ladder.

Her loyal Labradoodle, Chestnut, on the other hand, might have tucked it under his blanket to keep it safe from the bird in their ongoing interspecies skirmish. A third possibility was that Esmunda, a human guest at Mayfair House who was as capable of causing mischief as the two pets, had simply smoked too much Spice, or synthetic cannabis, and dropped it in one of the sixteen toilets scattered among the five stories of the rolling old pile. Then Ellie's phone had rung—her parents.

"Just stay with the car!" Ellie yelled during the first minute of panicked incoherence instigated by a video call which was displaying jittery and jumbled pictures of her parents' Reliant EV, her mother's soaked galoshes, and snowy ruts in a road somewhere. "Can you hear me? Why are you on video call?"

Her mother had again dropped the phone onto what looked like slush-covered gravel. Some of the slush must have gotten stuck over the mic as well as on the phone's camera lens because all she could hear was static and mumbling.

"I can't hear you. On the chance you can hear me: STAY WHERE YOU ARE."

She looked for her car keys as a flurry of images flashed on her display, terrible ones. She must have imagined it—a face and a mouth and pale eyes staring back at her. It must have been some jumble of shadows and her imagination working overtime. Then there was a crackle and a blip, and the connection cut out. As she tried to redial, she remembered Esmunda's one useful talent. "Ezzie! Where are you? You're a cracker with these smartphones. I need youuu, urgently."

She hit redial for the fourth time.

"Damn." Ellie could only get her parents' cheery voicemail, and her grip on the phone became so tight her knuckles blanched. She could call 999 straightaway, but what would she say? Perhaps they could trace her parents' phone. Did it have to be on when they tried that? Or could they tell where the last call came from? But come to think of it, still pictures often had geographic coordinates on them—wouldn't the same hold for videos?

And then there was that ghastly image, still flashing through Ellie's memory. What if it wasn't a winter's night mirage? Had her parents found some people who had been trying to keep warm inside their car and… and…

"Ezzie! Answer me this instant, you freeloading—"

"Why all the time you so cross… uhh, all the time?" Esmunda's mumbling voice came from way up the spiral staircase. She leaned way out over the railing, looking down at Ellie, who was on the second floor.

"Please come down, I've got an emergency. Need your help." Esmunda continued to stare down, unblinking. "I don't care if you've been smoking," she added. "I need your help, urgently!"

And why did the only other person in the house have to occupy a bedroom on the very top floor? Scratch that, it was obvious: Esmunda was in the midst of methodically dirtying up each bedroom and ensuite bathroom in succession and then moving up to the next clean one. The former London roost of dukes and Edwardian shipping magnates was starting to look like a student protest squat, but at present there was no sense worrying about the finer points of the infantile twentysomething's domestic demerits.

"Here," she said, thrusting her handset at the half-dressed girl. "See what you can make of this. I need to know where my parents are. They sent me this video call."

"Uh?"

"They're. Likely. Lost. Find. Them. We. Must." Ellie spoke at half speed to penetrate the inner fog that a lifetime of cannabis abuse had afflicted on the woman's brain. "They are possibly freezing to death on some backcountry road, right bloody now."

"Uh, hi." The monosyllabic greeting was delivered in a decidedly baritone and nonfeminine tone, and behind Esmunda came a bare-chested Asian man who smiled down sheepishly at Ellie.

"Oh, yes, Ellie, this is Jaiden. Jaiden, meet Eleanor Sato. We were rehearsing for the play, a musical really, The King and I; we're putting it on for the New Year's—"

"Hi, Jaiden, find a shirt and say bye, Jaiden. Ezzie, do tell me you can find them by looking at technical things on my phone."

After the pair of aspiring thespians had descended the staircase to Ellie's flight, and her The King and I co-star had been made decent and directed to his appropriate exit mark, Esmunda's long black-polished fingernails flicked through screens and apps faster than Ellie could follow.

"Ah, here it is, video call, mpeg files... Got it."

Esmunda rattled off a string of numbers.

"Wait, I'll take those down."

"No, I'll just copy and... paste into the map. There, they're right in the middle of this open field. Kore Energy property, but I don't see a road. Why would they drive into the middle of a meadow in an industrial park?"

Ellie looked at the tiny map. The location was somewhat near her parents' home and would at least give the authorities someplace to start. What extreme of cold could they be suffering without shelter on the exposed and windy countryside?

"All right, let's call 999."

Esmunda batted her hand away. "Hang on, why would they send a video call? That's an odd thing to do if you're in distress." She replayed the video file.

"Holy crap. What is that? Did they find someone frozen on the roadside?"

She froze the terrible image, and upon a closer examination, to Ellie's intense dismay, it really did look like a person.

"It's a woman," Esmunda said. "Why is she buried up to her neck in a snowdrift?"

The image of the presumably deceased young woman turned out to work in their favor. When they finally got through to the emergency operator, the operator's initially laconic tones of unconcern caused Ellie to fear the authorities were too busy tracking down villains perpetrating pronoun crimes to bother with two missing citizens. However, when Esmunda uploaded the screengrab picture file to the Met's online "crimes in progress" site, a chief inspector came on the line right smartly and advised them of the serious consequences of pranking the police and demanded they remain where they were.

While they received no assurance that a rescue operation would immediately be mounted, Ellie thought at least they'd got the first responders' attention.

"Lazy buggers," Esmunda agreed, after she'd voiced her concerns. "What are you going to do?"

The authorities had all the information they did. Ellie thought for a moment. "Well… we're not hanging about."

"We?"

"Put on some clothes, warm clothes. And while you're up there, grab some for me. I'll get the ignition fob for the SUV, unless our pets have nicked that as well."

Ellie didn't wait for a reply and ran down the stairs toward the key cupboard on the main floor.

Chapter 03

The lift down to the subterranean levels of Mayfair House was designed like a huge gilded birdcage. It would have been an elegant conveyance but for the astoundingly diverse collection of rubbish and bird droppings on the floor. Ellie kicked a French fry container out of her way.

"I thought you were going to be neater," she absentmindedly scolded Esmunda, who trailed behind with a selection of coats suitable for any season except winter. "Wasn't that one of your self-authoring goalposts?"

She set the antique ceramic dial for B2, machinery clanked, and they descended.

"I've been a bit preoccupied."

"I saw."

"My psychotherapist says I've got to have creative outlets or I'll go mental. I was nearly committed to Saint Barts NHS Psychiatric during the bloody pandemic. Besides, don't we have house-cleaning robots?"

"That's the thing, they don't take care of themselves. They need oiling and tipping out when their robot pouchy things are full."

Mr. Surghit, the one human employee who came with the mansion, had given his notice after a dispute with the new owner, a very rich, very obnoxious American. Ellie couldn't rightly complain since, as a favor to her and a reward for services rendered to the United States government, the wealthy eccentric had leased the 12,000-square-foot residence to her for one pound per annum.

"That was also on your self-authoring to-do list: applying your mechanical know-how to vital domestic purposes in lieu of paying actual cash money for rent, utilities, use of the cars."

"I don't even have a license, I never—"

"Don't even. The one thing I learned to operate was the house surveillance cameras. But I don't have to rely on them because the gas tanks and hydrogen tanks and battery cells are always empty when I need to drive, and I also receive and have to pay all the traffic and parking violation fine notices in order to keep our cars from being impounded."

Esmunda sulked. The lift shuddered to a halt; Ellie heaved the folding doors aside with a loud metal-on-metal squeal.

She sniffed the air. *What now? We've got to get going.* "Ezzie, why does the entire garage reek of gasoline?"

"Oh!" Esmunda motioned vaguely at the dimly lit ceiling. "Is that a spider? How we've let things go here, in the domestic sort of way, that is. As soon as we rescue your poor stranded parents, I've resolved a firm resolution to make a spreadsheet to assign cleanup duties. I'm sure Jaiden and the theatre company will pitch in."

"Really now, what have you been doing? Gas fumes are flammable." Ellie looked around for the fat button on the wall that opened the garage door to the street. She found it, then considered that an electrical spark could send the whole place up like a roman candle. Instead, she used the manual pulley. Twist by twist, and with a great squeaking of wheel and axle, it raised up the metal shutters. Immediately a blast of fresh but icy air blasted across her ankles. "Give me my coat."

Ellie stared Henkel cutlery sets at Esmunda as they waited, shivering, for the six-car garage to air out.

"All right, enough oppressive looks," Esmunda said sheepishly. "I get enough of those at the Jobseeker's Allowance office when I claim my benefits. So, now, on the topic at hand, as to the petrol fumes, what occurred, to the best of my current recollection, is this: I tried charging up my scooter via the outlet. But the breaker kept popping off. The wiring here must go back to the Crimean War, the first one, I mean. So then I thought I'd save you on electrical by using the Honda generator. Of course, that machine runs on petrol, and I had to get the fuel out from this old dinosaur gas-guzzling planet destroyer."

"The Bentley SUV? The only car we've got with tires that can drive over ice and snow? Go straight away and unsiphon the generator tank. We've got a hundred and fifty miles to drive, and the weather report isn't favorable."

Emptying the emergency generator gave the formidable SUV three-quarters of a tank of luscious, RPM-powering petrol, enough to get them to her parents' last known location, assuming Esmunda's calculations where correct.

"They're right there, right where you, uh, left them." She giggled. "You can trust me."

Inside the plush confines of the Bentley Bentayga, Ellie could smell acrid fumes of synthetic cannabis emanating from her companion's clothes as well as the cloak Esmunda had chosen for her, which was almost certainly a theatrical prop and, upon closer inspection, was found to be mostly composed of faux fur and feathers.

Esmunda shrank down in her seat as they sped up Piccadilly. "I hope none of my mates see me. They're real eco-fanatics. But man, I could get used to this seat heater. You posh people have all the best toys."

Unwilling to unbundle her arms from her heavy coat, Esmunda popped her bare and prehensile foot out and sent her painted toenails dancing over the dashboard controls until they found the heating gauge, which her big toe set to its maximum output.

"How many times do I have to explain? I'm not posh, and come January, we'll have to move unless you can afford about a million pounds rent." Ellie's American benefactor had prepaid all the household accounts until the end of the year, but a few months back, news reports had come out about an FBI raid on his office in New York, and since then, getting hold of him by any means had been impossible. For Ellie, Esmunda, and her merry band of theatrical players, the gay times at Mayfair House were coming to a close.

"What about that fellow you're dating? He's filthy rich. The one with the stupid toff name."

Ellie gripped the fat leather steering wheel. "No one's 'dating' anyone."

"He's always knocking about, and I see the way he looks at you."

For a homeless unemployed actress and vapeaholic, Esmunda claimed to notice a lot.

"Ranulph Oliphant is a widower and... we went through trying times together during that big conflict in the Middle East and then during the fiendish plot we foiled in Paris. I'm probably one of the few people he can speak to in total confidence."

She could feel Esmunda's laser-like pupils, which were ensconced under her gothic-painted eyebrows and lashes, boring into her neck. "No wonder you're a spinster. I thought all you Asians just wanted to find a man with a Mercedes minivan and pop out babies."

"I'm Eurasian, and I'll… be in full charge of any popping." Ellie made a harder turn than she had to onto the A4, a maneuver which snapped her companion smartly back into her seat. "And I'm not a spinster; I was nearly engaged, practically."

Esmunda screwed up her face as though trying to solve a trivia quiz. "When was… Oh, right the dead guy. The American."

This was no time to give a promiscuous Spice addict a primer in good manners, so Ellie merely said, "Well, look, let us get back to the task at hand, shall we?"

They tried the Satos' number a few more times with no luck connecting.

"All we've got is your estimate of their last location," Ellie said, her frustration building as they crept along behind a wide lorry. She couldn't very well call the authorities again—they'd asked her to wait in London. Like that was going to happen if her mum and dad were at risk of hypothermic shock on some deserted roadside.

"We've also got this." Esmunda tapped—this time using her hands—and fiddled with the way-too-complex-to-be-in-a-car computer protruding from the polished Tamo Ash wood dashboard. "Let me upload something from your phone to the car's media. There we go."

"Ack!" Ellie nearly swerved into the other lane as the frozen face of the young woman appeared on the big heads-up display. "Take that away unless you're eager for a demonstration of really expensive airbags when I crash."

The haunting face of the young victim—she had to be dead—disappeared, then they both jumped in their seats when a telephone rang.

"It's not my phone," Esmunda said. "It's not your phone. It's the car."

"What do you mean the car?" Ellie asked, at once befuddled and annoyed as she realized it was only her second time driving the largest of the vehicles that came with her temporary lodgings.

"It's got its own mobile."

"Who could be calling?" Ellie said. "Even I don't know the number."

Chapter 04

"Press this to connect the call," Esmunda said as she extended her bare foot under Ellie's nose in order to poke a garishly painted toenail onto one of the multitude of icons festooning the SUV's steering wheel. All about them, stereo speakers crackled to life.

The only cogent thoughts that mustered themselves in her head revolved around the possibility Scotland Yard might have tracked her down as she flagrantly disobeyed their directive to stay home. These notions were dashed away when she heard the caller's voice—it was refined, manly in an endearingly awkward way, and touched with pressing concern.

"Ellie, have I got through? Can you hear?"

"Yes, er, hi, Ran, I mean, Mr. Oliphant. I don't quite know how you managed it, but we're connected, and I am well and I, that is to say, we are a little preoccupied at the moment."

Beside her, Esmunda pursed her lips and made a swooning motion in an absurd and, given the circumstances, wholly inappropriate attempt to mimic romantic infatuation.

"Well, uh, good, then. I just wanted to find out how you were."

So he decided to randomly call one of the six leased cars registered to the company which owned Mayfair House? There had to be more to it.

"We've had a bit of upset," she said. "I'm going to locate my parents, who seem to have gotten stuck on the road up Hereford way. But perhaps you already know that, so I should ask you: How the devil did you know that?"

Ran sheepishly explained his tech conglomerate was a contractor for the UK's intelligence and cyber security agency, the GCHQ, which monitored all electronic communications in the country via an artificial intelligence system.

"I got my guy to program in some keyword alerts whenever they come up."

One of those keywords was her. So her longtime associate, and definitely not romantic interest, however rich or charming he might be, had hacked his own company's product to trace her whenever mention of her came up in the millions of phone conversations, texts, and emails continuously monitored by an ever-increasingly nosy and paranoid government. Ellie didn't know whether to be flattered or wonder at behavior that could be construed as obsessively stalkerish.

"You don't say, Ranny Oliphant. Or is it Randy Elephant? Heeeee," Esmunda butted in, always keen on talking tech. "But a serious programming question, what algo do you use to sniff out your key terms, Random Forest or Lasso Regression?"

"Uh… that's classified, and with whom do I have the pleasure of speaking?"

Ellie introduced her houseguest.

"Ran, have your contacts with the authorities got any updates…"

"Of course, sorry, should have said, that's obviously tops on your mind. The local constabulary has located Mr. and Mrs. Sato, and according to Lead Sergeant Taft, at present they're in great shape and currently warming up inside an emergency services vehicle." Ran's voice, she knew, always sounded more Scottish the more stressed he became. "Per'aps you should wait, meet them at the station."

"What is… umm." Ellie was a little flustered and annoyed that no one had bothered to keep her informed. If they were all right, why hadn't *they* called back on a borrowed phone? "Is anything wrong? Has anyone else been injured? Anyone at all?" She thought but didn't say: for instance, the young lady buried up to her neck in hard-packed snow?

"Anyone else?" Ran added in the tone he always used for gaslighting, a type of deception at which he fared exceptionally poorly.

Esmunda leaned over toward the steering wheel. "You know, the body in the snow; she looked quite young, poor thing."

"Oh, that."

"Yes, that little detail," Ellie added sternly. "You're dealing with Britain's foremost investigative journalist, you know."

"And her most able accomplice… Oh, that's not the right word, is it?" Esmunda broke into a spontaneous fit of wholly inappropriate laughter common to Spice devotees.

"It's a little more complicated…" Ran said in that rich person's paternalistic manner, which set Ellie's teeth on edge, largely due to the fact that in the case of such admonitions, he was nearly always proven correct. "Just consider discretion for once in your career. You're not even out of the city; turn yourself about. And if you don't want to wait at the police station, go to my townhouse. My staff will let you in."

Esmunda leaned over the microphone in the steering wheel, and at the same time fluffed her reeking mass of hair in a way that nearly caused Ellie to go off the road. "Oh, so you're tracking us in real time too. How absolutely dear," she said with a big grin while miming a motion with a crooked finger in the side of her mouth like a fish being hooked, indicating she thought Ellie had hooked a fine catch by, through no fault of her own, inducing obsessively possessive behavior in an eligible widower.

"Ranulph Oliphant," Ellie said in her most businesslike tone, "you might recall I was there every step with you and your hardened military chums when we faced down terrorists in the Paris Catacombs. I think I can endure a simple country road calamity. Good evening."

And with that, she hit an orange button. Except that one controlled the car's stereo music system. After she turned off the loud music, hitting the next button over set off the panic alarm. Tapping that again got rid of the screeching alarm sound.

Finally, she found and tapped an icon deceptively named "End Call" and rang off.

Chapter 05

"Where are we?" Despite her eagerness to follow the directions of the Bentley's navigation system, once they left the highway, Ellie had been forced to slow down and directed to take a turn onto a two-lane road bracketed by snowdrifts piled upon hedges bounding it; for long intervals the two-lane road contracted itself into a single-lane road canopied by low-bowed, ice-burdened trees and paved by sheer ice of every hazardous variety: white, black, gray.

Esmunda studied the glowing dashboard map and mumbled something about the River Wye and Tar's Brook. "But we're definitely on the right track." That was quite certain, as there were no other tracks, except those belonging to wayward cows and sheep.

Soon they came upon a cacophony of bright blinking lights, but these were not ones that gave Ellie's passenger any comfort or joy.

"Oh dear. Eleanor, uh, d'ya mind letting me off here? Anywhere is dandy." Esmunda unexpectedly started squirming in her seat as they approached the mass of illumination, visible for several miles on the otherwise pitch-dark country road.

"Why on earth would you ask that?"

"Well… in my youth there was a small bit of mischief with the Moldovan authorities on the continent, Transnistria, actually. No one's looking for me in the UK, but…"

They were close enough to the scene that reflections of flashing emergency lights competed with Esmunda's pupils for dominance on the surface of her ever-enlarging peepers.

"We don't have time to indulge your paranoia," Ellie protested. "My parents are out there somewhere. Did you not think in your wildest conceptions there'd be coppers on the scene, given the indisputable presence of the body of a decedent which has turned up frozen solid?"

"I just didn't think there'd be so *many*." Esmunda rubbed an aperture in the fogged-up side window and looked out with rising alarm. "That must be a convocation of every copper south of Scotland."

She had a point, Ellie thought. Even given the body of some unfortunate hiker caught in the latest ice storm, the dozens of vehicles and multitude of white plastic crime scene tents being put up seemed a bit much.

A fair half kilometer away from what seemed the center of intense official activity, they were ordered to halt by a bored-looking constable with a squashed-up bulbous nose, red from the chill breeze, and slightly drippy. Esmunda's neck and head retreated into her wardrobe like a tortoise sporting a shell made entirely of plush gray chinchilla fur.

"Road's closed," the bored copper said as gouts of steam came from between his clenched teeth. "Major investigation underway."

Ran had given them the name of the lead sergeant in charge of the scene. Mentioning that name got Ellie through to the next checkpoint, and the next, but with a significantly inconvenient caveat.

"But you'll 'ave ter proceed on foot and must remain in bounds of the flagged path," said the next bored copper, who was skinny in body and face and who had an enormous nose, just as red as the previous man's but of a sharp, protruding character; it gave him an uncanny resemblance to a flamingo.

Esmunda volunteered to wait in the Bentley. Halfway along the icy path, which was bordered on each side by long ribbons of blue-and-white *POLICE LINE DO NOT CROSS* tape, Ellie realized that while her friend's selection of light and faux-feather-laden outerwear was barely keeping her upper body from freezing, her footwear was even more atrociously badly suited. By the time she got to the top of the hill, she couldn't feel much below her ankles.

No one stopped her as she trudged up a slight hill past a sign that said Kore something-or-other. The intense activity was down the other side, where the entire road was blocked by multiple emergency vehicles and lit up like St. Paul's Cathedral before the national energy crisis. The display was so dazzling she walked right past an ambulance sheltering the very people she'd come for.

"Eleanor! Oh my Lord, how dreadful you've come!" cried a shaky-sounding voice from behind.

Not quite the greeting she'd expected. Nearly slipping on the mushy snow, Ellie rushed over to find the disheveled couple sitting on the tailgate of the rescue wagon. An officer in a winter jacket moved to stop her and was brushed aside by a handsome blond fellow wearing an overcoat with inspector's epaulettes featuring Order of the Bath pips.

"It's fine, let her past. I assume you're the daughter?" he said, thoughtfully taking her arm with a large hand clad in Chester

Jeffries bespoke gloves to help her over tire track ruts in the snow. "I'm Harrigan, City Police."

"Way out here?" Ellie instantly felt the fool. Of course this was no longer a local matter. The girl, whoever she was, had likely gotten lost on unfamiliar roads and byways and might even be the subject of a national missing persons alert. On the other hand, the City force was distinct from London's much larger Met police force. What could be the connection?

"There's awr Ellie," Mr. Sato said in a fatigued drawl. "Rode to the rescue fer us, eh?"

She ran over to the ambulance and skidded to a stop in front of the limp-looking couple, whose hair, faces, and clothing drooped and steamed, having been quick frozen by the sub-zero country air and even more quickly thawed out by the radiant heat lamps which shed an orange glow on their slumped shoulders.

"I thought I'd find you alone and forlorn in the woods. But... how did so many... and what is this place?" Ellie looked around. Leafless trees scratched at clouds hovering low in the night sky; the regimented flora bracketed a low-slung industrial complex and the whole area was lit by floodlights visible from about a half kilometer. "How could you possibly have got stranded out here?"

A large-faced officer with glaring blue eyes and ginger hair peeking out from his hat interceded. "Now look, miss, we'll be asking the questions here."

Inspector Harrigan brushed his inferior aside. "Thank you, Sergeant, this is the couple's daughter who, may I make a presumption, has driven all the way from the city, and unless you have grounds for suspecting Mr. and Mrs. Sato of involvement in these serious crimes rather than just by sad chance being on hand and innocently discovering them, there's no reason they shouldn't have a few moments of privacy. I'll take full responsibility."

With that gesture, which Ellie found quite gallant, she was ushered into the bright and warm emergency van. Her parents tried to explain how they'd gotten stranded way out there. With both of them speaking, Ellie was able only to gather that the ultimate responsibility for their stranded state lay with some star-crossed combination of the "bloody Reliant batteries," *The Great British Bake Off* competition, and former prime minister and reality game show contestant Boris Johnson. As to what they found blocking the roadway—

"That must have been a shock," Ellie said. "Do they suspect she died by foul play?"

"Canna really tell, can ye?" her dad said, looking quite pale. "I... I mean all of them arranged like that."

"All who?" Could hypothermia cause cognitive dissonance? Her father, being an Asian transplant, was at the best of times more inscrutable than the average English person, but he seemed to be rambling more than usual.

"The heads, dear," Mrs. Sato said primly, with the harsh exactitude of a bailiff denominating pounds and pence owing to obtain the release of an impounded lease car. "Five heads in a row, just planted there like, like... frozen cabbages. Cabbages, yes, and all directly across the icy road. If I hadn't grabbed the wheel at the very last instant, we'd have certainly squashed them under our tires. Like cabbages... all frozen like."

Mr. Sato looked far into the dark distance, mouthed the word "cabbages," and made a sound as though trying to swallow.

Then he fainted.

Chapter 06

Paramedics soon revived Mr. Sato. One wiry young fellow with a ponytail, who was perhaps a trainee eager to show off his skills, grabbed a pair of scissors and exuberantly sheared off Mr. Sato's down jacket, his favorite cardigan, and the top of his reindeer-patterned long underwear onesie. Ponytail Paramedic then insisted upon attaching a dozen ECG leads all over Mr. Sato's nearly naked and shivering torso. Her father's shredded clothes were replaced by a silver-and-gold foil blanket more suitable for wrapping a goose for the oven than draping over a middle-aged man.

As soon as the final ECG lead was in place and the medic proudly announced his accomplishment, a stout and humorless female medic informed him they had no monitoring device to which said leads could be attached.

"Well… it was worth checking the old boy out," the ponytail said.

Soon after the demonstration of advanced British emergency medical treatment was concluded, Ellie insisted her parents obtain legal advice before responding to any more questions from the dozens of uniformed and plainclothes officers who were beetling about what she, with her journalistic instinct for the macabre mass appeal, felt was about to become the nation's most sensational crime scene. They were allowed to leave with the caution, issued by the beefy-faced ginger officer, that they must remain available if further inquiries were deemed necessary. Their three-wheeler Reliant was to remain impounded.

"Not much use, out of juice," her father quipped as his teeth chattered and the corner of his mouth twitched while he carefully pulled off the leads attached to his naked chest. The ponytail medic had disappeared in a huff, perhaps intending to apply first aid to the five victims, who were of course beyond even that man's redoubtable skills.

"Get in the Bentley, Dad, and cover up, please. Esmunda's with me."

"Oh, is she?" Mrs. Sato crowed. "How nice of her to come all this way. She's such an amiable girl; good with the fellows as well, I'd expect."

"Are you sure you're all right?" Ellie said, looking at the line of emergency vehicles. "There must be a spare ambulance with a normal medic nearby."

Mr. Sato stubbornly insisted he had never felt better. He nodded to Esmunda, wrapped the metallic blanket more closely, sat down with a crushing crinkly sound, and offered to drive.

"Not on your life," Mrs. Sato said. "One crash up per evening is my limit."

"Hi, Mr. Sato, Mrs. Sato," Esmunda chirped as they got in and proceeded to gab in her rather indelicate manner. "What's all that about then with those coppers? Have they found out about the corpsicle? Who is she? What was she doing way out here?" Then she remembered to say, "And I'm so very much glad you two are alive, though I never doubted for a second. I said, 'Those two old birds would make it through the Flood.' S'mostly why I came along, to morally support Eleanor. She was on the verge of goin' mental."

Ellie was aware her father's lips were still colored a chalky hue, and she did not want him fainting again, therefore she recapped as few details as she could to her roommate. However, her mother divulged that there were not one but a grand total of five "corpsicles," represented only by the uppermost part of their anatomies, which had all been arranged in a row across the lonely country road in the middle of a blizzard. These salacious details only spurred Esmunda's wild speculations.

"So... these heads, you say they were arranged along the road, like, on purpose?"

"Mm-hmm, like cabbages," Mrs. Sato said distractedly while texting furiously to several people and social media at once. "Or really more like pumpkins."

"Mum!"

"Wow, d'you think it was kids? Y'know, a prank?"

"Out here?" Ellie asked as she turned the vehicle around and made sure the heater was set to maximum output. "That's a bit much. I mean, assuming these are genuine body parts, and not just ultra-realistic 3D-printed waxworks, these mischievous misguided cherubs would have had to rob multiple graves or break into a morgue, wouldn't you think?"

Esmunda pondered the issue. "Did any of them look foreign?"

"What? Migrant heads?" Mrs. Sato asked. "We only saw one clearly and close up, and she looked local. To be honest, a frozen English rose. Really sad, now that one has time to ponder on it."

Mr. Sato gave a low moan, but Ellie saw him raise his hand to signal he was still conscious.

"I insist you two stay over at Mayfair," Ellie said. "In the morning, we'll retain the most suitable solicitor and see when your car can be released from impound."

"Perhaps you might ask the nice inspector's assistance. What was his name? Harrigan. That's right, ask him personally how things stand," Mrs. Sato said, her antennae always able to detect the presence of possibly eligible men, even under the most exigent circumstances. "I mean, you are Britain's leading investigative journalist, a famous author, and proprietor in chief of Britain's most venerable newspaper. He should be happy for a chance at some good press, and you shouldn't be so shy about showing off your notable feminine attractions."

Ellie just had time to express mild irritation at her mother's ill-timed attempt at matchmaking when the SUV's phone rang.

"Oh," Mrs. Sato exclaimed and shook her head at her husband and gave him a poke in his ribs. "That's got to be the police telling us to turn back and surrender into custody. Why did you keep fainting, Gen? It's a sure sign of a guilty conscience."

"Stop it, Mum, it's for me. Hello? Is that you again, Ran?"

Ellie felt, rather than heard, a short intake of breath from the back seat—the billionaire was very high on her mother's list of whimsical candidates for son-in-law.

"I see you're moving away from the scene of the, er, accident. Everything all right?"

"Other than the otherworldly creepiness of you following my every move through some kind of AI computer hackery, it is; we're good."

Mrs. Sato burst forward between the front seats and waved her gloved hand at the audio microphone for no reason her daughter could fathom. Mrs. Sato practically trilled, "Mr. Oliphant, helloooo, it's Mrs. Satooo, proud mum of Britain's leading investigative journalist. Ellie's right, such a bright girl, she is. We're glad to get away from all the hullabaloo. It's not just a bit

41

grim back there. Some people have no regard where they leave things lying about, no regard at all. But hearing from youuu makes any occasion a charm, a simple charm."

"You don't say, Mrs. Sato. Ellie, may I ask, you were right on the property of Kore Industries, correct?"

"Now I remember!" As Esmunda interrupted, her head popped out from among the fur ensconcing her. "Dr. Kore, he's the mad-looking scientist with a technology that's supposed to be saving the world delivering unlimited geothermal energy."

Ran continued calmly but pointedly, "You didn't happen to run into any of Dr. Kore's security staff, did you?"

It seemed an odd question, and Ellie felt the weight, once again, of being the most responsible person in a complex situation and certainly the one everyone would blame if things went wrong. On the other hand, since her parents had chosen to travel along, of all the roads in the land, the one that harbored a major crime scene, humoring a member of Britain's financial ruling class like Ran was not the worst idea. His long-distance introduction to the sergeant on the scene had markedly expedited her recovery of her parents, and he probably knew every law firm in town, especially ones that might extend credit and allow fees to be paid over a decade or so.

As they drove away from the sound of mobile generators and the sight of rhythmic flashing of lights, she described accurately and succinctly what she'd seen and heard. Her parents also avowed they'd only dealt with uniformed emergency responders.

"That said, what are you on about, Ran?" she asked while at the same time neatly keeping the car from sliding off the slippery narrow country road.

"Nothing, really. It's just that I know Dr. Kore, you know, professionally, from energy conferences, so, uh… But as it's a police matter, that's that, then."

After extracting a few more assurances they were in immediate need of nothing, Ran rang off.

"Now there's a fellow who's keen on you like whiskers on a cat!" her mother exulted.

"Please!"

"But I wonder… I've been researching him online. Is he quite, *ahem*, right in the head?"

"He's a war veteran and a widower, and he loaned me money when the *Juggernaut* was in trouble."

"Yes, dear ; however, some articles I found… they talk about his twisted *sex* life." Her mother whispered the salacious word, which far from muting the salacious word merely made it sound still more salacious. Even Esmunda roused up from her Spice hangover doze and perked up her ears.

"Mum!"

"The worst report on that, *ahem*, ra-ther forbid-ding subject, *ahem*, was printed in the pages of your very own *Juggernaut*." Mrs. Sato's forced throat-clearing sound clearly implied that Mr. Oliphant's legendary penchant for perversion would, all things being equal, have immediately disqualified him as matrimonial material but for his very unequalizing tangible connection to an Alpine mountain-sized pile of cash.

While Ellie had been on vacation, and in hiding from Papal assassins, her editor Smitty had let loose with a series of articles connecting Ran to a franchise of lady-boy brothels in Thailand. "My staff made all that up about Mr. Oliphant because they were trying to compete with the *Daily Mail*, which had been running a series heavily implying Meghan Markle was in transition to be a man. That will teach you both." Ellie looked sternly at her father, who hadn't said a word. "Never believe anything you read in the general media, especially the *Juggernaut*."

"Oh…" Esmunda said dreamily. " I remember that, the *Mail* even published a picture of her, I mean his, Mike Markle's thing. I guess it was fake and turned out to be photoshopped pictures of her, or rather his, neophallus Frankenstein penis which Mike, I mean Meghan, was supposed to have had sewn onto their groin. It looked so real, I had nightmares."

They drove on in silence. Heavier flakes of snow rushed at the windshield, arcing down from the black beyond the headlights. Ellie turned on the wipers.

From the back seat, Mr. Sato looked out the side window and muttered, half to himself, "I wonder who they were, them victims back there, all stood up in the frosty road? Who was she, that poor girl?"

Chapter 07

On their drive into the City, Mrs. Sato's insistence on testing the limits of the upper band of the SUV's heat pump had turned the air from comfortable and cozy right through to hothouse soporific. By the time Ellie pressed the garage-door remote, each breath she took filled her nose with nauseating tropical humidity tinged with scents of wet leather and whatever body lotion Esmunda had rubbed on and was now exuding from her overactive pores. Ellie pressed the door remote twice more.

"It's not working." She banged it against the burnished wood dash. "D'you think it's frozen shut?"

"Look out there. All over, it's dark," Esmunda said from beneath her pile of fur. "Must be a rolling blackout. This climatic change energy apocalypse is getting really inconvenient."

"Go in and light up the generator," Ellie suggested. If she left the big gasoline vehicle in the alley, a parking violation enforcement robot would come along and send a triple-digit fine directly against her bank account, which at present couldn't withstand a single digit's worth of debiting.

"It's illegal to fire up a private generator during a blackout. Against climate regs. As a good global citizen, I just can't see abetting that kind of violence against humanity; it's genocide."

Since Esmunda was habitually possessed of every recreational drug along with matching paraphernalia for immediate enjoyment of same, Ellie was skeptical of her sudden conversion into a legally pedant conformist; she just didn't want to get out in the cold. "Ezzie, just go. You expect my folks to? After what they've been through? Out, out, out you get."

Her houseguest grudgingly got out, grumbling something about this being the last time she ever helped out on a desperate nighttime rescue mission. Luckily there was enough fuel left in the emergency generator. It could power most of the house lights, but only the servants' area's kitchen appliances worked, and the elevator was left dark. After confirming all of Esmunda's rat pack of thespians and cannabis aficionados had left Mayfair, Ellie was considering which bedroom would suit her parents when a raspy voice croaked harshly out from the dark:

"You are a very difficult woman!"

"Ah!" Ellie's dad gripped her arm as a pair of dark wings beat the air above their heads and then seemed to disappear up the dead blackness of the mansion's central circular staircase.

"Who... er, what?"

"That's just Magellan, a really wicked macaw."

"What is it saying? It won't attack us during the night, will it?"

"Don't worry, Mrs. Sato," Esmunda said. "He's harmless. He's just repeating lines from the play I've been rehearsing here, *The King and I*. It's a musical, you see. It's set in Asia with all sorts of Asian people in it. You'll love it. I'll get you tickets for the opening."

"If Magellan starts singing, out he goes." Ellie cast her voice up to where she knew the malevolent bird was lurking. "You heard me right. Straight out into the park where you can perch on the nearest icicle until your beak freezes off."

During the rest of the night, they got no more trouble from the bird or anyone else, and by morning the power was back on.

Ellie checked on her parents; they were still resting. She found Esmunda in the second-floor kitchen.

"Morn, Ezzie; what's it say on the stove?" she asked as she tried to turn on her phone, which of course she hadn't plugged in. "Every appliance has a different time."

"They go bonkers when the power cuts out. I can't really be bothered resetting them. It's just another way the government's oppressing my generation." Her phone had charge. "Virgin Mobile says it's 10:22. I guess that's accurate; I mean, do they have to pay someone for the time or is it just in the air?"

Ellie grabbed Esmunda's bathrobe. "Whatever you're smoking, just don't have any more until my parents are gone. I'm trusting you. Got to get to the office now. Give them my love."

Ellie walked out toward Grosvenor Park, sipping a coffee derived from a not-at-all-bad pot Esmunda had got the robot chef to brew. The lawns were covered by a crisp shell of snow, but there was barely any wind; the thick trench coat she'd grabbed would do until she got to work.

The *Citizen Juggernaut* was England's oldest paper by many accounts and traced its lineage back a century before the advent of the printing press, or at least that's what it said on their website. Like all print media, it had fallen on hard times, and its physical edition was basically an insert that Tesco supermarket employees (human and robotic) wedged between egg trays and milk jugs at checkout. Under Ellie's stewardship, the newsroom had moved offices more than once as their fiscal situation had become more and more precarious. The demise of thousands of UK pubs since the Great Energy Crunch had presented an opportunity of a reasonably priced lease not far from where Ellie resided.

The Iron Baron was a former drinking establishment located on Avery Row; a dusting of snow covered the horned helm of the eponymous statue of the Iron Baron, which still hung over the entrance which had, in more booming times, been the gateway to good fellowship, full pint glasses, and honest mirth. A long counter still dominated the interior décor, with a massive top supported by carved pillars. The narrow space behind the row of vintage beer taps had been claimed by Smitty, the *Juggernaut*'s managing editor, as his office.

"Where have you been hiding?" he bellowed. His bald head and bushy eyebrows poked up above the worn wood which had seen the pouring of how many million beverages? "Your policeman friend Harrigan called looking for you. Why is your phone always off?"

Normally much more cantankerous on account of his chronic back pain, Smitty's greeting struck Ellie as positively merry.

"Dare I ask why you're so cheery?"

"While you were napping, we've managed to scoop every other London daily paper: Telescam, the Snarkian, even the bloody Daily Snail as well."

Smitty slid a tablet computer down the bar; Ellie caught it before it fell. The *Juggernaut*'s home page read:

EXCLUSIVE!

HEREFORD HEADSMAN STRIKES!

Partial remains of Five Climate Activists uncovered on rural road!

Police baffled.

Locals apoplectic with fear! "I'll never leave my house until these mad killers are caught," said one resident. "I sleep with a shotgun and haven't fed *my wolfhound in a week. Let the b***tards come at me!" declared another feisty resident of cow country.*

Home Office alarmed; Parliamentarians in Westminster demand action!

The unspeakably horrendous scene of the crime was discovered by a hapless retired couple who blundered on the butchered remains in middle of night, possibly complicating the investigation. The suspicious pair, one of whom is foreign-born, was held for questioning but then released without bail. "This doubtful pair seems to be the only lead Scotland Yard has, and it wouldn't be the first time culprits have pretended to discover their own crime scene," a criminology expert told the Juggernaut. "It's quite possible they were released far too quickly by our naïve local constabulary."

Was this terrorism carried out by Islamic Jihad or the Far Right or Far Right Scientologist Jihadis? Sign up HERE for Breaking Bulletins via email, text, or neural implant.

"Your chum from Old Bill gave us the tip," Smitty said. "We were four, dash that, closer to five whole minutes ahead over every other outlet breaking the story, including those bottom feeders at iTV."

"I've got a scoop for you, Smitty," Ellie said, her annoyance making her cheeks flare with warmth. "The people you've painted as England's answer to ISIS are named Sato, and they weren't hapless or blundering. So go into the web-coding html thingy and change these patently libelous headlines before my parents see them."

Ellie only had time to briefly explain the mind-bogglingly uncommon events that had beset her normally staid and respectable family members the previous night when a ruckus came from the rear of the newsroom. The venomous shouting came from a badger's den depression in the floor, which had previously been an area reserved for competitive darts play. Her only other employees, John and Ed, were having a go at each other.

"Someone's got to pay it, or we're cut off in two hours. Less, if I have to use the scanner," John shouted.

"It's you climate fanatics who've sent this country back to the Middle Ages," returned Ed with like vehemence.

"If you'd have only listened to Al Gore and Prince Charles back in the 1980s, we'd have sorted everything. The weather is killing us... we're killing the planet... and it's-it's-it's killing us back!"

"What? The UK, with one percent of these bloody carbon emissions, CO_2? Totally harmless, by the way, and China and India and Russia and all Africa spewing out in a single day what all sixty-odd million Britons produce in a whole year? Did I mention CO_2 is what you fanatics produce every time you yell out loud about CO_2? You cucked zipperheads have lost the plot!"

Ed straightened himself up behind his flimsy deal-table desk and said, in his most sanctimonious voice, "One percent, one tenth of a percent, or one hundred and ten percent, we all must do our part. For the planet."

"Ninety percent of the planet thinks you climate loons are flat bonkers. Two hundred million Chinese people would like to eat more food each day; three hundred million children in India would like their lives not to suck because they're dirt poor. No one's on board with your self-flagellating civilizational 'See-Oh-Two' suicide cult."

"Gentlemen." Ellie saw the immediate need to exert managerial authority. "I couldn't help but notice, our small part of the world, this former publican establishment, is rather chilly. And what's that about the electric meter?"

After another brief rant over rising sea levels, John admitted the former owners had only completed part of the heat pump installation, as required by city regulations.

"So, what you paid twenty thousand quid for only pumps air, unrefined by planet-killing processes. Therefore, we get cold in winter and hot in summer," said Ed with a triumphant climate-skeptic tone.

That explained the refrigerator-like atmosphere in her newsroom. However, for Ellie, a more pressing matter was the prepaid electric meter—it needed prepaying or all their gadgets would cease operating.

"Wasn't there an excess of five hundred pounds on it a day ago?" Ellie said, aghast when she saw the remainder prepaid was an anemic and rapidly depleting £42.62.

Smitty mumbled something about "surge pricing" and "London's consumer subsidy funds running dry" and "small business always gets the shitty end of the wicket."

"Also, on account of the cold, we had to plug in space heaters," John said, unrepentantly shielding his small coils of life-preserving warmth with his broad muffler-clad torso as though she were going to snatch it away.

Oh, toss buggerfutz, Ellie thought, longing for the days when you could just throw a nice heap of coal into a cheerily blazing fire behind a cast-iron grate.

"And no use trying the phone app to pay the meter. That dodgy app's always out of service," Editor Smitty said, rolling his orthopedic chair over to where they were conferencing. His lower body was covered with possibly every blanket he owned. "Someone has to take the plug-in fob out from the meter and pop down to the Payzone office down the street. It's nearly the end of the year, and they said the new relief fund will kick in on the first of January. At commercial rates, let's see now... we should get by with about two thousand. Twenty-two hundred to be safe."

Fortunately, Smitty had put aside £2,900.00 in a contingency fund.

"That sum seems to ring a bell," Ellie said.

"Well, it is the same nominative number as, er, numerical terms would express to be, to put a fine point on it—your salary," Smitty admitted, staring at and addressing his words to the ceiling. "In point of fact, it is your salary."

After all mandatory deductions and advance proprietor's taxes payable, if she paid the power to keep Britain's oldest newspaper in business another week, she would be left with remuneration accruing to senior management in the net amount of £153.89.

Feeling the need to leave the oppressive—and increasingly costly—environment of the business she owned, only five minutes after having arrived, she volunteered to take the meter's smart key down the street and top it off before their electricity was cut. She kept warm by dodging charity muggers hungry for commission, who joyfully assaulted her with picture placards of starving Arctic nematodes that would certainly be the next endangered species destined for extinction but for her £25-per-month donation. Twenty minutes later, she returned to the *Juggernaut* having secured their crucial connection to Britain's precarious electrical grid. Her mobile rang.

It was Esmunda. "'Lo, Ellie? Uh, really sorry about this, but this is verifiably not my fault in any way—you'll agree with me when you know all there is to know about the facts surrounding—"

"What?"

"The police have just been round. They've taken your parents away. Under arrest."

Chapter 08

E llie was familiar with a few areas of the big, imposing, sensibly square building on the Embankment. A stout uniformed lady showed her into a waiting area, which opened onto a hallway and doors leading to public washrooms for both gendered and nonbinary individuals. She sat on one of the hard plastic seats, strenuously hoping the complications that had ensnared her parents wouldn't require bail money, at least not totalling more than the £42.62 in her bag.

At the end of the long hall, a door opened. The sign next to the door read Victim and Witness Services. An officer led out a distraught-looking woman with bushy brown hair tinted pink at the ends, directing her to the washrooms. As she passed, the woman's red-eyed gaze fixed on Ellie for a few seconds. Something about the woman's haunted expression made it mesmerizing, and for a few seconds she felt transfixed and unable to turn away. Just when the silent encounter became utterly uncomfortable, the bushy-haired woman's face sank down into the sodden fake fur collar of her overcoat, and she shuffled toward the loo.

What was odd about the woman? Did she recognize her from a book signing? Even so, that look was not a "You're my favorite author, after George Martin" stare, it seemed so much more intense and needy. Ellie was still pondering where she might have encountered the stranger when a disinterested-looking duty sergeant gave her a visitor's lanyard and badge.

"That'll be interview room five. Just knock."

Inside the starkly lit room, she found her parents wearing overcoats over their bathrobes. They were sitting behind a desk with built-in handcuff restraints. Fortunately the desperate criminal couple was not, for the moment, restrained in shackles. They looked quite stunned and had that terribly guilty look which only completely innocent people can achieve when they are unjustly detained by the Man.

While he had not shackled his prime suspects in the sensational multiple murder case, the inspector interviewing them looked as though he was not above applying a little physical coercion to get a full confession. Like most English coppers, he had no firearm. However, his taser and extendable steel baton were at his fingertips should the desperate Sato gang he'd nicked give him any game.

"Ah, you would be…" The glowering policeman consulted a fat ring-bound notepad and then continued in a droll and dramatic voice, the intended gravitas of which was undercut by a mild speech impediment. "The daughter. Yes, the daughter, the journawist, I bewieve. All three of you are here. Have a seat, if you pwease."

He was a ruddy-faced man whose upper lip sported the bristling ginger attempt at a moustache. He informed her that Mr. and Mrs. Sato had been taken in because a search of their internet history had turned up some disturbing evidence. "Possibwee connecting them materiawee to this very vicious crime." He inhaled with a slight nasal wheeze, possibly to underscore the gravity of his insinuations. "Under caution and having waived their right to counsel, Mr. Sato has freewee admitted 'thumbs upping' a cer-tain online post. A cer-tain post most critical of Extinction Rebellion, the widewee-known activist group."

He slid a sheaf of printouts across the desk.

"Oh my," Ellie said involuntarily.

"Ah, so you freewee admit how it appears, in the prima facie sense, huh? We're convinced these two are not being entirewee forthcoming about their chance arrival at the horrific crime scene, one featuring multiple homicides." The manner in which the policeman hissed out the final word in an unmistakably accusatory manner raised Ellie's hackles to full height, or that's how she would describe the sensation if this unpleasant episode ever found its way into one of her best-selling memoirs.

"That may well be," Ellie said, trying not to lower herself by showing her anger outright. "But what I was reacting to was the subject matter of the post, which someone may or may not have 'liked' or given a 'thumbs-up' or a smiley emoji." She read the quote of the comment. "The posting says: 'I have to take exception to anyone lighting their genitals on fire during a tennis match. This is not an appropriate way to express one's concern over the serious debate over climate change.'"

The posting was accompanied by a picture of a deranged protestor setting his groin on fire on center court during the Wimbledon final.

"So you say," the inspector said, nodding sagely while he scribbled furiously in his notebook, pausing only to stare at her visitor's pass, presumably to make certain he was spelling her name correctly for further investigation. "Perhaps we should check into your thinking as wew."

He furiously licked his thumb and flicked to find a fresh notebook page. "What are your Internet awiases? And would you consent to us making a copy of your phone's hard drive, just to ewiminate you from suspicion, of course."

Ellie's forceful retort was cut short by the sudden opening of the interview room door, which sudden opening was immediately followed by the entry of an ample stomach and a comparatively short arm, either one equally likely to have pushed open the aforementioned door. Behind the belly, and indeed its custodian and author, came an elderly chief inspector, and behind him, brimming with manly robustness, the assertive figure of Inspector Harrigan. Despite the exigency of her circumstances, Ellie noticed, for the first time, the charming dimple in his right cheek.

"Grantham, Grantham, Grantham," the senior officer drawled as he looked at their ginger-haired Inquisitor, the senior man's thin lips gyrating over teeth that were either grotesquely grown natural ones or horrendously bad-fitting dentures. "You'll excuse us, please, Grantham. Priority matter here, you see, straight from the commissioner and Home Office."

Grantham stuttered and shook his ring-bound notebook in the air. "But, sir, I was just getting though the gwaring inconsistencies in their awibis… They were about to crack."

Harrigan stepped forward, his imposing solid bulk essentially sweeping the eager inquisitor out of the room. "The only thing cracking is you, Grantham, you old prune. C'mon, then, I'm sure the duty officer has a nice shoplifting case for you."

"There's a good 'un, be a good 'un, very good man," the elderly chief inspector mumbled, and the door closed behind Grantham.

Ellie was glad for the relief, if relief it was. She and her parents were still deep inside the Met's headquarters caught in some Kafkaesque bureaucratic jumble. The Juggernaut even had a weekly feature: "Brits guilty until proven innocent—the Law's Increasing Incompetence, Ignorance, and Malfeasance. And what's with those Benny Hill uniforms anyway?"

The chief looked over Mr. and Mrs. Sato with squinty, watery eyes, as though they were potato salad when he was certain he had ordered the shrimp. "They seem quite, uh, how would one phrase it? Actually, one in my position would not phrase it, anyway, anyhow. Well, now, Mr. and Mrs. Sato, you were on the scene. Yes, yes, yes. Uh, Harrigan, what do you say?"

"The GPS data recovered from their Reliant verifies every word of their story. There is no evidence they didn't come upon the scene quite by chance. In fact, it's beyond a doubt they did just that."

"Then my apologies for your inconvenience," the chief said, condescendingly addressing the erroneous side dishes of innocuous non-suspects he'd been served. Ellie's parents just stared, possibly not following the quick turn of events. "I say, Harrigan, do they speak English?"

Moments later, the handsome young man shouldered the doorway open, and Ellie, along with her parents, walked out of the interrogation chamber to inhale the air of freedom and stale coffee. She read Harrigan's business card.

"I recall now. You said at the scene you're City Police, didn't you?" Ellie made a popping sound with her cheeks and lips, her signature sound, which she made when nervous and with which she had been annoying people since primary school. "That's different than the Met, right?"

"And you call yourself Britain's leading investigative reporter?" Harrigan offered, with light sarcasm and heavy charm.

"That's just something my editor made up to impress people who can afford £39.95 for hardbound deluxe editions of my books," Ellie said, blushing in the full glow of Harrigan's gaze and hoping it came off as winter cheek flushing.

As he led them out from the labyrinthine building, their liberator explained that the City Police were an entirely separate and smaller force.

"We only have jurisdiction, officially, in the square mile of the City of London. City Police has about nine hundred officers compared to the thirty thousand the Met boasts, and the Square Mile has only eight thousand permanent residents, but as it's the center of the country's financial business, on weekdays half a million people commute to work there."

"That must keep you on your toes," Ellie said with a spontaneous giggle that made her feel even more like a muppet than her daft reply.

"We're never bored." He held the final door open, and they were greeted by a damp, icy wind and speckles of sleet. "Libertas reddita," Harrigan said with a flourish.

Just then, a medium-sized harried figure brushed past them, nearly knocking over Mrs. Sato and flatly hustling into Ellie. She recovered her balance and heard a muttering that sounded like an apology, then the indistinct figure hunched down, tucked her bushy hair underneath a flipped-up coat collar, and was gone. Despite the mysterious figure being clearly at fault for the bipedal collision, Mrs. Sato felt the need to apologize on behalf of her daughter.

"She's usually not that clumsy," Ellie's mother said while beaming at Inspector Harrigan as she breathlessly added, "She's normally quite graceful. Six years of dancing before she decided to concentrate on academics, become a world-famous author, and become sole proprietor of Britain's oldest newspaper. And with all that, you'd think she'd be snooty, right? Not so! Not a bit. Very approachable, our Eleanor, or Ellie, as she for some reason prefers, or even Elle which sounds a bit French for our taste, but—"

"Thanks, Mum. I think the inspector has some murders to solve." She turned to the bemused-looking policeman. "Thank you ever so much for clearing that up in there."

"Was nothing. Grantham's not a bad old stick, but he's of the school that thinks forcing a confession out of the first bystander is the quickest way to close a case."

Mr. Sato politely pointed out their Reliant was still in impound.

"Just call my secretary. She'll get the paperwork ready. The car's not involved in the crime; that's fundamentally plain."

Ellie absently wondered what angle the Juggernaut should take on what would clearly be a major story for weeks, an angle that didn't name her parents as the prime suspects who had narrowly escaped justice due to Met incompetence. "Don't worry about us. Now I've got my folks back for a second time in twenty-four hours, I'm determined not to let them out of my sight."

"Take care, ladies, sir." The inspector gave them a warm nod and went back inside. Ellie reached for her wallet to make certain she had enough money to pay a cab and instead found a bit of torn paper; it definitely did not belong to her and hadn't been there when she put on her coat because it was where she had warmed her gloveless hands while walking. She unfolded it; wet snow dropped on it, making splotches on the hurriedly handwritten note. She stood, rigidly hunched over, and read it again and took a hurried glance at her watch.

She spun on her heels and, turning back to her beleaguered parents, said, "Oh look, there's a cab, here's some cash. You go on, I'll meet you back at the house when I can." She dashed away.

Chapter 09

Confidential sources often got cold feet, so all world-class journalists know they have to get a move on and be prepared to meet them whenever and wherever. She looked back and made sure her parents were getting into their cab. They were indeed entering the conveyance, Mr. Sato with a look of mild bemusement on his kind, sanguine features and Mrs. Sato with pursed lips and the raised eyebrow of disapproval. Whether her mother's angst was spurred by her dashing off, or more likely, Ellie not insisting Inspector Harrigan meet her that very afternoon at the English Rose Café and Tea to discuss the case and whether he was seriously romantically involved, heterosexual, or at least bisexual, was not clear, though she felt certain she'd soon enough hear volumes on the latter topic.

Guarding it from further despoiling by the ubiquitous damp and droplets of half-melted snow, she once more read the note which had mysteriously appeared in her pocket.

"Postman's Park, noon, you alone, you are the only one who can—" the next word or two were smeared beyond recognition.

The weather was becoming increasingly foul, but Westminster Station wasn't far, and the underground was the safest way to get to the appointed location on the other side of St. Paul's in time. Postman's Park was not impressive even in spring and summer; in December, with a looming dull gray mist above the city, not a leaf on the few lonesome trees, and melting snow clinging to the facades of the surrounding townhomes, Ellie felt the urban park was downright dismal.

Another heavy wet flake fell on her eyelash, making her wish she'd brought an umbrella. Then again, she didn't want to be one of those odd people sloshing along the street with mounds of snow sliding down the sides of their black brollies. She made for a small structure with a slanted roof. A sign read:

The material prosperity of a nation is not an abiding possession:

The deeds of its people are.

G.F. Watts's Memorial to Heroic Self-Sacrifice

With a shiver that turned into a clarifying catlike shake, Ellie shook off as much freezing wet as she could. The place was still. There was the drip of water, the slurping disgorging of a drain somewhere, and over it all the steady static hum of metro London traffic.

The woman was standing so still Ellie hardly noticed her initially, her mind perhaps registering the shape as a statue, until they were only a few feet apart and she moved.

Ellie gasped, and the figure's head swung toward her. Twin realizations struck Ellie: this was the woman from the police station, the one with bushy hair and rumpled coat. Of course. Who else could have slipped the note into her pocket? Secondly, now that she saw her face straight on, a chilling resemblance of her features, especially around the eyes, stunned her to silence.

A nearby bell tower chimed the hour, and the stranger approached.

"You've come," the middle-aged lady said with resignation, which seemed tempered with a note of solemn resolve. "I know the police will do nothing. You must help me, Ms. Sato, help me find out who killed my Miriam."

Miriam. That must be her name. For an instant, all Ellie could think about was the picture of the girl's face, the face of the victim of the Hereford massacre. The woman went on speaking, but Ellie didn't catch a word. Not wanting to admit she'd zoned out, she disguised her lapse of concentration by pulling out her Moleskine notebook and trusty fountain pen.

"Could you say that again? I'd like to be certain of getting it all down correctly."

The woman, whose name was Mrs. Goldsmid, blinked back tears that were welling in her eyes and told her story in short, intense bursts interspersed with long pauses. Her daughter, Miriam, had been a top student at the London School of Economics, and after college had got an accounting accreditation. She had also become heavily involved with a series of student ecology and climate groups. To her mother, each activist organization seemed more radical than the previous.

"She was always an intense sort of girl, never halfsies in anything. But she weren't no lawbreaker. You'd never see her befouling a painting in a museum or hangin' upside down from the Tower Bridge givin' honest workin' folks heart attacks. No, not 'er. My ex-husband nearly hit the roof when she decided to change her name, but what was there to do? She's an adult. At some point... y'just have ter let them be who they are."

Three years previous, Miriam Goldsmid, Chartered Management Accountant and avid climate protestor, legally changed her name to Green Hope. As Mrs. Goldsmid said this, she paused for a brief awkward moment. Was she watching Ellie's face to detect whether she thought this small eccentricity of her late daughter was ridiculous?

"I'm so sorry for your loss," Ellie said. "She was clearly a brilliant, hardworking woman whose innocent life was cut brutally short by a foul crime. Do the police have any leads?"

"This is why I wrote that note," Mrs. Goldsmid said, speaking most sharply. "I saw you in the lobby, recognized you from your GB News interviews. Then I recalled my aunt in Israel sent me your book on the Ninety-Six Hour War. She said your account was the only one even close to what she experienced in Jerusalem. I knew I had to take a chance, so I wrote the note and pretended to bump into you at the doorway. From what the police asked me, they have some tomfool notions about neofascists or Islamic terrorists, which means they haven't got a clue. I haven't the money to hire a detective, but I could pay some of your expenses, if only you'll look into it with your connections, the way you've uncovered those other international scandals."

Ellie felt the unexpected burden of the grieving woman's faith come down on her shoulders like a physical weight. She immediately felt a fraud. Should she decline and admit her past exploits had merely arisen from chance placing her in the middle of wars and intrigues? Should she confess that any reportage she'd managed to scrabble together came out of the same source that let her escape those deadly situations with her life: dumb luck?

But if she did, what might this lady do in her desperation? There was a full brace of charlatan private investigators afoot in the country, preying on people let down by a criminal justice system in tatters. On the other hand, was it right to give false hope? What could she do that the whole British police force could not accomplish in pursuing the largest investigation undertaken for many years? She might even end up interfering with official inquiries. There was only one prudent, responsible choice: politely as possible, she had to decline.

"Mrs. Goldsmid... I really..."

The haggard figure of the bereaved woman, soaked in melted snow and shivering, seemed to waver then stiffen as though bracing herself for another cruel disappointment.

Then Ellie thought of something: of all the roads her parents could have been on that night, what were the chances they'd be first on the crime scene? And the likelihood they'd be taken in on nonsense charges just when Mrs. Goldsmid was at Scotland Yard? Could it be some convolution of fate had brought them together? Besides, due to drastic cutbacks of police budgets, barely half the murders in the UK were solved last year. Miriam, Green Hope, deserved justice, and whatever was in her power to do, Ellie resolved right there and then to strive to obtain it.

"I'll... really, really try."

That's all she had to say to cause Mrs. Goldsmid to move with surprising quickness, for a portly middle-aged lady, and embrace her. Ellie was not a hugger but was carried over in the emotion of the moment and gave the woman's damp fuzzy jacket a few pats until she left off.

"I knew you had a kind face. You're Oriental, right?"

"Eurasian. Japanese on my father's side."

Mrs. Goldsmid then burst forth with various details all jumbled together that she thought might be relevant and spur a quick resolution to the heinous crime. Having only the *Juggernaut*'s jumbled account of the official version of the crime in her mind, which was quite possibly worse than having no information at all, Ellie was hard-pressed to sort out from the plethora of details the ones that might prove useful.

"You say she worked at Kore Energy? That was where..." Ellie got fresh chills just thinking about the fiendish minds—it had to be more than one person, didn't it?—that had arranged the macabre crime scene.

Her companion's stout body became rigid, and her lip trembled. "Where she… Where it happened? Oh! Who would do such a thing to my poor baby girl!" she said with great bitterness and started sobbing once more.

On parting, Ellie insisted they use hand-delivered letters to communicate, the recent incident with her billionaire stalker Ran Oliphant having put her on guard as to how easily electronic communications could be intercepted. All that would make Ellie's week perfect would be for that overbearing prig Inspector Ginger Grantham to haul her in for obstructing his official investigation, which seemed primarily disposed toward collecting social media posts in order to incriminate her parents rather than the much more taxing direction of gathering relevant evidence in the real world.

When she opened the swinging doors into the *Juggernaut* newsroom, the blast of warm air that hit her made her think of pound notes blazing away on a bonfire. A comparison, given the ruinous electricity tariffs that were making the people of Great Britain "Great Depression" broke again, was not altogether inapt.

"Smitty! Who turned up the portable heaters? Aren't we limited by law to five degrees Celsius or thirty-nine Fahrenheit? It must be near double that."

Her editor waved a pink form. "Got a health exemption. The cold makes my back muscles seize up something awful. If you try to lower the thermostat, I've every right to drag you in to an Employment Tribunal for hazardous working conditions and possibly forced labor via duress and torment under the Modern Slavery Act."

She put aside thoughts of witty rejoinders to Smitty's threats of prosecution, which were only half serious even when he was being most grieved by his lumbago condition. She banished dread of impending bankruptcy—she had to rally her team to her new cause.

"Everyone, gather round! Shift all the daily pages over to content generated by AI wire services and freelancers, by which I mean lancers who work for free. I've got an inside lead on the crime of the decade. From now on, we're working exclusively on one story."

Chapter 10

"**B**ut... but... but," Smitty sputtered in exasperation, which, sputtering as a direct consequence of his reclining position in his mobile orthopedic chair, sent little spittle flecks straight up at the newsroom ceiling. They hung in the air a moment, and he tried to wheel out from their descending path, never leaving off objecting to Ellie's executive decisions. "But 'Hereford Headsman' sells papers. Everyone's taken up the term—which I coined, by the way."

"Those were actual people who were dismembered," Ellie chastised her lumbar-challenged editor, thinking only of the distraught look on Mrs. Goldsmid's face, so blotched by her tears and melted snow. "It's disrespectful. I don't care what they do at the Telescam or the Daily Snail, at the *Juggernaut*, they're to be collectively referred to as the 'Hereford Five,' and that's final. As for getting punters to click, and the few subscribers we have to renew, everyone knows it's celeb tits and ass that sell. By the way," she said, tapping her finger on the master layout computer screen, "Duchess Giselle Fontenbra's boobs are nowhere near big enough in that picture. When I come back, I want to see those tanned sweaty globes proudly dominating our Life and Arts feature page."

Only two days had passed since the grisly discovery outside the Kore Energy property. However, being in the news business meant finding innovative ways to accommodate the public's ever-shrinking attention span. If one only went by the raw sewage of fake news and blatant propaganda that spilled through the wire service news feeds, it would have seemed two months had passed. The initial public shock and horror at the mass murder had been knocked clean off the front pages of all the daily papers by fuel riots in Belfast and a government thermostat rigging scandal in England.

While the public was freezing under maximum temperature mandates suitable for a walk-in freezer, it was revealed that the nabobs of Westminster and Whitehall had rigged their heat pump displays to show 5°C/39°F while the system was actually putting out a tropical 26°C/78°F.

After two reasonably restful days at Mayfair, her parents had taken the train back home. She was ever grateful they hadn't, on that fateful evening, been physically injured by an accident or come upon the scene earlier than they had. What would the villains have done had they been surprised by a middle-aged and defenseless couple in the middle of nowhere? The thought made her shudder.

She'd promised her mum and dad she'd look after their impounded car. According to a text from the enigmatic Inspector Harrigan, the Met no longer required the Reliant for their investigation. However, when she got to the impound lot, she found the electric conveyance's batteries utterly out of charge.

"But you must have some sort of cables here," she said to the sullen-looking lady sitting behind the security glass. "I could pay, of course."

"Nothing like that going on here. Drive er tow, tha's how't goes here," the bundled-up official replied, causing small puffs of steam to escape her barely moving lips. "An' 'undred fer the flatbed bring in. 'Undred surcharge, tha' is. Won't tow regular, these eee-lectric Reliants."

"It's only got three wheels," Ellie complained, "and I'm supposed to pay extra so none of them touch pavement?"

The reigning nabob of the impound yard shrugged, huffed steam, and checked the clock on her desk.

"Tow, then," she said with resignation. Had they been closer to Mayfair, Ellie might have been tempted to try pushing the toylike conveyance.

After the two-mile journey through London's clogged streets and byways in the overheated sickly fake-pine-tree-smelling cab of the tow truck, she was handed a tablet with the invoice.

"Three hundred?"

"And tax and enviro charge and ULEZ-Ultra waiver fee. This here ol' flatbed conveyance being required to be a diesel, miss, on account o' it actually hauls stuff."

She was forced to text, of all people, Esmunda to bring out the emergency household funds from her desk, and to cap it off, they had to push the Reliant into the garage, as the operator refused to venture onto private property.

"Liability rules, y'understand." At least he left off with a cheery, "'Ave yourselfs a better one tomorrow, eh!"

By the time they rolled the garage door shut on the frost-covered alleyway, Ellie was both flushed and sweating as well as frozen to the core. Esmunda seemed in a chipper mood. In fact, she was positively glowing, and something about her was different…

"You've cut your hair," Ellie panted, sitting down finally and rubbing feeling back into her frozen hands. "It's short and darker." The style was oddly similar to her own.

"You noticed," Esmunda chirped cheerfully, which was unusual for her after being pressed into any sort of useful activity. "I've decided to turn over a new leaf, y'know. Make a new chapter and… I felt I needed a role model, and since you've been so kind to me, ever since I interned at the *Juggernaut* and you let me stay here and room with you even though the newspaper business wasn't suited to all I've got to offer, I decided there's no better exemplary example for my brilliant future success than *you!*"

"I'm, er, flattered," Ellie mumbled, hoping that wouldn't oblige her to share whatever cold-water flat she'd be renting when they had to leave the Mayfair house with the endearing Spice-smoking layabout. Of course, that was weeks off, and who planned that far ahead? They had immediate problems to solve. "Have you any idea how to put electrons into the spot where this car needs them?"

Esmunda was surprisingly technically inclined when she put her mind to it. Perhaps that was the way of her generation. Ellie was only ten years her senior, but her conservative upbringing and time studying in Japan seemed to add a century between her sensibilities and those of the average British twentysomething.

"Here it is!" Esmunda explained. "Under the front bonnet. But it looks like a proprietary plug. That way they make you buy an adapter or you're limited to charging up at their branded kiosks, which limits you to the Shetland Islands. Lemme think… There's probably something in the kitch I can use." She ran off.

"Don't electrocute yourself," Ellie called up the stairs after her and leaned on the car, which had started dripping melting snow as soon as it was brought in from the cold. "Or worse, bugger my parents' car. They've had shocks enough to last them an age, and Dad claims this model is nearly vintage or some sort of collector's item that might one day appreciate in value."

There had to be some redeeming feature to the awkward conveyance, she mused. The butt-ugly bug-eyed hulk looked like something not entirely out of place among a pile of rubbish left behind by gypsies who had decided to move their caravans down the road.

Esmunda returned with an expensive-looking carving fork to which she attached charging cables and then proceeded to jam into the Reliant's socket. As she did so, a mound of gray slush fell from the front wheel well onto her shoe.

"Bugger all!" She kicked it away, then leaned down. She grabbed and held out a bit of metallic rubbish.

"We agreed you'd charge the battery, not disassemble the car. I hope that's not an essential part," Ellie said, wondering why plug-in cars had to be so much more perplexing to operate than cellular phones. "After that towing expense, I can't afford a mechanic or an electrician."

"Naw, look, it's a little Gaia medallion." Esmunda looked at it closely. "The top looks odd. I wonder... I think I've seen this somewhere."

Ellie stopped and stared. She, too, had seen that design featuring two crescent moons on either side of a figure with arms circled above its head. It had to be part of the pair.

"I... know where... it must have dropped from Miss Goldsmid's, I mean Green Hope's ear. It's part of an earring." This bit of jewelry had been dislodged from the ear of the poor girl's frozen severed head.

Chapter 11

"How did that get there?" Esmunda looked closely at the piece of jewelry. "Let's see if it really is the same one as in the picture your mum accidentally snapped. Where's your phone?"

Ellie gave her handset over, and her roommate brought up the macabre screenshot, then zoomed in on the victim's right ear. "That side's missing... though not altogether."

There was indeed, Ellie could see, a portion of metal left in Green Hope's earlobe. What she held in her hand was the bottom part, which had somehow come off the shepherd hook that remained in the piercing hole.

"Why would it break off?" Ellie wondered aloud, suddenly feeling uneasy about having any portion of the murdered woman's property, however small. Was it evidence? Should she turn it in to Inspector Harrigan?

"Maybe it didn't break; let me try something," Esmunda said and pressed the end of the trinket onto the trim of the Reliant's bumper. It stuck. "There, it's a magnetic breakaway join."

During the commotion surrounding her parents' arrival at the crime scene, or even possibly prior, the detachable end of the Gaia earring had come away and at some point been lodged in the wheel well of the Reliant. Since the vehicle had been parked outside in the impound lot, a layer of snow had kept the fragment in place, only melting here in the warmer atmosphere of the garage.

"But why would anyone want to wear a piece of jewelry like that?" Ellie asked. "If you took off this bauble, you'd still have the hook in your ear. Why not just take the whole thing out?"

Esmunda was paying her no mind and studiously examining the bottom of the Gaia charm. "There's holes on the bottom. Umm, that's a nano USB that is."

"You mean like a computer plug thingy? Do they make electronics that tiny?" The possibilities made Ellie somewhat dizzy. "Would it have recorded anything, like sounds of the crime?"

"That's not what it is. It's like a very tiny hard drive for storing data. This girl would have wanted to be able to plug it into a computer and then quickly disguise it back into an earring when she was done copying data onto it. This could be evidence, and Old Bill don't have a clue it exists. But you're not keeping it?" she said with a souring expression reserved for people who had just revealed themselves as an embodiment of the distinct opposite of fun.

Ellie told Esmunda about her meeting with Mrs. Goldsmid.

"Ohhh, I knew it!" Esmunda squealed, brightening, as she cleaned off the bottom of the tiny data device with a makeup remover pad. "We'll be like Miss Marple sleuthing sisters, except we shall crack mysteries while being really hot, fashionable, and not even a shade of dried-up old biddy."

"I don't know how far we should go along that particular avenue." When Esmunda became enthused, Ellie's natural caution flared up like prickly heat.

"Oh, don't be a dry old biddy. It can't hurt just to have a wee peek at what's on it. I mean, we're just looking, right? Oy! What's that smell? D'ya smell that? It's like… it's…"

Ellie had been so distracted by the completely unexpected and somewhat macabre discovery that she hadn't noticed it till then. A thin trail of acrid smoke curled up from the make-do car-charging adapter Esmunda had fashioned from a carving fork. She jumped as the other woman yanked the cord out of the Reliant, causing a flurry of sparks to spray all over the garage's dark interior.

"Ezzie!"

"S'all right, s'all right, uh, it should have enough charge to get to a service station," she said with her usual hapless, and entirely unreassuring, enthusiasm when smoothing over near-fatal disasters.

After poking around a vast but also vastly stuffed dimly lit garage, making certain nothing else was likely to catch fire, she prodded Esmunda upstairs, excited and somewhat puzzled over their discovery. She was familiar with powerful miniature magnets that were sometimes used to secure bracelets and necklaces.

"But are you sure this is a data device?" she asked as they climbed the stairs. "Wouldn't a magnet interfere with it? I once had to give away a perfectly good Louis Vuitton wallet because the clasp kept erasing the stripe on my bank cards."

Esmunda assured her modern SSDs, whatever those were, were nearly impervious to magnetic fields. Under a clutter of astrology charts, tarot cards, and bong-smoking paraphernalia, her houseguest found the extension cord she needed, and they were soon looking at the data contents written on the secret earring storage device: reams of utterly boring figures.

"Spreadsheets and relational databases," Esmunda said. "They seem all mashed together as though they were copied in a hurry from different sources. Without that girl's help, you might never make sense of it. Was that really her name? Green Hope?"

"Her birth name was Miriam," Ellie said absently, thinking about what else Mrs. Goldsmid had told her. "See if there's anything about Kore Energy—that's the company she worked for."

"Kore? Let's check them out." Esmunda opened another browser window next to the perplexing jumble of figures. "Right... Largest company in Europe by market capitalization, twelve thousand employees... worldwide operations developing unlimited clean energy from ultra-deep geothermal drilling. Two fully operating pilot plants, one in Ethiopia and one in Hawaii currently producing scads of megawatts and gigawatts."

Had Green Hope stumbled onto some embezzlement or insider trading scheme? Even if it were motive for murder, what could the other four victims have had to do with it? And how did the partial remains come to be placed on display right outside the company's headquarters?

Esmunda looked up, and Ellie followed her gaze up to the top of a cupboard. At first there seemed nothing there, just a shadow, then one malevolent speck glinted over a wickedly curved beak; the pernicious macaw Magellan was glaring at them with one sinister black eye.

"We should just turn it in, right, to the authorities?"

"You want to do that? After they tried to railroad your parents? You didn't see how they jackbooted their way in here and took them off like they were terrorists or somethin'."

Yes, there was that, Ellie thought. If only there were someone she could confide in, someone who wasn't a chronically unemployed actress. Two alternatives came to mind: the familiar, sometimes comforting, sometimes uptight and starchy Ran

Oliphant, and the somewhat younger and intriguingly mysterious Inspector Harrigan of the City Police. On the one hand, she had known the ex-soldier and businessman for years. He'd proven very trustworthy, but he had always seemed enigmatically distant.

Harrigan, on the other hand, practically oozed warmth and solicitude, though that could be a skill they taught senior officers to employ when dealing with members of the public in harrowing situations.

Before she could mull the knotty issue through, her mobile rang.

Unknown number. If it was a bill collector, they would have to get in the queue.

Ran Oliphant's face, looking uncommonly morally upright, appeared in the video call window.

"Ellie, stop poking around in Kore Energy business." The rather shockingly intrusive demand was made by the aforementioned billionaire without the benefit of preamble. "I don't know how you get muddled up in these matters, but I assure you, this is not something you want to pursue." He sounded extraordinarily emotionally uptight and starchy.

"Hi, Ran, I was just thinking about you and what to get you for your birthday. Perhaps a set of manners to go with your OBE. Why weren't you stalking me so enthusiastically when my parents were arrested and hauled out from Mayfair? Right, right, thanks for asking. They're fine, I'm fine. As a family of habitual criminals, we're used to being pinched, cross-questioned about our social media posts, and we know how to keep our pie holes shut when being given the rubber hose treatment by the Man."

The dead silence that followed made her grin—a sharp dose of sarcasm always stopped that man in his tracks. "And how could you possibly know about my interest in the Kore company? It's been less than five minutes since I learned anything about them."

"That's my business. I mean, never mind that. No, that didn't sound the way I meant... I'm only looking out for you."

"As you may have noticed during our spelunking adventure in the Paris Catacombs, I can look out for myself when I'm not called upon to keep others, including you, from extreme peril." Ellie looked around as though she could spot a hidden camera. "If you've bugged my home..."

Ellie scanned the light fixtures and ventilation shafts of the room where she was seated. They all looked innocent enough, but what did she know about sophisticated spying devices?

"I haven't bugged anything. It's you who's intruding." Then, perhaps realizing how dumb he sounded, he quickly added: "This much I'll tell you: I've a meeting with Dr. Kore this very evening. I don't want him canceling it because your amateur sleuthing buggers delicate negotiations that have been weeks in the making. There are larger stakes at play than you realize."

Ellie felt her ears become quite warm, and not just from brain-frying 5G cellular signals emanating from her phone. She was at the point of getting bitterly angry and sounding off as to what stakes could be larger than justice for the murdered Green Hope and the other activist victims, when a thought occurred to her.

"So... you have an important meeting that would very much be buggered up if I called up Kore Energy's press agents and publicists right now, pestering them for an immediate interview with Dr. Kore to deny details of a very salacious, and highly embarrassing, front-page story on his company set for release in tomorrow's *Juggernaut?*"

"Balderdash. You have no such story."

"Give my guys a pitcher of beer and twenty minutes, and you won't believe the nearly libelous, muck-raking fecal matter we can make up on the fly. We're journalists, you know."

Silence and manly heavy breathing.

"Well, then it's settled," she continued. "I'll be joining you for that meeting. Otherwise, I might be busy doing something that inadvertently causes a panic and gets it canceled."

"Heh, fat chance of you attending," Ran said with some relief. "We're meeting at the only place Kore feels he can speak candidly: my club, White's. No girls allowed, I'm afraid."

Did they actually still have such places? "Are you taking a mickey? When dodgy, pervy trans women with a rudely throbbing plonker can legally insist on going to the loo with six-year-old schoolgirls? You exclude natural-born girls from your posh boys' club?"

"We don't call it fair, we call it the last bastion of English manfulness."

"What if I identify as—"

"Nope, nope. You have to have, er, a, y'know, the dongle." The way he whispered *dongle* was ever so endearing. In their previous conversations during their adventuring, when, solely for medical purposes, genitalia had come up, Ran always looked genuinely uncomfortable. Perhaps it was as a result of having gone from a boys-only boarding school straight into the Royal Marines that, when dealing with girls in their capacity as girls rather than adventuring buddies, he became unfailingly shy and awkward. She had to tease him further.

80

"Actually, surgeons are doing wonders with neo-dongles. What about…"

"They have to, um, fulfill the function of… it."

The redder Ran's face got, the more she felt the need to press on the attack.

"Recently, the *Juggernaut* published a story on this Swiss surgeon and robot prosthesis expert who's managed to implant dongles, which many dongle experts couldn't even distinguish from the naturally grown dongle."

"Ellie, enough. It states quite clearly that to be a member or guest at White's, you have to have had a… *member*, which works, from birth!"

Ellie noticed Magellan land indelicately on Esmunda's bed, then he used his sharp, curved beak to pick apart fake jewels glued to her theatrical top hat, which she used in her drama plays and musicals. Her stage equipment and costumes were strewn haphazardly all through the house.

"One of these days, Ran, you'll come up with a real dilemma that a media mogul and celebrated author can't vanquish in less time than it takes to pose said entirely made-up chimeric dilemma. White's Club won't be a problem. When should I be ready?"

Chapter 12

The appointment with Ran Oliphant and his fellow energy tycoon Dr. Kore was set for eight p.m. at White's Private Members Club at St. James, a fuddy-duddy boys-only social club. She had to trust Esmunda to gather the items necessary to make that outing a success because in the meantime, Ellie had to dash off on an urgent errand—she had received a note from Mrs. Goldsmid, which needed immediate action. It read:

Fiver Rebel (that's the only name I know for him, sorry) at Dancing Hare Ecovillage (I haven't a proper address, sorry), ex-boyfriend, hates all members of what he calls: nazi government oppressors. Only one I know of for certain. Your kind help is my only lifeline, Bless You, Eleanor Sato!

This was in reply to Ellie's own note asking Green Hope's mother if she knew any of her daughter's close friends, especially ones not known to the police.

"Esmunda, you're certain of having everything sorted by six at the latest, are you? I don't want to make a fool out of myself." *Any more than I absolutely have to*, she added in silent postscript, trying to hide her own sense of impending multiple-front failures by harassing a subordinate. She felt heavily burdened by Mrs. Goldsmid's completely unfounded faith in her abilities.

"Trust me," Esmunda said. "I minored in theatrics at college, mostly 'cause there were extra stipends from the government for taking anything listed in the anti-Colonialism curriculum. But it's really working out now that I can use my very special skills to help you. Y'know, you've been such a role model to me. You've been such a great friend, nicer than most of me family, really, letting me stay in this huge magnificent place while I get myself back on track. I wanted to... Er, but I see you're busy, huh?"

Ellie could tell her housemate was bursting to confide something to her. In addition to emulating Ellie's hairstyle, the younger lady had borrowed her bathrobe and beauty products. Hopefully, Esmunda's secret wasn't some variety of a lesbian crush.

"I've got to see if I can find this Extinction Rebellion fellow. If you're still up by the time I get back from White's, we'll have tea and a chat."

Dancing Hare Ecovillage was located on the outskirts of a council rubbish heap thirty minutes by cab from Mayfair. This fellow, who called himself Fiver, presumably after the clairvoyant bunny in *Watership Down*, lived off the grid. She guessed it would take the authorities a few more days to track him down, and she had to find him first before he lawyered up, clammed up, or bolted. Ellie used the drive time to reflect on the very minuscule chance that she could accomplish something the proper coppers could not.

Scotland Yard had set up a special task force dedicated to solving the mass killing, and at the bottom of the press release, she had noticed Harrigan's name as City Police liaison. There might be a time to reconnect with the charming inspector, but first she wanted to get as much information as she could on her own.

Snow-capped lampposts slid past her fogged-up cab window. Everything she was able to learn from public records, social media, and a folder of personal documents from Mrs. Goldsmid, all of it indicated Green Hope had possessed an exemplary civic spirit, a stellar academic record, and had no known enemies.

"Ah... ma'am, this the place?" the cabbie said as he turned sideways, one large bloodshot eye distending out like one that would not be out of place on the head of a flounder. "It's a rubbish tip."

"Best place for a quiet walk. Actually found all my drawing room knickknacks in city dumps. Shocking what people throw out, simply shocking. Could you go along a bit? There should be an entrance to a sort of commune."

The driver chortled to himself as he let the vehicle creep along. "Mayfair to a squat, n'er seen 'at before."

"Well," Ellie said, looking around at the deserted, unlit area and wondering whether she should ask the man to wait until she was inside the chain-link fence, which was topped by rusted razor wire dotted with the remains of decomposing plastic bags. "At least it's a gated community, right?"

The man looked back at her as though she was off her head and about to run off without paying the fare. She astonished him by paying with a hefty tip, which meant her return journey would include walking to the nearest Tube station, but after that idiotic episode with her parents at Scotland Yard, she refused to countenance losing even a sliver of face. Ellie stepped out onto slush-covered gravel that churned up as the cab drove off. A sign by the commune gate had half fallen off its support posts. She turned her head sideways to read:

Visitors Welcome

EXCEPT: Cops, Tories, and fascists

To which someone had added in fading black Sharpie lettering: + *Russian spies!*

"Hello?"

There was no buzzer to press, so after aiming a second brief verbal salutation in the direction of an ice-covered assembly of sunflower plants that had dropped their petals off their blackened bulbous heads and which blackened bulbous heads were pressed onto the chain-link fence, Ellie pushed the gate open as far as it would stretch against the negligently tied rope holding it not completely closed. She walked in.

The grounds were filled with snow-covered protrusions, the unmistakable signs of abandoned gardens: dangling trellises supporting withered vines and an enormous moldy pumpkin that nearly captured her boot when her foot slid against and partially through its outer husk. The only sound was the hushed roar of an elevated motorway and the squeaking of a rusty wind turbine, which had given up trying to generate electricity but soldiered on, serving as the community's weathervane. A puff of smoke and the faint smell of cooking gave her a clue as to the location most likely to harbor residents wintering over in the commune.

Deep ruts in the twisting path forced her to keep to one side; unfortunately, it was the side where heaps of rotting vegetable matter had frozen in place yet was squashy enough if stepped upon. As soon as she was able, Ellie took a side path along a line of rusting appliances. The retired washers and dryers ran past an alcove that contained an outdoor showering station; by the scorch marks covering the bottom of the boiler, there was no doubt the contraption functioned by burning wood fuel. A faded sign read:

Taking A Shower:

Please do not burn painted wood. If wind is FROM the WEST, wait until it shifts in order to be KIND to our NEIGHBOURS. This stall is

GENDER NEUTRAL—save water, shower with a buddy!

P.S. No one needs to bathe every day.

P.P.S. Many colonial BIPOC oppressed individuals have never had the privilege of showering! Honestly evaluate your hygiene habits for implicit cultural Imperial bias, residual privileged patriarchy patterns, and ESPECIALLY White Fascist Supremacy.

Beside the shower installation there slumped a broken toilet with a plastic food-scraps bin jammed into the bowl. A sign above this said *Hraka Station BYOB bring your own baggie.* Ellie's growing sense of sanitary horror was sharply interrupted by an angry-sounding howl followed by a series of deep-throated barks.

"Who is that? I have a dog!" shouted a hoarse voice from the direction of the smoke plume.

"Uh, sorry to intrude," Ellie said in the direction of the voice. While the barking continued, the human speaker remained hidden. A few moments later, it became obvious that the "dog's" barking kept repeating every few seconds in exactly the same cadence and timbre. "I'm not on the list of banned persons, you know, the list at the gate. I'm with the *Citizen Juggernaut,* Britain's oldest continually published paper. And we are most liberal and ecological minded. We were also the very first London daily to come out against slavery and smog. May I come closer?"

The not-very-convincing guard dog noise abruptly ceased mid-bark, and a youngish fellow with a thin face and a straggly man bun carefully approached down the path. He was wearing a hugely thick sweater, which made his skinny and quite naked legs look even more preposterous, as he tromped forward with his feet shod in loosely tied desert camouflage combat boots. His ferret-like eyes darted left and right. As soon as he satisfied himself the unannounced visitor to the commune was alone, he quickly hid the rusty golf club he was holding behind his back.

"Are you the proprietor or head comrade of this spacious and extraordinary commune? I'm wondering if you know Fiver Rebel?"

It turned out the nervous twentysomething was the only inhabitant of Dancing Hare Ecovillage. He had decided to tough it out during a profoundly chilly winter, and his appellation in the Extinction Rebellion community was Fiver.

He invited Ellie into his dwelling, which was a two-story affair cobbled together out of plywood and sheets of metal and plastic. The whole affair seemed like a poorly planned architectural fusion of a garden shed with a Mongolian yurt hut. The interior was only a few feet square of canvas-covered floor space and felt as hot and humid as any sauna due to the unfortunate combination of a leaky roof and a blazing fire in the wood-burning stove.

"Please excuse the mess, heh, I wasn't expecting company," Fiver said, taking another cautious glance out the door as she shut it nearly closed on creaking hinges.

"But perhaps you were wary of unwanted visitors? Of the constabulary variety?" Ellie used her most empathetic tone, which was not difficult after her experience with the Met police.

"Well, uh…"

"My paper has been covering the killings of the eco-activists. I'm not surprised your group has taken precautions. The terrible crime seems aimed directly at terrorizing members of your community. I'm told you knew one of the victims. Green Hope?"

The phone in her pocket vibrated, and she switched it off. She had found her quarry, and he was as nervous and flighty as his namesake; it wouldn't do to distract him by taking a call or texting.

At the mention of the slain woman's name, Fiver burst into tears and buried his narrow face in amongst the copious sleeves of his sweater. Out from the frayed bottom of the garment sprouted two knobby knees above gaunt shins, which plunged into the comically large boots, their laces dragging along the refuse-covered floor. Ellie had the distinct and somewhat discomforting impression that these were the only items of clothing he was wearing. She sat lightly down on a wobbly ottoman as Fiver slowly recovered himself.

"Sorry, but it was... Oh, how could anyone do that to a... such a pure-hearted... I mean, she'd gone corporate, for certain, no denying, but after she left Dancing Hare, every now and then we'd find baskets, y'know, of stuff she knew we needed, toothpaste and the like, and I knew who'd left them." He reached over to a lopsided shelf set into a wall covered with aluminum foil, almost touched a jumbled heap of woven Easter-type baskets, paused, his hand frozen in midair, and then broke into a moaning wail.

Minutes passed before Fiver again settled himself. Ellie thought she should steer the convo to a more neutral subject, one less prone to eliciting sensitive-male waterworks before venturing on a more pointed line of inquiry.

"So, Mr. Fiver, you grow most of your own food here?"

"We do. I mean, in season," he said and shoved some Dominos and McDonald's food wrappers under the skirt of his easy chair. By the amount of fast food debris festooning every corner of the compact abode and the crushed state of the cardboard wrappers, Ellie concluded the eco-warrior had been raiding food waste bins and heating up the discarded, but not yet spoiled, food on the hob attached to his stove.

"Many people living here? In the season?"

Fiver nodded. "Up to twenty, but that includes part-timers who mostly sleep at their parents'." Fiver's vague brown eyes quivered as he recollected something. "*Juggernaut?* Was it your paper did the series on the London sewer protests?"

London's sewer system had not been upgraded since Queen Victoria's time, so every bounteous rainstorm sent millions of liters of raw sewage over and out of the system's ancient confines and straight into the tidal Thames. Eco-fanatics demanded the multibillion-pound public works project be entirely re-engineered toward the construction of facilities for composting and methane capture.

"That was your group behind that? Well, the *Juggernaut* was proud to chronicle your efforts. Not many activists would have the high level of commitment to submerge themselves in 'first flush' from sewers in heavy rain riding in kayaks and plastic barrels with a not-insignificant risk of being swept out to sea."

"It was the greatest moment of my... We were, were..." He burst into tears again. "Sorry, sorry, Green Hope was there too. She was so hard-core, y'know, back then."

The fact the *Juggernaut* had refrained from ridiculing the sewer protestors with as much satiric venom as the *Daily Mail* and others had, calling them Poop Jihadis and Brown Greens, seemed to put Fiver more at ease. Truth was, by the time Smitty got around to editing the story, all the good jokes had been taken, and the photographer they had hired to cover the event no sooner got on the scene when he started vomiting so uncontrollably he had to be taken away in an ambulance. As a result, there were no pictures under which to put captions mocking Fiver and his band of smelly rebels.

"When was the last time you saw her?"

Fiver had last seen Mrs. Goldsmid's daughter a month or so previous; they had met for tea, and she presented him with the oversized Shetland sweater he was now wearing.

"I know I said she went corporate," he added with a note of contrition at the thought of having slighted his deceased friend. "But I think her heart was still with XR. She also brought us a load of firewood. The stuff we can scrounge, it's often shite for burning."

Green Hope had been one of their founding members, meaning she was intimately familiar with the Dancing Hare squat. "Although—and this is the only really serious argument we ever had—I'm... I'm so ashamed to say it almost got..." He half whispered and half sobbed the word, "...violent."

That was probably not the wisest admission to make about relations with someone who'd recently been sadistically murdered. Ellie measured the distance to the exit, then looked again at the underfed man's arms and legs—the parts that showed were about as thick and imposing as hairy albino string beans. Fiver, she was certain, was no lunatic killer capable of dismembering one person, let alone all of the Hereford Five.

"I'm sure it wouldn't have come to blows," Ellie said. "You seem so spiritually peaceful. What was the row about?"

"She didn't quite agree with the community's founding principles being based on *Watership Down*."

"The children's book about bunnies?"

Fiver nodded, which in his case was a sort of nervous vibration made primarily with his chin, a motion which nestled his unshaven face even deeper into the folds of his sweater. "I mean, yeah, it is a deeply fascist, racist, misogynistic work, possibly imperialist because how do we know the Down wasn't the home of moles before the rabbits decided it was theirs, y'know, and also how in the book the males treated the females as objects of bunny rape. They even call them 'does,' and the total lack of bunnies of color and zero representation of gay and trans rabbits, which any rabbitologist will tell you can be found in great numbers in any warren." He said this with bitter indignation. "But even with its faults, which the author couldn't help because of his whiteness, *Watership* spoke to me in a profoundly spiritual way nothing ever has, or ever can."

Ellie pointed out it was published in the seventies, before the issue of transgender rabbits had received much attention.

"So I did compromise, and we settled on calling this place Dancing Hare rather than Sandleford, which I still think would have been better because of the notion of impending doom which we face along with the whole planet."

"Did she live here?" Ellie glanced up at the sleeping nook near the ceiling.

"Only during summer vaccy, and then she got an internship with those Kore people."

"You're not keen on them? As I understand it, and believe me I know next to nothing, they're on your side, clean power based on geothermal energy, no?"

"Bloody corporate capitalist sellouts." Fiver scoffed. "Dr. Kore, y'know, richest bloke in Europe, does he dare part with any of that filthy blood lucre to support the movement? Wankers, all of them. I always told them not to get mixed up with those types."

"Them? Who besides Green Hope…?"

Fiver opened his mouth, waggled his tongue without allowing it to produce any intelligible sound, and looked left and right. Ellie had seen this facial sequence many times when an interviewee realized they'd just blurted out something they meant to not blurt out. A moment later, Fiver realized it was useless to try to walk back his involuntary admission. Instead, he again peered over her shoulder and out the other two small windows that adorned the circular residence, which was about the size of a large broom closet.

"You won't use my name?"

"I've never divulged a source against their wishes."

"Even to police? They're all corrupt, in the pocket of the nazi quangos. Look at what they did to Assange and Snowden, and for that matter, Russell Brand."

Ellie was about to explain the number of levels of appeal the authorities would have to win under the Human Rights Charter in order to legally force any incriminating information out of her, but Fiver seemed to have the attention span of a video-game-addicted gnat. She shook her head in a way that expressed sincere firmness. "If it comes to that, I'd rather go on the lam, probably seek asylum in Russia. They owe me a favor, a real solid one. I helped Vladimir Putin out of a rather monstrous balls-up he'd got himself into."

"Really?" The prospect of her exiling herself to the Arctic Circle to protect her sources seemed to encourage him.

"Really. It's all in my book *The Pangea Protocol*."

Fiver explained that one of the other Hereford victims was known to his circle of eco-activists. "When I saw his name, I got chills."

When he said this, the long dark hairs on his skinny ivory legs actually started to lift off his skin. Fortunately, when she noticed this behavioral oddity, Ellie's mind became frozen between mirth and revulsion, so in the end neither a giggle nor a yelp escaped her lips. She merely stared glassy-eyed as the equally bristly hairs on Fiver's forearms also joined their panicky brethren.

"I mean, when they published his ordinary name, the poor chappie. We knew him as Oppie, short for Oppenheimer. Y'know, the atom bomb fellow…"

Her increasingly loquacious source explained Oppie had been a legitimate nuclear scientist, a genuine prodigy taking post-graduate courses at the University of Manchester where, decades before, the first nuclear reaction was studied. At some point during his PhD candidacy, Mr. Peirpoint, Oppie, became radicalized and changed his name to fit in with his new friends in the XR and Just Stop Oil movements.

"Last half year, I saw him lots more often than Hope, even though Oppie was never steady here—he had some other gigs and mates we never knew about. Last time I saw him was seven or eight weeks ago. He didn't say nuthin', but I saw a Polish phrase book in his bag, so I mean, y'know, what else was there to think but he was going on a trip to the continent, huh?"

Two people out of the five decapitated victims had an association with this particular eco village. That had to be worth following up, Ellie thought while she tried to maintain a facial expression and body language that would radiate sophisticated journalistic competence to Fiver. This was becoming difficult, as the side of her face nearest the piping-hot stove was beginning to perspire and was likely developing an embarrassing red flush.

"Would you know any more details? For instance, the date when Oppie left Britain or any company he was working for?"

He looked around, seemingly perplexed, and then a moment later it seemed as though he was about to weep again. He reached for a faux-fur bunny-themed rectangle. Ellie thought it was a tea cozy of some sort, or a plushy stress comfort toy, but it turned out to be a laptop cover.

"I keep it turned off to save battery," he said, pulling the cover off by its protruding pink ears. "In winter, we never get enough sun for the solar. They let me charge it at the coffee shop as long as the gaffer ain't about. Lemme get you the exact information. Oppie asked me to pick up his mail at a bird's place. They weren't talking anymore by the time he left, but that email should have some details... old thing." He shook the laptop. "Takes forever to boot."

As they waited, Ellie took the opportunity to get up and step across the narrow room to where a cool draft was coming through a crack in the wobbly doorframe. Behind her, the computer came to life with the familiar chimes of mail and news update alerts. Just outside the foggy glass, she could see a small speckled bird hopping around the unkempt trail which ran through the eco village; it picked at the leavings inside a Subway wrapper.

A guttural grunt from Fiver's direction made her slowly turn around, her thinking and reactions having been made a bit dull by the heat permeating the little living shack.

"Sorry, wha—"

"Who the fuck are YOU?" Fiver screamed. The knuckles on his hands were blanched white with the death grip he had on the long metal shaft of his golf club as he raised it and came lunging at her with the clear intent of bashing in her skull.

Chapter 13

Ellie quickly raised her hands to ward off the blow and at the same time stepped back, which, in the tiny dwelling, pushed her back against the outside door; it was not latched and gave way immediately.

Too fast! Her heel caught on a raised threshold meant to keep out ground water and vermin. Fighting for balance, she latched on to the only thing she could grab—the handle of the door, which swung her to the side as she clung on to it, her heels dragging in the muddy slush, sending her sliding sideways.

The unintended maneuver undid Fiver's rabid golf club melee attack. Carried by his forward momentum, he flew right out the empty doorway. As he exited, the head of the club caught on the top of the frame, causing the shaft to bonk him straight on his forehead. Just outside the door, three feet away from Ellie, he collapsed, and his thin frame seemed to sink into the puffy mass of his ungainly Shetland wool sweater. Ellie regained her feet, spared his insensible form a glance, then looked around for something with which she could strike the raving man if he renewed his attack.

The only object at hand was a rusty horseshoe hanging next to the entrance. She pulled it free and loomed over her downed assailant.

"Fiver!" she yelled down at him as sharply as she could. "I've had punch-ups with trained killer cyborgs far bigger than you, and I survived to write best-selling nonfiction about it, so stay there and explain yourself or I'll thrash you and call for the police and then thrash you some more while they take their jolly time getting here."

As though he were an enormous turtle with a crocheted shell, Fiver's head slowly made its way out from the neck of the sweater.

"Don't hit me! But ... police? You can't call them. You're with the killers, the ones who killed Green Hope and the rest!"

Ellie kicked the putter out of his reach, and then, displaying what she felt was an admirable amount of sufferance, explained she was no such thing. "And dare I even ask why would you think that I'm with the killers?"

"Th-the news, the real Eleanor Sato, newspaper owner and author—she's dead!" he panted. "Just been killed. You did it! You took her place so I would trust you. Oh, I'm so dead now." His head, which sported a bloody welt in the center of his forehead as a consequence of the backfired assault, threatened to retract back into his oversized garment.

Now it was her turn to feel a raving loon. "Explain. More slowly now. And keep your head where I can see it. You've really broken trust, you have," she said, feeling more confused than scared or angry as she studiously menaced Fiver with the grimy horseshoe.

"It's breaking news, y'know, the headline popped up when I turned on the computer. Look, there's even a picture. They're taking your body, *her* body, out of some posh digs down in Mayfair."

"You just... stay where you are." Ellie edged over to where Fiver's laptop lay. Turning her head to match the upside-down screen, she saw the surreal headline from, of all outlets...

"The *Daily* bloody *Mail*," she whispered between clenched teeth. What was going on? She read on in disbelief that became something closer to alarm.

"Murder in Mayfair? Armed police and emergency personnel rushed to the home of notorious author and self-styled newspaper magnate Eleanor Sato… reportedly arriving too late … officials would not rule out suicide, bringing a decisive end to a dodgy career marked by well-known episodes of aberrant behavior…'"

Below this snippet was an animated picture of someone with short dark hair lying on an ambulance stretcher being taken down the steps of a house that had regal lions topping the copings. Those were her very own regal lions. It was definitely her home, but who could that be?

"Oh fuck. Esmunda!" Ellie dropped the horseshoe, made sure she had her bag and notepad, then ran along the path out from the eco commune without a backward look at Fiver the eco-warrior.

By the time her ice-cold hands gripped the chain links of the commune's outer gate, she was clean out of breath and her half boots were squishy with melting snow. She finally looked back, but the lapine-obsessed nutter was nowhere to be seen. She slammed the gate shut behind her and leaned against it.

The headline flashed in front of her eyes: *Murder in Mayfair?* It was a journalistic trick to assume the worst to get people's attention but then qualify it way down in the story past some clickable advertisements, that was the purpose of the question mark. Also, she thought, as she recalled the ghoulish paparazzi-style pictures, didn't they cover deceased bodies completely or draw chalk outlines around them before moving them? The Ellie Sato double at her house, which could only be Esmunda, was clearly visible in that grainy video clip.

She dialed the newsroom. Ed answered the editor's line.

"You're alive?"

"Don't sound so disappointed. Where's Smitty?"

"It's just, we all just got through contributing to your obituary. We had to set the record straight after the stitch-up the Daily Snail pulled, y'know, to quash the 'failed TV presenter' and 'controversial author' bits they had in their story. We pulled together an astonishingly good piece, best we've done for years, really. I was just about to post it online."

"Sorry to put you out. Next time I'll try harder to please. Listen, I need to know where they've taken, er, 'me.'"

Calling the office was the fastest way to get updated news on the case. The *Juggernaut*'s computer system had a chat line set up with media relations officers from every important government department.

"Looks like they've taken the victim of the brutal attack, which you claim is not yourself, to NHS Nightingale London."

"In Battersea?"

"I suppose all the regular emergency units were full up; it's been quite a night for machete and machine gun fights between Albanians and gypsies."

"Travelers! Travelers, you bigot!" Ellie could hear John shouting in the background. "How many times must we tell you they want to be called Travelers!"

Ellie rang off and looked for a cab. After the pandemic and, even more so, the massive side effects of the experimental gene therapies given out to nearly everyone in the country, the public health service NHS had become even more of a crock-up than before 2019. Surgery waiting lists stretched on for years, and queues shortened, not by procedures finally being done, but rather by patients on the waiting lists obligingly ceasing their years of agonized suffering without further annoyance to NHS central planners by dropping dead.

Following the Purge of the Starmerista Socialists in Parliament, revanchist Corbyn Marxists seized power and established Soviet-style field hospitals, giving them the hopeful and utterly misleading appellation "Nightingale Clinics." The one in London was located in a decommissioned power station, which had seen successive service as a failed Pakistani mall, a failed Chinese mall, a failed North Korean mall, and then had become a social housing development intended for seaborne migrants, none of whom ever moved in, citing mold, bedbugs, and no ensuite laundry facilities or the free nanny services they'd been promised by the people smugglers who shipped them across the Channel. What remained of these residential units had devolved into squats for drug addicts and the lower rungs of the City's multicultural criminal element.

The first cabbie she managed to flag down wanted extra to go to the reviled NHS Battersea address.

"It's just the hospital I'm off to," Ellie protested. "I'm not buying narcotics. Can't you tell?"

The driver looked at her soaking-wet pantsuit and her hair, which, during the melee with Fiver, must have become quite deranged and gotten covered in bits of spatter, which hopefully had only come from rotting pumpkins.

"Actually, I can't tell. Not judgin' or nothin', just can't tell what your game is, which isn't ma business, and the particulars of which I can't tell nothin', s'all I mean."

After receiving the benefit of the doubt as to what her business at Battersea might be, they settled on a flat rate, which the driver greedily agreed to take in the form of five times the face value in the form of Shop-N-Fly gift bonus points. Her years of compulsive online bargain hunting had finally paid off, because her journey would basically be free.

The big black EV's motor made sounds like a vacuum cleaner digesting steel nuts and bolts but quickly maneuvered through a noontime lull in traffic over to the south bank of the river and up to the monstrous brick building, which still sported its four huge smokestacks, redundant edifices which last saw use during the facility's inaugural heyday as a coal-fired power plant. A pair of lazy-looking security robots ignored her as she rushed into what appeared to be the hospital's receiving area.

Inside, Ellie dodged an elderly woman pushing a mop through fresh, semi-coagulated, and thoroughly dried blood drippings as well as unidentifiable green blobs, all of which speckled the floor along with not a few discarded needles and bits of charred tinfoil. The no-man's-land of the outdoor receiving area was huge, about a hundred yards wide and fifty deep and poorly lit; huddled figures lurked in corners illuminated only by a constellation of propane lighter flames as they cooked their drugs of choice.

"Excuse me, could you please point me to the admitting window or kiosk or bunker?"

The cleaning woman looked up, startled, as though she went days without being spoken to by another human. Mutely she indicated a kiosk with a dimly glowing "NHS" logo. Before Ellie got there, she pivoted sharply around. Someone was calling out her name. "Ell-ie—Ell-ie" in a raspy voice, which she barely heard over the hum and clank of machinery coming from the bowels of the former industrial power-generating monstrosity. She looked over, and through the gloom made out a pale hand waving in her direction.

"What are you doing out there?" Ellie said, half to herself, and rushed over toward a waiting area that looked more like a triage collection point she'd seen in some of the war zones she'd visited. Some people sat with forlorn expressions, their battered, bruised, and bleeding limbs propped up on plastic chairs. Others had slumped to the stony ground, too feeble to sit upright. A few, toxically animated, stood jiggling and dancing to tunes only they could hear while their brains were penned up in various stages of opioid bliss.

One dazed fellow, an African-looking man in a business suit, tried to maintain a posture of dignity and decorum while the thick gauze he held against his head wound bloomed crimson, likely an assault or accident victim waiting his turn to be called into the inner workings of the Nightingale facility.

She was nearly upon the prostrate form of her roommate when she noticed the upright and broad-shouldered form of City Police Inspector Harrigan. He stood along with another man in casual-sporty civilian clothes, this one with a stethoscope round his neck.

"Oh, I'm sorry," Esmunda gasped. "Made a mess, I have." Her quavering delirious tone caused Ellie anxiety and not a small amount of bitterness.

"What's going on here? Why am I, I mean, is she in the lobby? And look at this place. This… this filth… this is…" She lowered her voice to mute her politically incorrect epithet and hissed, "Bloody Third World shite."

Harrigan stepped forward and put a reassuring hand on her upper arm. "We drove here as soon as the call came over the emergency channel. I brought Morton. He's an Army CMT Class One; I'd trust him with a first look at any injury I received over any just graduated resident unlucky enough to be assigned to Battersea Emergency Clinic."

"'Lo, Ms. Sato." Morton nodded at her while looking at a digital monitor he'd placed around Esmunda's upper arm. She lay on a mobile stretcher, presumably the same one on which she'd been placed by the ambulance paramedics who had rushed her away from Mayfair.

"How is she?"

"Ohhhh, I'm so fine, a bit light, y'know, bit bubbly in the upper, er, what is it now…"

"She's possibly concussed, and she inhaled some kind of fast-acting anesthetic," Morton said, his narrow forehead wrinkling. "I'd say it's similar to chloroform, but no way to know without a sample or lab bloodwork."

"How'd this happen?" Ellie asked, equally aghast at her friend's neglected situation and relieved at her not being comatose or dead.

Harrigan quickly explained that persons unknown had broken into Mayfair House that afternoon and during their search for valuables had encountered Esmunda in Ellie's room. They surprised and swiftly subdued her, but ruckus caused during the criminal intrusion drove the pets, a dog and a large, possibly predatory, bird into such a frenzy that the intruders knocked over a hotplate, which triggered a fire alarm.

"The villains had managed to subvert the burglar alarms but had completely forgotten about the fire systems. Nothing really caught flame, but a batch of cheese toasties produced as much smoke as a good-sized tear gas grenade," Harrigan explained, then raised an eyebrow and crinkled a dimpled chin at his colleague. "Let that be a lesson, Morton, if you ever indulge in housebreaking."

Harrigan spoke with such clarity and genteel manly authority that Ellie was strangely put at ease, even as images of the violation of her home filled her imagination. Prominently featured in those mental reconstructions were a sudden barking, biting, a flapping of wings, the tearing and gouging of a sharp curved beak, likely accompanied by gratuitous foul language issuing from Magellan, the verbose macaw.

When the fire and police had arrived at Mayfair, they found Esmunda unconscious next to Ellie's ID, which had been on the desk. Esmunda's face was still red and puffy from whatever chemical concoction they used to knock her out. In all the confusion and the smoke-filled interior, it was easy to see how the misidentification occurred. But what had the housebreakers been searching for?

Instinctively, Ellie's hand tightened around her purse, Green Hope's Gaia earring with the Kore Energy data still in it. What should she do? She glanced at Harrigan's handsome lantern-jawed face. Twice, he'd intervened. Once to assist her parents, and now had rushed to what he had thought was her bedside. Could she trust him? Should she turn the whole dangerous mess over to him? Her idiotic attempt at investigating this major crime was certainly beyond the scope of her abilities and might have gotten Esmunda killed.

Just then, her phone rang. It was her other platonic boyfriend, Ran Oliphant.

"Hello, it's me, I'm alive." Ellie waited for an awestruck gasp or at least a mild outburst of profanity and went unrewarded. "Are you not even the least bit shocked?"

"Not the least. They mistakenly checked in your batty roommate under your name. And don't ask how I know. I just called... to, er..."

"Right, uh, appreciated." Was Oliphant tapped into the hospital's CCTV system? London had nearly one camera for each of its ten million residents. She looked at the ceiling; a few of the hooded camera boxes were covered with a dried brown substance, which she hoped was not organic. Others had been cracked open and scavenged for their components, but three or four looked operational. "Really, it's a great comfort being spied on night and day. I'll let you know if there's anything..."

Just then, semiconscious Esmunda mumbled something from atop her stretcher and reached out, likely intending to grasp her by the arm, and only managed a boneless flopping motion in her painkiller-induced delirium. "One sec, Ran. Yes, Ezzie? Didn't quite catch that."

"S'why I needed to turn meself around, y'know? Everything in my sorry-assed life, stop clanging up like I have. You're my example, Miss Sato, the sssample I'm going to patter after and the reason I decided to keep it... my baby." Esmunda jerked her hand toward her midsection in a manner both pathetic and endearing and startling in equal measure.

"Shhhhite," Ellie swore under her breath and checked Ran was still on the line.

"As a matter of fact, my dear," she said in her most charming man-compelling voice, "there is one thing we need urgently: a spot of that posh private healthcare you enormously rich people take for granted, including a medical air ambulance to get us out of this feculent NHS bunghole. Ugh!" That was the only exclamation she could muster as she found her half boot stuck to an oozing roll of used gauze bandage from which protruded the pointy business ends of at least two used syringes.

Chapter 14

As they were loading Esmunda into the helicopter, she waved Ellie closer. What now? If it weren't for Harrigan flashing his credentials they wouldn't have even persuaded the surly looking Nightingale staff to let them up the elevator to the rooftop helipad.

The wind up there was furious; she shielded her eyes against blowing snow crystals and yelled over the whiney roar of the aircraft's engines: "Quickly! You're definitely concussed, possibly mortally poisoned, *and pregnant!* What do you need?"

"Your things! I laid all your things in your room!"

Ellie made a grimace, which she hoped conveyed her confusion.

"Y'know, White's Club, your dinner with the possible killer?"

In all the tumult, she'd forgotten. "I'll try."

"Go, you gots to," Esmunda pleaded, and, concussed or not, the wily slacker could still lay on heapings of guilt at will. "If I hadn't been preparing your costume, I wouldn't have been home. You gots to go." The grimacing smile Esmunda managed was a sight of uncommon gruesomeness due to her features having gotten all red and puffy from the chloroform substance the housebreaking fiends had used to subdue her. "The snow must go on!" The prone girl cackled deliriously as a wash of rotor-borne flakes whirled over everyone and everything.

"You just take care."

The helmeted attendant pointed to a spot out of the way of the scything blades just above their heads and advised her she should get on or push off.

Apparently, in twenty-first-century Britain, the chronic rudeness epidemic had also infected private healthcare. Ellie pushed off, ducking low and ending up bumping into the very dapper civilian overcoat of Inspector Harrigan; it was a long, navy-blue cashmere car coat that made him look more like a stockbroker than a policeman.

"Steady on, Ms. Sato," he said, steadying her on the slippery surface of the roof walkway by placing a firm hand under her elbow. "May I offer you a lift wherever you have to go?"

Like many strikingly handsome men, everything Harrigan said had a bat's squeak of sensuality. But for his smoothly respectable Southeastern English accent, he'd sound positively indecent.

"Uh, oh, yes, certainly," Ellie stammered. As they descended in the lift, she felt the silence becoming fairly awkward, so she reverted to the subject in which she was most experienced. "That's not an English cut."

"Huh?"

"Your coat, I would have said Huntsman & Sons from the quality of the wool, but the back slit and slanted pockets are a dead giveaway of a continental origin. Fashion and leisure were my first assignments as a junior reporter."

"And now you're a media mogul and sharply observant too. I'll have to watch my step around you. No, it's, er, Austrian, bespoke." He fastened the bottom button and smoothed the front of his costly bit of couture, possibly with a touch of remorse at having laid out three thousand pounds for a seasonal fashion item.

Ellie smiled to herself. She'd been there and done that, before falling into the indentured servitude of being a business owner. The elevator door jiggled then reluctantly creaked open to reveal the dreadful lobby of NHS Battersea.

"I also have an ulterior motive for being your chauffeur," he said. "There's something I have to tell you."

Really? It was quite a day for revelations, she thought. As they made their way to the service vehicles car park, Ellie wondered whether she had anything to divulge to Inspector Harrigan.

"Where to?" he asked, holding the door open for her.

"Where else? Scene of the crime... the most recent one."

Chapter 15

The gently wafting hot air put out by the Jaguar's vents warmed Ellie's extremities so quickly they pricked and tingled. She glanced at Harrigan as he confidently navigated his way toward Mayfair. Despite the toasty temperature, he kept one hand in the folds of his jacket, possibly to keep the hem away from her garments, which were soiled with suspicious brown and orange stains garnered during the brief struggle with Fiver.

She had no intention of turning in the eco lunatic for assault. Friends of his had been killed in a most brutish manner, and the violence surrounding this mysterious case had also landed in Ellie's own home. She clutched her purse, again mulling over how much to tell the reassuring but mysterious man beside her. Of course, Harrigan had secrets too; best to pry his out first.

"You mentioned a confidence? Perhaps you'd best tell me before we arrive."

"That, yes, quite." A pause carried them half the length of a city block. "You understand that my branch of law enforcement reports directly to the Lord Mayor of London."

"Right, I learned this in civics. There are really two mayors here, aren't there? The big mayor whom everyone hates and is responsible for buggering up the lives of nine million people with his wretched ULEZ robo-Stalin cameras, and then there's the Square Mile fellow who's so obscure he might as well be a hermit."

Harrigan smiled. "True as that might be, I wouldn't mention that aspect of his office to the lord mayor when you see him. He's taken an interest in your interest in the case of the Hereford Five."

"Really? It's quite out of his jurisdiction."

"Yes, but Mayfair's much closer. He heard of this latest outrage at your home and requested I pass along a request for you to attend a confidential interview with His Lordship."

"Confidential" and "interview" did not generally go together in Ellie's lexicon, but she wasn't going to snub such an unexpected invite. All she knew about the current office holder was that he was a titled aristocrat, wealthy, and fairly eccentric.

Harrigan handed over a card. "That's his private line. He never answers voice calls. Text only."

Harrigan seemed reticent, or at least unenthusiastic about passing along the invite. He noticed her noticing.

"He's a bit of a fellow, not quite a card, much too respectable, but he's definitely a fellow, the mayor definitely is. Odd, but very pleasant." He shrugged apologetically. "You're under no obligation to go. I'm passing on a completely unofficial back-channel inquiry. If you'd like me to decline on your behalf…"

"Any idea what he wants?"

Harrigan made a manly and nearly musical humming sound, which Ellie interpreted to mean: *That's for you to find out.*

A constable was on duty out front of the steps up to the Mayfair townhouse. Her escort halted the car directly in front. He turned to her and said in a fastidiously neutral tone, "Now, Ms. Sato, is there anything else you would like to share with me?

Even something you would care to share with me, and me alone, not necessarily the department? Anything at all?"

Ellie had to consciously resist the temptation to clutch her purse to make certain she could feel the bulge of the data fob. Nevertheless, she answered without hesitation. "Not a thing except... unending thanks for your latest rescue efforts."

Her lovely oak door was festooned with crime scene tape and a surveillance camera on a tripod. A quick word from Harrigan to the lady officer got Ellie through without being frisked.

"You've been such a help, you and your medic friend, won't you come in? You must be famished." Police guard notwithstanding, the place had a dozen bedrooms, and Ellie felt not a little creeped out going back alone to the scene of recent violence.

Harrigan beamed her a reassuring smile from the driver's side of his car and declined. Ellie propped the front door open despite the chill afternoon air streaming in—that way there was a better chance of being heard if she had to shriek in terror.

"Ah!" Ellie jumped as a shape slinked around a corner behind her. She heard a low growl and caught sight of white canines flashing in the shadows.

"Oh, it's only you, Chestnut." The growling stopped, but the curly-haired head of the Labradoodle remained in a low, guarded position. Very unlike him.

When he finally came forward, he was favoring his rear leg; on his side was a bloody welt about the size and shape of the toe of some beastly swine's boot. One of those ghastly intruders must have kicked him during his escape, kicked her pet hard enough to cut his skin. She bent down to have a closer look.

"You poor thing. Well, if you're limping tomorrow or I hear you have trouble breathing, I'll take you next door. I'm afraid the mad dog lady is the only veterinarian we can afford to look you over."

She found Magellan perched on the second-floor banister; the excitement seemed to have worn down even the hyperactive, foul-tempered macaw. Instead of threatening her with his wicked beak and prolific cursing, all he could manage was a desultory flap of a wing and a lazy squawk.

"Yes, Magellan, I'm also glad to see that you survived."

As soon as she flopped gratefully down onto a sofa opposite her bed, she noticed the time and recalled her appointment with Ran at his club. "Do I really have the energy?"

On her bed and makeup table were spread out, in surprisingly meticulous fashion, everything necessary to temporarily change her gender. Esmunda had put quite a lot of work into those preparations. Had Ellie's digging into Green Hope's past and the information stored in her secret earring data fob really been the reason for the attack at Mayfair House? The brief interval of time between their discovery of it and the violent home invasion made it improbable the two events were not connected. If so, shouldn't she drop the whole damned dangerous thing? Just hand the information she'd gathered to Harrigan and let the authorities sort it all out? Seemed simple enough; but she could have done that anytime while he had been driving her home.

And if she were about to dive more deeply into these hazardous waters, how could she pass up an invitation to covertly spy on a meeting between two of Britain's most reclusive billionaires, Ran Oliphant and Dr. Kore, the latter of whom owned the property on which the dreadful massacre had occurred.

Chestnut laid his head on her lap.

"Well, I guess you'll be safe with a constable on duty all night." His expressive brown eyes looked questioningly up at her. "Really, for a petite girl with a dress size I'd say was about a size eighteen, the girl looked quite fierce. I'll wager she knows karate."

After studying the objects Esmunda had laid out for her and watching the helpful video queue up on the tablet computer on the makeup table entitled "Uses and Abuses of Spirit Gum in Theatrical Makeup," Ellie felt confident enough to start.

First, she banished all makeup from her face. *Are my lips really that pale? Where have my eyes gone? They look like squinty little Hershey's kisses.* Thankfully her hair was short enough to style into a roguish swirl with something called Monster Hold Gel.

Next, the tricky parts: a lace-backed moustache with matching sideburns, which she stuck carefully on with spirit gum.

"When Ezzie and her friends do their plays, they do all this bosh before every performance?" She looked in the mirror, cringed at the result, then dimmed the light and sighed. "Well, most of the old codgers at White's Club will be near-sighted."

The result, when augmented by a man's suit with shoulder padding, wasn't half bad.

"I'd certainly date me." After peering around the corner and sniffing the air, Chestnut limped cautiously toward her. She pointed him to his basket. "Oh, no you don't. All I need are doggy hairs adorning my trousers. Go and have a lie down while Magellan's too exhausted to harass you."

She texted Ran to meet her around the corner, not relishing the prospect of explaining her transformation to the officer outside her front door. The wingtip shoes she'd been provided with looked very masculine but were far too large. Trudging up the stairs to the side entrance from the garage, she felt as though she were wearing flippers and held fast onto the handrail.

"Oh my," was all Ran said as he peered at her from the back of his limousine.

"Let me in, it's freezing out here. I don't think I've been given the proper type of men's underwear."

After jiggling his beefy but not jowly head, he apologized and opened the door. "I was just having, uh, a moment to… You're a strange sight, s'all I can say."

"Next time we'll dress you up in heels and a corset and see how you like it." The bottles in the minibar in the spacious rear compartment gave a tempting tinkle, but Ellie resisted their call. She needed all her wits about her this evening. While she'd been transitioning, her curiosity had been in overdrive, generating a plethora of questions. She couldn't hold them in any longer, so she spewed them out while at the same time trying out her man voice: "Hoow do you know Dr. Kore? Doo you think he's involved in this business? Have youu heard if the police are making any proogress? It was a quintuple hoo-mi-cide, they moost be going mental under pressure from Hoome Office and the Mayoor."

Ran, the former Royal Marine, still burly and athletic looking even in his dinner jacket, opened and closed one broad and scarred hand, put the other over the lower half of his face, and burst out giggling.

"Oh-ho-ho," he said, finally catching his breath. "It's too much! I've got to take a video of you—just let me catch my breath—for blackmail purposes if you ever dare slander me again in that rag you publish." He gasped out some more hearty chuckles. "*Hooow do you know*—no man in the history of men has ever spoken like that!"

114

While one of Britain's foremost captains of industry was incapacitated with a paroxysm of laughter at her most sincere efforts at temporary gender transformation, Ellie calmly asked the driver to continue on to White's Club, as the hour was approaching eight p.m.

"So... no talking?"

"Not a word. That voice you are attempting makes you sound like a Eurasian chipmunk who has imbibed too much cough syrup."

"Thanks for the vote of confidence." She fumed, hoping any perspiration would not unglue her moustache and sideburns. "You men! I'm glad I'm only among your ranks very temporarily."

The dusk-shrouded urban landscape slid past the limousine's tinted windows. Despite Ran's disapproval of her sudden transformation, she felt quite comfortable sitting next to him. Being attacked by Fiver and then rushing to find out whether the false Eleanor Sato had been killed had her absolutely knackered, so much so she was in danger of falling asleep. She roused herself by considering their upcoming meeting. "I read up on Dr. Kore and his company. He's not fond of interviews. How is it you convinced him to meet?"

"It was he who phoned up my office. Rum thing, considering for the last few years he's been trying to put my nuclear energy company out of business. He's put pressure on politicians and bureaucrats to cancel our permits, tried to sabotage our funding, and secretly given money to eco-fanatics to protest at the site of our pilot project. He even paid off newspapers to publish tommyrot about radioactive waste pollution."

"Really? We'd never take foul payoffs like that at the *Juggernaut.*" Then she recalled their prepaid power account would run out in a day or two. "I mean, no one even asked me about it. Any idea how much he was paying?"

When they arrived, Ellie set her jaw and lower lip in an attitude that would announce to all and sundry that here was a masculine man of the "strong and silent" variety. She adopted the manliest stride she could manage, marching up to the steps of the dour Victorian edifice which housed one of the last redoubts of pure testosterone-oozing British manhood. She copied her friend in carelessly clomping his feet free of loose slush on the stoop; she had to curl her toes so her over-large shoes would not come flying off to reveal nylon stockings, and then followed Ran inside.

A stout security man sat reading a paper; her vivid fears of instantly being outed as a fraud and tossed out went unrealized. The air was humid, warm, and redolent of something ineffable… money? Amiable disdain for the working classes?

"Don't gawk," Ran whispered to her as he led her toward the attendant guarding the dining area. "Evening. Ran Oliphant and guest to dine with Dr. Kore. A private room, I believe."

"Ah, yes, the gentleman is waiting," said an angular man with a huge Adam's apple and a tiny waxed moustache. He looked searchingly at Ellie.

She wondered whether she should have pressed her boobs down more, but the jacket Esmunda had picked had so much padding in the shoulders, they hardly bulged more than well-developed pectoral muscles would have.

"Would your guest care to sign in?"

Gosh, she hadn't really thought of a boy name. Improvising quickly, she filled in the guest card:

Ellis Satoni, Portsmouth. BritEnergy Corp.

"Mr. Oliphant," the White's man said in an unctuous tone which morphed into an ever-so-slight unctuous sneer when he added, "and Mr. Satoni, please come this way."

They walked through a cloud of foul cigar smoke issuing from a dark-paneled side room. Ellie shrugged her shoulders and made a pantomime of puffing. *What gives?* she thought. Luckily she and Ran had shared enough life-and-death perils over the preceding years so that he instantly comprehended the meaning of her gesture.

"One of our board members is a KC for the largest legal firm in the City. He's filed a human rights case on behalf of the traditionally smoking-enabled, a very disadvantaged and oppressed class under the Equality Act, I'll have you know, and that fine pettifogger has managed to get an injunction against prejudiced and possibly racist indoor smoking laws."

"That's taking the piss," Ellie mouthed.

"Really, the Justices of the Supreme Court, in their infinite wisdom, actually called our winning arguments in the case 'very progressive and anti-colonial.' Did you know the majority of Micronesians of Kiribati are smokers? They have suffered terrible colonial exploitation in the past. It's not right we should take away one of their few pleasures. Our lawyers will fight the tobaccophobes and stand up for the civil rights due to Micronesians and smokers everywhere."

Her raised eyebrow sent Ran into another transport of privileged mirth.

"Exactly, nothing tops fighting the good fight on behalf of filthy-rich nicotine addicts."

Dr. Kore was a balding, red-faced man with free-range sideburns hanging over his starched collar. Fortunately he seemed so distracted by his thoughts he barely spared Ellie/Ellis a glance except while saying, rather abruptly, "I thought we'd be alone, private room and all that."

"This is Ellis, my confidential secretary. Don't worry, he's under a pile of nondisclosure agreements and enough Official Secrets Act declarations to crush an elephant. So confidential is he, he's a gentleman's gent. He has my complete confidence, Ellis Satoni does."

Kore's blubbery-lipped mouth paused a moment, then parted in a dry laugh revealing splayed yellow teeth. "Heh hee, crush an elephant! Pretty funny, Mr. *Oliphant*."

Three of the walls of their sequestered room were lined by floor-to-ceiling glass cabinets holding hundreds of wine bottles. A chandelier hung over seating for eight, and they made themselves comfortable at the end farthest from the door.

Dr. Kore had ordered a set menu. Perhaps he was a controlling old geezer, or he didn't want waiters popping in and out more than absolutely required, Ellie thought.

"Of course, Ran, you and your confidential secretary may have what you wish."

"Nothing extra for me. How about you, Ellis?"

She pursed her lips and widened her eyes, the hearty smells from the nearby kitchen reminding her she hadn't eaten anything since hours before her tumultuous meeting with Fiver at the eco squat. She made a noncommittal humming sound.

"My secretary will have whatever you're having." That turned out to be a Sunday roast special featuring beef, potatoes, vegetables, and Yorkshire pudding.

118

"Bad business at your headquarters," Ran said as the famous scientist and entrepreneur tore into his fare with carnivorous enthusiasm. "Police told you anything?"

"One dead body is one too many, Ran, wouldn't you agree? But five, and vivisected like that? Disgusting and deplorable. It smacks of ISIS or some kind of fanaticism. They're looking into Iranian terror cells that might be operating in Britain."

"Ellis, take that down." She brought out her notepad, but instead of writing down what she already knew, she wrote something else and slipped the page to Ran while their host was pulling the cork out of another bottle of wine.

Ran brightened a bit, and Ellie reflected that men always needed to feel they had one up on one another, even in the most tangential and obscure concerns.

"But of course, there's the matter of a member of your own staff among the victims." Ran glanced at her note. "A Miss Green Hope, if that's her correct name."

Dr. Kore made a choking sound, and it was his turn to look out of sorts and surprised. Fortunately, no chunks of roast came flying out from his mouth. "Of course, yes, p-poor girl. She let me call her Miriam. She was a real supporter of our work, dedicated to eradicating the existential crisis of climate change. And so bright, a born organizer and administrative leader. Irreplaceable. Avenging her brutal killing is why I've personally offered a million-pound reward for information that leads to solving this beastly crime. Of course, a true fitting memorial to her and the others would be the success of Kore Industries and true reliable and constant green energy powering Britain and the world without suicidal fossil fuels."

It was obvious to Ellie the mention of Green Hope's name had disordered Dr. Kore's blustery self-assurance, and he had attempted to recover by changing the subject.

"How's that going, by the way?" Ran asked in a mild tone.

That got Dr. Kore started off on his favorite subject: his own worldwide giga-project. As he rambled, Ellie pretended to make notes and quietly ticked off the facts she had researched earlier and also referred to a printout of a screenshot saved from Green Hope's earring bauble data cache.

Kore's geothermal drilling division had apparently perfected ultra-deep drilling, which would release heat from deep inside the earth.

"When we started, the deepest anyone had drilled was a mere eight miles," he said, stabbing his fork into his vegetables. "Our first test maxed out at ten times that depth. And as for the thermal variance, ha! People couldn't believe it, and some fools in the fringes of kook science, all climate-denying scum, still do not."

He mentioned the two Kore pilot projects generating electricity at the same rates as medium-sized nuclear reactors in Ethiopia and Hawaii.

"Naturally I was inundated with many offers on where to build my first plant near major population centers. The Saudis made a most generous proposal, but since we started in Britain, I said: 'Let us do it right here.' And we are doing it right here. Unlike solar, wind, and other types of intermittent energy, geothermal is steady, always there when you need it, just the thing to generate baseload current to a complex international grid."

The fare at White's was really good. Holding her knife and fork in what she considered to be a manly full- fingered grip, she shovelled food into her mouth without the slightest regard to whether she was making a pig of herself. Some aspects of manhood were just plain fun, she thought. Then she suddenly stopped eating. In her gastronomic enthusiasm, had she swallowed her moustache? She quickly raised a napkin to her face. The feathery thing was still there, only now it was slimed with gravy. Gently, she patted it down, hoping to tidy her fake follicles without pulling them away from their adhesive.

Annoyed by Dr. Kore's smug lecture, she recalled one of the file names on Green Hope's device. It sounded technical and so might make their side sound more informed than they were. She jotted it down and slid a second note to Ran.

"I've seen the data from your pilot projects, very impressive, but I've been hearing rumours about these Benioff Dilatancy waves. I'm no geophysicist, but—"

"Of course you are not, and even if you were, most of our work is beyond what has heretofore been taught at universities."

As he interrupted his guest, Ellie noted a peculiar cascade of expressions cross Dr. Kore's florid and pugnacious face: first surprise, then what she could only have described as sneaky annoyance.

"But here's something I trust you will understand: money, Ran. Hard currency, oodles and oodles. Your company BritEnergy is generously valued at sixty billion. I wish to buy it, but I want to forestall any competing bids and make you an offer only a lunatic could refuse. How does an even one hundred billion pounds sound, my friend?"

Ellie snarfled into her wineglass and narrowly stopped herself from making ultra-gauche choking noises. What was going on here? No one had ever offered her even a measly billion pounds for the *Citizen Juggernaut*. Her life's work, to date, now seemed severely undervalued.

"I like round numbers," Ran said with a casual glance at her and an unreadable expression on his face. "My debenture investors' cash costs are only twenty. Let's say I persuade them to merely get their money back plus interest, and you pay me eighty for the intellectual property which, as it happens, is in my solely owned private company?"

The perpetual flames of greed and hope lit up in the dark, close-set eyes of Dr. Kore. The two industrial titans bantered over billions a bit further while Ellie finished her meal and wondered why she'd ended up as an honest but broke journalist instead of a shifty and horribly rich businesswoman crypto mining in Mongolia or running a vast empire of relentlessly oppressive apparel sweatshops in Tibet.

"Well, Doctor, thank you for hosting us," Ran said, shaking the older man's hand. "I'll be in touch."

As Ellie, her thoughts in a whirl, turned into the corridor leading to the exit, she nearly bumped into a middle-aged gentleman who was so startled by the near collision that his monocle popped out of his eye and dangled down his stiffly starched shirt from an impeccably polished silver lanyard.

"E-excuse me," Ellie stuttered in a gravelly mumbling tone after spending a second or two thinking that saying nothing would be more suspicious than speaking two words, which she must be able to without sounding like a chipmunk. The older man barely glanced at her, said something noncommittal, and toddled off.

A moment later, she recalled who it was—he was the lord mayor, the minor one in charge of the Square Mile. And right beside him hovered a dark-faced Indian man who looked down at her with an expression of cutting annoyance. *Oh drat.* It was Mr. Riffi, the former prime minister of the whole bloody UK.

"Come along, Ellis," Ran said, pulling her along by her elbow and nodding to the distinguished pair. "Evening, Your Lordship, Mr. Riffi."

"Oh my word, it's Oliphant," the mayor said, turning around as he replaced his monocle. "We're just going up to the games room. Fancy a rack or two of billiards? Bring your man too; it'll make four. We'll have a jolly tourney."

For a terrible moment, Ellie saw Ran toying with the idea of further tormenting her by accepting the invite. She turned her back to everyone else and made her "seriously miffed" face, which only Ran could see. One half-drunk, near-sighted scientist she could fool, but under the apparently sober gaze of two of the country's most astute politicians, not likely. Come to think of it, Sanjay Riffi might even have a grudge against her and the *Juggernaut*. When the Tories ousted him as PM over a small scandal involving a car accident, her paper had heavily implied the real cover-up involved Riffi's somewhat incestuous affair with his underage first cousin. And Riffi was a man known to hold cruel and terrible grudges in business and politics.

"As a matter of fact, I've been wanting to even the score with Your Lordship since the sound thrashing you dealt last month. Shall we say double—no, treble or nothing? I must warn you, I've been honing my game, received coaching from the All Commonwealth billiards champ, so consider yourselves both duly cautioned."

Just as her facial muscles began to cramp in "seriously miffed" aspect and the edges of her false whiskers started to peel away, Ran relented. "Actually, I'm so sorry, but my assistant feels unwell. Not used to spirits and cigar smoke, poor fellow. Look, I'll see him off and be right up. In fact, Dr. Kore's here. I'm sure he'll join to make four."

As Ran held the door of the limousine open, Ellie asked, "What was all that about? I thought you said Kore was trying to ruin BritEnergy. Now he wants to buy it for some astronomical sum?"

"Interesting, eh?" Ran's eyes narrowed as he looked toward the city lights in the distance. "And notice how Kore got even more enthused when I suggested we conspire in ripping off my own investors? Which I would never do, of course."

For a second, she thought: *At least not in front of a famous journalist,* but then she banished the idea. Ran was the most respectable oligarch she'd ever met and had rescued her and her friends from many a tight spot. On the other hand, no one quite knew exactly how an ex-Royal Marine with no family connections had made such a beastly amount of money so quickly.

Before sending her off, Ran kindly reminded her not to try entering Mayfair House through the front door to avoid being arrested by the constable on duty for appearing to be a strange man trying to enter a crime scene. "I amend that," he added, "to very strange, mute, nonbinary, nearly passable man trying to break in."

The driver closed the door softly, and she was off.

Dr. Kore, BritEnergy, what could it mean? thought Ellie as she reclined in the huge puffy leather seat. The overheated air in the car and the rich meal she had just gobbled down sent her head spinning with waves of fatigue.

Chapter 16

After a night of fitful rest plagued by dreams of facial hair which no amount of tweezing, shaving, or waxing could remove, she woke up to the sound of very real footfalls outside her locked door.

Thankfully, these were accompanied by the click-clack of Chestnut's toenails on the polished marble of the hallway. Ellie blinked, yawned, and rose. She had just enough time to get to her appointment. The mayor's office was on the other side of Canary Wharf, and she wasted fifteen minutes wandering around trying to find a cab. The first three she encountered were empty but had their "Low Charge - sad smiley face" lights on and were themselves desperately seeking a charge-up station that was not out of service and had not used up all of its daily ration of electrons. As a result, she arrived at a hideously lopsided blob of modern architecture on Kamal Chunchie Way a mere two minutes before her appointment with the lord mayor.

Really hoping not to be outed as the previous evening's cross-dressing interloper at the men's club, Ellie had piled on her makeup and put on a frilly dress she had once absconded with after a Ditzy Girls in the City–themed fashion shoot. She immediately regretted the low cut because temperature regulations meant government offices were nearly as cold inside as they were out in the street, where pebble-sized hailstones were pelting down on hard-packed snow.

"Looks like we're in for a bit of a blow," said the Right Honorable Viscount Jacob Tempest, who was also the Right

Honorable Lord Mayor of the City of London, as he ushered her into his rather modest office.

"Some storm brewing in the North Atlantic?"

"Not just a storm, my dear girl, a cyclone." Lord Tempest was so delightfully eccentric, he was one of the few people in the country who could refer to women as "girl" without fear of legal action. "Hasn't a name yet, but it's out there, seething, growing. I've got to get to my house on the coast, make certain everything's battened down. A handful of years ago, Storm Eunice, that destructive harridan, tore the roof off the stables, right off and away! We never found it."

She sat down when he did and waited while he polished his monocle with a monogrammed silk handkerchief. He gazed at her a bit too pointedly for comfort and said, "Have you a brother who works in the City?"

"No, sorry, just me." Ellie smiled, laughed gaily, and fluttered the extra-long eyelashes she'd pasted on in an effort to put even greater distance between her and Ellis Satoni.

"Just, you look… Oh, I'm dithering, aren't I? What may I do for you?"

"You had actually asked to see me." She batted her lashes, hoping they stayed on. "Inspector Harrigan passed on your confidential request."

"Oh, oh, oh, yes, Harrigan. Good man. Har-ri-gan. Solid police worker, very politically in tune, if you know what I mean. Most people know him and not a whisper to his discredit. He'll go far, mark my word."

As he spoke, Lord Tempest tapped something hidden behind a stack of papers on his desk: a manila envelope, a fat one. To Ellie, it seemed he was trying to make up his mind about something. The mayor gazed out the window.

"Do you ever feel you're, how shall I put it…" His lightly jowled face took on for a moment a mildly pinched expression. "…out of your depth?"

"Me? Just every morning when I'm forced to realize I own Britain's oldest newspaper. The pressure of historical legacies can be off-putting. I needn't tell you that; the Tempest family peerage goes back to the *Magna Carta*, and you've got the Square Mile to manage in the bargain."

The reference to history seemed to put Lord Tempest instantly at ease. Ellie found him to be in life as he seemed in news clips: possessing the bemused and off-beam quality of having just walked out of a nineteenth-century photograph onto the modern street.

"Oh, but you're too modest, Miss Sato." He pointed to the shelf behind her, and she turned and felt her face flush as she stared at her very own collection of titles, all in hardcover binding. "I've read all your books. Chronicles of hazards and derring-do right out of Rider Haggard and Jules Verne, what?"

Had His Lordship summoned her to get her autograph? The true purpose of the interview still remained a mystery.

"I even signed up for your newsletter to keep up with, as the sign-up page put it: 'The Greatest Lady Adventurer since Amelia Earhart and Lady Stanhope.'"

That really set her cheeks on fire. "My publisher bounced me into that, contractual publicity obligations, y'know."

"You're bolder than I, I'll say that. Tell the truth, I never wanted to be in public life before all this." He waved his hand at the chain and seal of office dangling over a red velvet cape below a black three-pointed hat and a powdered horsehair wig, all of which were stashed in a corner of the room. "I had a cozy tutorship all arranged at Merton College, but the marquess, my father, would have none of it. Not even being the product of his third marriage got me out of 'being somebody.' His exact words. I'll never forget the exact words the night he told me off, and mind you, this was in front of his valet, or at least within earshot. Yes, right, he said, 'I'll not have a dithering moralizer, some detestable imitation C. S. Lewis in my family. You, my fine sir, are going into politics. That's the way to thrash any morality out of any old soul.' Or anyway, that's the wording I recollect, of course, being in a somewhat shaken state at delivery of the dictum," the mayor concluded with polite bitterness. "At least I was able to bargain my success down from aspiring to be London's grandee mayor to standing for this less-exalted post."

His face split into a childish grin as he added, "There was a time when the lord mayor had much heavier duties." He pointed to a model ship beside the bookcase. "During the 1600s, command of the Royal Navy was deemed too important to commerce to leave to the monarch. What days those must have been."

As much as Ellie enjoyed reminiscing about the nation's centuries of mercantilism and general pillaging, she was just about to look at her wristwatch to signal she was, what with avoiding being killed and crime solving, pressed for time, when something in his tone changed, became more serious.

"Today we're still, you could aptly say, yes, still a country dependent on the moon and the tides. Not literally, but tides of finance. And those seas, too, gestate their own cyclones, laying waste to economies, the livelihoods of millions of people, with a violence that seems to thunder out of nowhere. Today the fortune of every citizen depends on the ebb and flow of dollars, pounds, yen, and yuan.

"I'm sure you know the world economic turnover is about 100 trillion dollars, but the financial world is much, much larger; adding in stocks, bonds, gilts, derivatives, no one with any sense marks it at less than a thousand trillion: a quadrillion dollars. Imagine that sum. And here's Britain, a little brigantine with a turnover of barely three trillion per annum, afloat, some would say adrift, on that." He pointed to an animated wall screen with a jumble of graphs and numbers with labels reading LSE, FTSE, NYSE. In the corner was a calendar, that day's date highlighted in green with a red square which was a Monday three days away from that very day.

"What's that square? It looks ominous," Ellie said, thinking it would at least seem ominous to people with some market savvy and invested savings. Thankfully, she was secure on that score, being savvy-free and savings-free.

"What? Right, annual Quintuple Witching Day. Nothing to be worried about, happens only once a year. It's when a whole slew of financial instruments called 'derivatives' all expire at once. Of course, the larger the proportion of derivatives to shares and shares to actual assets becomes, well, it does make worrywart investors nervous, always fearing another 2008 when the whole thing nearly ground to a halt. When those American firms like Lehman Brothers failed, banks stopped trusting each other, and when that happened, the whole financial system teetered on the verge of collapse. Teetered and tottered, for days on end; people literally threw themselves out of skyscraper windows."

Having previously been on the personal precipice of extreme financial embarrassment, in fact, really never having managed to back more than a few steps from the edge of said pecuniary cliff, Ellie could empathize, sort of, and felt compelled to counterbalance the sensitive-seeming man's worried tone. "But it all turned out well, er, back then. I was a bit young to follow it all, but you printed gobs of pounds and dollars and yen, and things went merrily on."

That seemed to cheer him, but as he continued to chuckle dryly, she felt she hadn't quite hit the point she had been aiming at.

"Merrily, yes, that's one word for it. But, some fear—and in my darker moments I am among those pessimists—some fear that one day printing money won't put Humpty Dumpty back together again. What if exporters of real things, things that you can't create by typing zeroes into a computer—exporters of rice, wheat, oil, uranium—what if they stop believing these fiat currencies like the pound are worth anything? I tell you, it would be most unpleasant. Banks would fail, payroll payments would bounce, exporters and importers wouldn't get paid, rich countries would sink into a decades-long depression, and in poor countries millions of people would simply die of starvation, lack of energy, and be cut off from even basic medicines. Did you know a billion and a half people in Africa import more than eighty-five percent of their food? They'd get the worst of it.

"Back in 2008, at the very last hour, governments stepped in and saved the system, essentially guaranteeing institutional solvency. Of course, they did so with fiat currency, just notional money generated in ones and zeroes on computers. They simply wrote bigger cheques due in the future to cash the ones that were due presently, and it all worked because it had to. Since 2008, the financial world has grown much, much larger, into that quadrillion figure we mentioned. The question is: Would anyone still trust government guarantees again if another emergency arose? What would happen if no one had any faith in the guarantees of the fiat currency issuers like Britain and America?"

Ellie nodded in what she hoped was a sage and comprehending manner, one which would utterly obscure the fact her competency in finance began and ended with having to reply to rude letters from her banker about her overdrawn accounts. "But how could they not trust government? They have all the money and gold and what not reserves, er… don't they?"

The mayor shook his head sadly. "Not since 1971. That's when America went off the gold standard after the French." Lord Tempest's sanguine features creased into a small but very distinct disapproving Anglo-Saxon frown. "When French President Pompidou demanded America exchange several hundred million worth of its paper dollars, then in possession of the French, for cold hard gold bullion, and since America had printed more money than it had gold to back it, Mr. Nixon quite understandably told the Frenchman to stuff it. Only very recently, China and Russia have decided to back their currencies by commodity reserves, which include gold."

Ellie continued the sage-like nodding and idly fidgeted with the only item she possessed that was reassuringly backed by eighteen-carat gold, her wristwatch.

"Well, my dear, is anything the matter? You looked perturbed for a moment."

"Oh, uh, nothing. I was just…"

The easily distracted peer followed her gaze to her wrist. "Oh, I say, is that a George Daniels?"

"It is. You have it exact. It's a gift from my parents. My father's first occupation was apprentice watchmaker at the Daniels' workshop."

"Of course, of course, right. I am reminded." Lord Tempest's eyes narrowed. "Was it not your very own parents who discovered the terrible Hereford crime scene?"

Ellie affirmed it and emphasized they'd been well taken care of by the authorities, including Inspector Harrigan. She omitted the rather precipitous arrest and accusatory interrogation at Scotland Yard and the unintentionally fortuitous lack of access to a charging station at the impound garage while reclaiming the Reliant.

"Horrific crime. These terrorists, they're more than just... I fear they are out to discredit or sabotage Kore Energy itself. The firm is an international behemoth, site-planning operations in eighty-nine countries. Every financial firm and pension fund in Britain is invested in their common shares and their Triple A-rated bonds up to their eyeballs. I've loaned some of my finest officers to help with solving the case before the New Millenium's Jewel in the Crown of the British economic empire. But, ho, tut tut, never say that in front of former Prime Minister Riffi; he'll think you're having a go at India, the previous Jewel, you recall, before Ghandi and all that independence business."

The mayor's lips compressed, and he set his jaw more firmly, seemingly resolving a debate he had silently been having with himself. "I believe the situation demands of us that we use all means to catch the fiendish perpetrators. All means and every means, yes. Perhaps means and methods which, strictly speaking, would appear irregular."

The odd man's monocle-enlarged eye, as well as his life-sized one, looked hard at Ellie. He then rose and picked up a silver tray holding the fat envelope Ellie had glimpsed. Lord Tempest held it out to her. She'd been a journalist long enough to know when someone was leaking important information. She snatched the documents off the tray before the offbeat fellow could change his mind. The mayor smiled with polite aristocratic pomposity, then escorted her the few steps between her interview seat and the exit.

She hurried out of the building, utterly disregarding the biting cold wind, and found a streetlamp that was in working order, and by its light she flipped through the sheaf of papers. They appeared to be the entire police file on the Hereford Five case, including autopsies and lab reports. She exhaled a great gust of breath, which turned to a gout of steam, and looked behind her more than once as she searched for a cab. What now? In the mystery novels she'd studied at her publisher's suggestion and with a view to writing something that would earn enough money to avoid bankruptcy, which the Daily Snail would report with almost as much glee as they had shown publishing her obituary, in those stories, the detective like Mr. Holmes or Miss Marple always seemed blessed with the knowledge necessary to interpret highly arcane clues. One glance at the leaked documents forced the realization upon her that she had no such requisite skills.

Even if she should take her immediate circle of friends and colleagues into her confidence, and thereby expose them to unknown danger, no one at her newspaper, and not even Ran Oliphant, had the technical knowledge to quickly and quietly sort through this mass of data for relevant details. However, there was one last alternative, and according to the elegant George Daniels timepiece on her wrist, it was still visiting hours.

Once she had tried to flag down and then obstinately chased a rusty and squeaking EV pedi-taxi until the lazy git stopped at a light and could no longer plausibly act as though he did not see her furious hand waving, she said to the driver, "Please take me to St. Bartholomew's Hospital for the Criminally Insane."

Chapter 17

Ellie teetered on a duct-taped, cushionless slat of plywood which served as the single seat inside the rickshaw-style ride. This seating area was encased in likewise patched-up plastic sheeting. While sightseers would not have been thrilled by the nearly opaque dirty covering, the small electric heater powered by the bicycle's battery warmed the tiny passenger space sufficiently for her to take off her gloves.

Her driver was a shapeless and sexless blob of many layers and many scarves; he or she or it alternated between coasting the e-bike on slight declines and furiously pedalling up inclines. At the speed they were going, the six miles between Kamal Chunchie and the hospital might take an hour, if the poor gig worker didn't keel over from myocarditis.

She decided to phone Barts Health NHS Trust just to be certain her trip would be fruitful. Predictably, she encountered an artificial intelligence service, which bounced her between voice-activated queries and touch-tone menus.

"Maybe the Luddites had a point," she muttered and rang off, hotly frustrated.

After pondering who might best help her, she settled on the not entirely disagreeable option of calling Inspector Harrigan. The Barts facility, with its medical museum, teaching hospital, and high-security ward, was in the City's jurisdiction, so perhaps he had some pull. He picked up right away and kindly inquired in a most sincere and manly way after her well-being and that of her roommate. She couldn't tell him the exact nature of her errand, considering it part of the confidence between herself and Lord Tempest, so she merely mentioned the name of the patient she needed to see straightaway.

"That, um, individual? Are you certain?" he said. "I should have thought you'd have had enough upset for one year."

Her incarcerated friend was infamous among members of London's police due to numerous escapes and enthusiastic, albeit patriotic, homicidal tendencies.

"She's not as bad as all that, Inspector. She's never tried to kill me." Then she remembered that assertion was directly contradicted in her own last book. "I mean, while she certainly put me in situations where my chances of survival were nearly nil, she never did so with much forethought. So could you please get me into St. Barts?"

"If you're determined to go, I am bound to assist a lady in need." After putting her on hold for a few minutes, he informed her all was arranged.

Ellie paid the muffled-up creature who had brought her by e-gifting him a pet tarantula from PurpleCreepies.co.uk, which accepted payment from her crypto wallet, and the fine arachnid specimen was judged a fair exchange for his/her/their/zher efforts by her energetic and enigmatic chauffeur. She walked over to the hospital guards' hut. The security screener merely took a cursory look inside her handbag and let her pass through the final Underground-style turnstile into the recesses of the formidable and grim facility.

The corridors were all painted pastel peach along the wainscoting, with lilac above. Generic music played which, far from having a soothing effect, set her teeth on edge. The air smelled a mixture of lavender essential oils, unwashed humans, and disinfectant. No one took any notice of her until she raised her visitor's badge and stopped a nurse.

"Could you direct me to the visiting area?"

"Wot?" the heavyset older woman said in a voice that conveyed mild surprise and end-of-shift lethargy.

"Miss Sato—"

"No one here by that name."

"Wait, please, no, that's me, I am Sato, the person who is here visiting," she spoke slowly and distinctly in a manner compatible with the public employee brain. "I, Miss Sato, wish to see a patient of yours: Annunciata Romanov China."

Had she jabbed a hatpin into the older woman's ample behind, she could not have straightened up and started wide awake any more rapidly than she did; that name got the lady's attention. She also covered the nametag hanging from her pronounced bosom, and with the other hand pointed sheepishly down a side hallway before soundlessly scurrying in the opposite direction, trailing her mop like an enormous wet gray tail. Like fear-inducing mildew, her friend Annunciata's aura had permeated through the high-security madhouse. Some people were just destined to be queen bees wherever they landed up.

At the place indicated, there stood a single, solid-looking door with a square window of laminated glass. Ellie edged around the corner, and from the other side she heard a shuffling, as though something were being pushed across the floor tiles. She looked in.

"AH!" She jumped back at the sudden appearance of a gray-haired old hag's face.

"Lucy," came a voice from behind the hair, "let her in."

The door creaked and was held open by the hag, whom Ellie guessed to be a senior inmate; she was a wild-eyed woman wearing a purple jumpsuit with a mad shock of greasy hair curled on top of her head like the grossest turban ever. This hirsute appendage framed a deeply lined, elongated face, the puckered lips of which looked frozen in mid-suck.

"Now leave us," said an ice-cold voice from the shadows in a tone barely above a whisper.

Lucy bowed her head, as though the words from her mistress had scored her hunched back like unforgiving fronds of a cat-o'-nine-tails, and she shrank away.

"Well, Anna, I see you've been winning friends and influencing people, as always," Ellie said, feigning a bolder confidence than she felt being alone with Britain's most accomplished poisoner. "How have you been?"

Annunciata Romanov China was a severe-looking woman five years Ellie's senior who exuded orders of a magnitude more seriousness. What first appeared to be sweat beading up on her exposed skin, Ellie knew to be mystical Rosicrucian symbols tattooed in micronized silver and gold. Her pupils were also augmented. She watched Ellie sit down opposite her with three dark elliptical shapes in each eye as she said, in a bored voice, "How have I been? Incarcerated."

"I see you've got the staff eating out of your hand, er, so to speak." Ellie smiled nervously and looked at the gray-haired Lucy, who had retreated out into the hallway and had just snuck a peek in at them, which Annunciata did not fail to see.

"Off with you, or no more extra Valium from my allotment." She shook her head. "Bloody halfwit, Lucy is, and a firebug, although she has a lovely singing voice when they get her med mix spot on. After the last round of staff cuts, they made Lucy a trustee with street privileges. Pfft! I have more medical degrees than the chief of staff. *I* should be running Barts."

Ellie suppressed a quip about inmates administering the asylum.

"Maybe some days out could be arranged," Ellie said pleasantly, wondering how best to broach the subject of the favor she badly needed Annunciata to grant. "Recently, I can share with you, in quiet confidence: I've got the ear of the mayor, Lord Tempest, and of course my first thought was to pop in to see whether you needed anything."

Annunciata's astonishingly decorated eyeballs stared at her unblinkingly.

Lord Tempest's name prompted a sound halfway between a hearty throat clearing and a derisive chuckle. "He's a nutter. In fact, if there was any justice, he and half his inbred family would be in here instead of me." She sat up and leaned forward, which motion made her cheap plastic chair creak in a way Ellie found a bit creepy and menacing. Then her friend added, with enough delight to be more than a little disturbing: "Speaking of justice, I heard someone tried to kill you. What a diversion that must have been from your normally drab spinsterish life."

"You needn't sound so cheery about it."

"I would never, ever be cheery if they'd offed you," Annunciata said with a dash of indignation. "You're my only civilian visitor. But it is an opportunity. You know, as part of my personal journey to redemptive and restorative rehabilitation, I've decided to use lethal means only on people who deserve it. Morally, I mean, not just because the government sanctions an extra-judicial execution."

She'd first met Annunciata in the Middle East, where MI6 employed her talents eliminating people they disapproved of.

"So whom do you suspect? That's why you came, right? You've so little experience in wet work. From what I've read in your books, in your whole career you've never intentionally offed anyone," she said with a touch of pity and condescension.

Ellie gently shifted the conversation from premeditated "offing" toward her actual area of needfulness. At first, when handed the file Lord Tempest had leaked, Annunciata's tattooed lip turned up as a teenager's might when confronted with extra homework, but she soon found her groove.

"Oh my, this is marvelously macabre. The papers, even the trashy ones like yours, hardly do the work justice," she said after a few minutes leafing through police pictures of "the work," also known as the Hereford Five crime scene and the autopsy reports. Ellie didn't bother to mention her parents hadn't found anything marvelous about the scene of the work at all.

"Oh, oh, oh," Annunciata mumbled to herself with growing glee. "What knobs these Met detectives are, utterly clueless." She rapidly scanned through the fat sheaves of paper. Her delicately tattooed fingers returned most of the pages to the folder but selected a few for extraction, which she placed in a neat pile to her left.

Well, that was an easy sell, Ellie thought. If Annunciata had balked at helping her, she had prepared a whole guilt-inducing tirade about one of her previous visits to Barts during which the devious villainess had drugged her and escaped by switching places with her, a prison break which left Ellie trapped inside the madhouse with the Croydon Cannibal.

"How is the Canni— I mean, our dear friend Harry?"

"The Cannibal? He escaped months ago, helped by his Russian girlfriend. The board of directors used the Secrets Act to keep it all hush-hush. Now you hush. I'm trying to concentrate, and I'm just getting to the most gripping and dramatic parts of the coroner's report."

A slowly dripping faucet in the next room was the only sound accompanying the turning of loose-leaf pages, until finally Annunciata flipped over the last one and let out a breath.

"Now I suppose you want my insights."

"It would really help me redeem my professional disgrace of having printed, as you so sagely pointed out, all that balderdash about the case up till now," Ellie said sarcastically.

"Before I forget," she said, digging into her brassier, which was made of black lace inlaid with patterns of dozens of black widow spiders. With a proud flourish, she brought out what appeared to be the tops of two syringes. "Got a present for you."

"Anna…" She cringed involuntarily and retracted the few parts of her skin that were bare.

"Not to stick you with, I promise. Something in case those people try to harm you again, a really quite special something if I do say. Most people think it's easy to put someone into an instant coma. They read about the von Bulow affair and start squirting insulin into their spouse's veins." Anna shook her head at their folly. "Doing it reliably, and not fatally? Sooo much more complex, and doing it so only you can reverse the process—*ein Meisterstück*. Here you go. I call it the Injucunda Somnia duo; the red needle puts 'em down, the blue one brings 'em back when they're tied to a chair and you've got all your interrogation tools out. Have fun."

"That's so thoughtful," Ellie said, carefully accepting the gifts. "And now I feel horrid for not bringing you anything."

"But you did. This was a fun read, but not exactly a mystery requiring Miss Marple to solve."

"You know who did it?" Ellie gasped.

"Don't be a ditz. But I can tell you a few things… Well? Get out one of your annoying fountain pens and some paper. Good. Firstly, I won't have the pleasure of any of the murderers' company in here. Any resemblance to a mad, cult-inspired ritual massacre, which some of the local rags are playing it up as, is entirely superficial.

"Next, the staging on the rural road with the lopped-off heads and what not, was improvised, not meticulously planned. I'll bet anything when the scene was fresh your parents could have gathered enough evidence to pinch the lot of the sloppy wankers, tire tracks, footprints, even cool stuff like fingerprints frozen right on the surface of eyeballs."

She let out a startling peal of laughter, which rebounded faintly from the bare, moisture-dripping walls of the asylum. "Eyeballs! That reminds me, Harry, the Cannibal, he shared a singular story one time during a group therapy session: he had taken his dirty perverted nonce of an uncle to a machine shop and, using a motorized bench vise…"

Ellie's former roommate probably noticed her face turning a pale shade of green to match the walls and relented sharing her fond reminiscences of their mutual serial killer buddy.

"Never mind, I'll tell you when you're in a better mood. Look at the time, visiting hours are over soon. What I meant to say, before you interrupted, is if no one's been pinched for this decapitation caper, either Scotland Yard has really let standards fall or they're not trying."

"Why wouldn't they try?"

"Been told not to," Anna said with an amused glint shining in her tattooed eyeballs.

"By whom?" Ellie said, astonished.

Her friend leaned forward. "By the people who tell underlings to do things, or else someone like me, just not as attractive, gets called to make them go poof." Annunciata flicked her razor-sharp fingernails in the air, then stared at Ellie in the creepy, intense, and perfectly motionless way she had before concluding: "So, despite the danger to you personally, you're not going to let it go, are you? Trying to catch the killers all by your nonlethal and unintimidating self?"

"I've, er, made a promise."

Anna's finely inscribed cheeks glittered as she made a my-poor-naïve-chum grimace. "And people wonder why photos of you sane normies always end up on the sides of soy milk drinking boxes pathetically advertising for leads to the whereabouts of missing persons." She spread out selected pages of the police file on the stained and nicked surface of the rickety deal table. "Besides the hasty execution of the crime, the cause of death of four of the victims is obvious."

"I should say so."

"Ahem, Miss Clueless. What I mean to say is they were not decapitated while they were still conscious or even alive—the incisions are too neat. Have you ever tried to lop someone's topper off while they were struggling?"

Ellie assumed that line of inquiry was rhetorical.

"Look here." Annunciata impatiently flipped over the pictures the coroner had taken. "Their skins are all lobster red, obvious sign of carbon monoxide poisoning. The exception, the one without a boiled crustacean makeover, is the girl, the one you're interested in: Green Hope. By the by, is that really her fucking name?"

"Miriam, Miriam Goldsmid's her old name before she got involved with eco-fanatics, and Anna, I didn't say anything about being more or less interested in her as opposed to any of the others."

"When I was leafing through the file, you purposely avoided looking at her pictures, so I assume she's your main interest for some squish-squashy bourgeois savior-complex reason. But wait, there's more, as they say on the shopping channel, which besides *Bake Off* reruns are the only things we get to watch on telly here."

She picked out one of the presumed asphyxiation victims. The picture of the severed head was that of a young man with a strong jawline and a very fine head of hair, which was stylishly shaggy even though it was matted down with melted snow. "This fellow, he's quite a hottie, heh-heh, in more ways than one. Whoever killed him did him a favor, saved this bloke from one of the most agonizing deaths in the inventory: slow liquefaction of all his internal organs due to acute radiation poisoning."

"Huh?"

"Fellow was fairly glowing in the dark." She pulled out a page with lab test results. "His tissue was rife with radionuclides, including a rare vintage Iodine-131, as well as the more commonplace Cesium-134 and a heaping dose of Cesium-137."

"Could he have been involved in an accident at work or while he was trying to steal some radioactive material?" Eco-terrorists had moved on from vandalizing artwork at museums, shutting down commuter traffic for hours, and setting themselves on fire at tennis tourneys to sabotaging oil refineries and other traditional power-generating facilities. A dirty bomb was an exponential leap up the extremism scale, but not unthinkable given their twisted beliefs.

"Eleanor, we've only got his head, and even I couldn't make him talk." Annunciata's eyes narrowed and looked up, flashing catlike in the glow of the overhead fluorescents. "But come to think of it, you may have—entirely inadvertently, to be sure—grasped something useful. Sources of primary nuclear radiation are unique, like fingerprints. One look at the radioactive nuclides and an expert can tell which sort of reactor or laboratory the sample has come from.

"That reminds me, I've always wanted to try offing someone that way, ever since I read about a Russian dissident who was poisoned with polonium hidden in a pot of tea in the mid-2000s; I just haven't had the opportunity, not yet anyway, though I am hopeful. In strict confidence, I can share with you I've sent a coded message to my former boss at MI6 and offered to take out their top three Most Wanted terrorists, totally pro bono. Yes, it's a bit humbling, but you see what I've been reduced to here." Annunciata snapped her fingers at the doorway. "Lucy! Stop eavesdropping!"

Ellie turned around just in time to catch a wisp of gray hair disappearing around the corner.

"Where was I? Right, totally pro bono. How can they refuse after all I did for them in Syria and especially how I saved the day during the Ninety-Six Hour War? They are taking their time responding. Whitehall's muddled bureaucracy, I expect."

Ellie tried to block out her disturbed friend's homicidal ambitions and consider whether her unique advice could somehow assist in unravelling the astonishingly tangled mystery she'd taken on. "Cesium-134, Iodine-131, what could that mean?" Ellie whispered her thoughts aloud.

"It means," Annunciata said with a gleam in each of her six pupils, "you've once again plunked yourself way over your head in dangerous mischief. What you need is a capable sidekick, someone with everything you lack: technical knowledge, sinister connections, and zero tolerance for decency and ethics. If someone were to arrange for me to be an outpatient…"

"Oh no, Anna, last time I helped you, we had to chase you all the way to America."

"I'll promise to behave."

Ellie sensed she'd gotten all the help she was going to get without substantial reciprocation and the risk of abetting a murder spree. "Best I can do," she said as she collected her papers and kept out of range of Annunciata's often-envenomed fingernails, "is put in a wholehearted endorsement personally with Lord Tempest."

The public address system announced visitors had to clear security within ten minutes. It seemed impolite not to accept the needles with the coma-inducing toxin, so Ellie stowed them in her bag.

"Don't expect anything else for Christmas," Annunciata cautioned grumpily. "They pay me twenty pence an hour to work in the dispensary and the labs. However… I could help you with your spinsterhood problem. Get me some Washington State magic mushrooms, and I shall whip you up some of my Amor Fortis love potion; with regular applications the hallucinogenic effects are guaranteed to last longer than the average UK marriage."

Ellie thanked her chum and declined the generous offer. The significance of what the former government assassin had told her reverberated through Ellie's mind. Was the investigation into the killing of the Hereford Five being squelched and suppressed by sinister powers? Why? And how did Lord Tempest fit in? The killers—Anna had said there was more than one—had already claimed at least five victims. Such people would not hesitate to kill again.

As though reading her mind, Annunciata stopped at the doorway out from the recreation room and said, quite sourly, "Good luck to you on your solo adventure. Tell your staff to keep your obituary handy."

Then, as is possibly the habit of severely schizophrenic patients, she immediately seemed to regret uttering that resentful sentiment. Annunciata started weeping with shame and remorse, and through her gushing tears she added, "Oh! I didn't mean that. It's just... I've been so isolated since the Cannibal escaped. We used to put on theatrics. Now I'm stuck here with this mousey old loon Lucy who sits in a corner pulling out strands of their own hair and then chewing on them all day."

Ellie turned around, and through the open doorway of the interview room saw the pitiful sight of the formerly hair-beturbaned wretch squatting beside a mop pail. Lucy had unwound the snakelike coil of greasy gray locks, revealing a large pink patch of her scalp, which had been plucked quite bald on one side. Selecting one delectable strand at a time, she spun it around her finger, yanked, and then sucked it off and commenced to joylessly chew. The thought suddenly popped into Ellie's head as she patted her chum's sagging, quivering shoulders as Anna hugged her: even an amoral serial killer deserved a better class of company.

Once she had regained the city streets, she walked away with far more questions buzzing through her head than when she had entered St. Barts asylum. She had just begun sloshing through frozen muck when a geo text popped up on her phone. It was a prearranged signal that a note from Mrs. Goldsmid was waiting for her at a place tagged *Winter Redoubt #16: An Official Point of English Invincibility.*

Chapter 18

Winter Redoubt #16: An Official Point of English Invincibility turned out to be much less impressive than it sounded. Located on the bank of the Thames opposite the Isle of Dogs, it was the government's response to the complaints of impoverished native Britishers (those who still could complain, not being among the number of elderly, infirm, very young, or just unlucky, found frozen to death each winter) who had to choose between heating and eating. Working-class citizens lucky enough to obtain any manner of council housing often warmed food on antiquated radiators in a pitiable attempt to stretch their slim energy rations.

"At least the poor in Victorian times were allowed to burn coal dust pellets, what?" a red-faced greeter, who might have been old enough to remember, fairly shouted at her as she entered the big army tent. The air was shockingly humid; the surplus moisture rose in wafts of steam up from melting snow-festooned coats and sodden mittens.

The Winter Redoubt greeter and member of the vanguard of English Invincibility took no mind of her gasping like a landed trout as she inhaled one part oxygen to four or five parts water vapor. He waved his arm at two wooden tables set along the canvas tent wall behind which sat a sputtering diesel generator that was connected to a yard-long power bar which, in turn, had a dozen power cords emanating from it like some electronic squid creature. "Phone charging's got a long queue, but you can have some tea straightaway. Donation cup's behind the desk now. Buggers kept nicking it."

Ellie explained to the fellow, whose breath smelled strongly of rum, that she was there to retrieve a written message.

"Oy, Ada!" the greeter yelled at a lady wearing a crocheted headscarf standing behind a steaming cafeteria-style hot water boiler. "Anythin' for a Miss Alice Toklas?" Ada immediately consulted the array of alphabetical pigeon holes in front of her. This was a service for London's lowest caste of homeless wanderers as well as elite drug runners, those who, by choice or involuntary penurious status, were without a device capable of receiving emails or texts. Here, they could receive messages. Ellie's code name had received a note. She read it:

Fiver sends his sincere apologies, would like to meet @ my residence, 3 p.m. if you can.

Ellie walked away from the Official Point of English Invincibility, then tossed the note into a burn barrel where a few shivering souls were gathered, warming their hands. She had memorized Mrs. Goldsmid's address but had secretly hoped she'd never be called upon to go there.

The driver of a commodious and clean black cab clearly shared her prejudice. "Tow-her 'Amlets? Are you taking the piss? After dark?"

"It's still light out," Ellie protested weakly as she looked at the diffused disc of the sun hanging a finger's breath over the rooftops.

The cowardly cabbie departed rapidly enough to festoon her boots with a fresh coating of messy slush kicked up by the cozy-looking vehicle's winter tires. The escapade prompted chortling laughter from a bundled creature hunched over the burn barrel. "Oy, lookin' for a ride ta Terrible 'Amlets, missy?" he or she said with a leer on their withered face, the mouth hidden by a moldy tattered item that had once been a scarf, then informed her about a cousin who ran an unlicensed cab service.

It was nearing three o'clock, and Ellie concluded her chances of being mugged, or worse, were slightly less inside the offered conveyance than walking to the notoriously dodgy part of the city.

The bundled creature inserted filthy fingers into its toothless mouth hole and produced a surprisingly loud and melodious whistle. A minute later, her chariot appeared. Its driver was a youngish-looking fellow, most of his face covered by copper-tinted dreadlocks that looked as though they had been machine washed when the instructions they came with specified "dry clean only." The only part of his anatomy clearly visible was his protruding and bobbing Adam's apple.

The chariot in which he rolled up was an astonishingly hideous electric car. The back was full of jumper cables, a hundred yards of industrial extension cords, and a dozen plug adapters likely used to steal electricity. She hesitated, getting in the front after noticing the floor littered with burned foil wrappers.

"Aw, don't mind that, ah don' let no one use needles in me car. Smoke, only smoke, that's the rule." Copper Dreadlocks checked his mirrors and rear-facing camera, presumably looking out for coppers. "In or out, lady. 'S'cooold." Here was a man who knew the value of keeping on the move in London's urban jungle.

After weighing the urgency of her journey against the chances of receiving an impromptu jab featuring HIV and a selection of currently popular variants of hepatitis, she sat down as lightly as she could on the passenger seat's supposedly needle-free upholstery, then she told him the address.

"That'll be double."

Despite the man's shaggy mane, which made her question whether he could see the road at all, he drove the absurd-looking EV with deft efficiency up to Tower Hamlets borough.

Under the "15-Minute City" directives, the borough had been somewhat randomly sectioned off into twelve prison-camp-style subdivisions. Some local wags had painted over the fingerpost signs with witty nicknames for each section: Colditz, Stalag 17, and Mordor. The one containing Mrs. Goldsmid's council row house was shut up behind an electronic gate. The isolation of each unit and the difficulty of police responding to crimes versus the ease of access for criminals via cuts in chain-link fences and a network of abandoned man-sized sewer pipes made it a dubious place to walk after dark.

"Daft climate lockdown. S'far as we go. Cash or e-rubles, if y'please," her driver said, nodding his sheepdog coiffure at the wireless payment module duct-taped to the dash. The third card she tapped against the RFID knob, a Russian Mir card she kept on hand for jaunts to the other side of the New Iron Curtain, was accepted.

"Would you mind waiting until I'm inside the gate?" A grunt issued from the shaggy mop of hair, and Ellie walked to the intercom system which, of course, was broken.

Suddenly out from a darkened corner, a figure lurched out right at her. "Gawr!" was all she was able to say as her gallant cab driver sped off, his high-revving engine making a grinding whine as it disappeared down the stark lonely avenue, leaving a trail of snow crystals, which could have been electron exhaust, in his wake.

"Miss Sato!" The words came out from the shadows in a hushed whisper. "Sorry to frighten you."

Ellie regained her footing and tried to act unfazed, as a respectable adventuress in the mold of Amelia Earhart would most certainly do. "Ah, Mrs. Goldsmid, how kind of you to come out. And please, send any apologies toward the direction in which my faint-hearted cabman fled."

"I had to sneak about," she replied meekly. "Our section's in climate lockdown—no cars in or out and only one person per household to nip out for fifteen and a half minutes on foot. I used my allocation sending you the note. Just as well, the gate's in a bit of a state, won't open from either side even on Freedom Days."

Ellie's heart sank when she saw the nervous and expectant look on the poor lady's face. What news had she to tell her? Practically nothing, worse than nothing; everything she learned only deepened the mystery.

Mrs. Goldsmid led the way up a narrow winding cobbled path, requesting her to watch her footing where the irregular-shaped paving stones were decorated with a generous topping of ice.

"Hello, just bringing in a guest," the middle-aged lady said, apparently to no one. Then Ellie noticed she was facing a tall metal pole that had on its top a surveillance camera, the dark cyclops eye of which was tracking their movements. "I hope they don't fine me for going out of bounds; they've become quite strict with us. But what can y'do? We've all got to do our bit to save the planet, right, Miss Sato?"

Mrs. Goldsmid's council house was actually the basement portion of a townhome that had been split into eight one-room residences to cope with the chronic housing shortage. A plywood barrier had been nailed over the passageway to the upstairs, but this rude renovation had nearly no effect on the loud music and smells of cooking and marijuana coming from the neighbouring micro suite. Inside the former storage closet, which was now the kind lady's living room, sitting room, and bedroom, they came upon, of all possible creatures, Mr. Fiver. The violence-prone eco-warrior had his gloved hands pressed against an old 1950s-style radiator running under the narrow single pane of glass that framed a view of a featureless alleyway.

"It's you," he exclaimed, in a rather redundant manner. He glanced in her direction for a moment, then settled onto an ancient couch covered in a hundred sewn-together doilies. He still had on that idiotic bunny sweater, and she was quietly glad to see he was also sporting a good-sized hematoma swelling above his eyebrows, fair payment for his rude assaultive behavior.

"I think you two have been introduced," Mrs. Goldsmid said with a shy smile.

"We had a memorable interview earlier," Ellie said, giving him a fierce glare, then turning around to face their hostess. Fiver said nothing but smiled awkwardly and then, most astonishingly, he looked behind Ellie and burst into sobs. Was he that much of a snowflake that the very sight of someone who'd given him a thrashing—and on that account, a much lighter thrashing than he had asked for—that just seeing her could send him into hysterics? Was this the sort of wet laundry which called itself today's British male youth?

Ellie glanced around to the other side of the narrow room and noticed rows of shelving with pictures of a girl, a teenager, and the same person as a young lady, always with a bright winning smile, posing with prizes, awards, accolades, and graduation certificates. The early ribbons for sporting achievements and science fair projects ran sequentially right up to Secondary graduation honors. Where the name showed on these mementos, it was the name Miriam Goldsmid. Only the last few, including a photograph of her posing with a pair of thin and cadaverous men, who could only be chartered accountants, featured certificates with the name Green Hope. In that final picture, the cadaverous men were presenting her with something called the ICAS Gold Medal.

Mrs. Goldsmid immediately set about trying to comfort the distraught Fiver as he wailed. "It's impossible to think of!" He pulled on his filthy sweater as though it were causing him physical agony. "I wake up every night in shivers. Who could have done that to such a lovely person? She was noble, kind, and did so much for us; other people said she had sold out, gone corporate, but I stood by her... alwaaaaysssh." The last syllable turned into a tortured hiss and not insubstantial geyser of saliva and tears.

The actual bereaved parent, their host, prodded Fiver to take some fresh tea and a tinned biscuit. Ellie declined her offer. Judging by the lack of visible food in the house, Mrs. Goldsmid was one of the millions of Britons whose penurious existence was ever so much more difficult during winter months. Ellie rather wanted to slap the self-obsessed eco-nut, who was very fortunate she wasn't in possession of a horseshoe.

"Miss Sato," Mrs. Goldsmid said, patting Fiver on the rumpled back of his sweater, "the police haven't been in touch with me at all. Have you, er..."

Ellie held on to her packet of gruesome data contained in a now slightly damp manila envelope. That was not something the poor lady should see now or ever. However, she had to say something. "I can tell you that certain official persons have not been altogether unhelpful, Mrs. Goldsmid. There's certainly more going on than they're letting on to the public."

The intimation that her daughter's murder had not been brushed aside seemed to hearten Mrs. Goldsmid, and she looked a bit less gloomy. Even Fiver forgot his own suffering and stopped snivelling long enough to munch on an all-butter shortbread finger.

Ellie keenly wanted to ask him about the nuclear expert victim, that fellow Anna had said was riddled with radiation; he must be the same one Fiver called Oppie. Rather than bring up the topic of autopsies and body parts, she decided to ask after Green Hope's tenure with her last employer. Mrs. Goldsmid was quite forthcoming and, thankfully, the change of topic muted Fiver's howling. He sat relatively quietly, making only a whistling, wheezing sound through stuffed-up nostrils and occasionally touching the angry red-and-purple boil swelling on his prominent forehead.

Green Hope had worked for Kore Energy for just over twelve months. In that time, she'd risen from an entry-level situation compiling accounts payables to an executive position reporting directly to the audit committee and Chairman Kore himself, Mrs. Goldsmid said.

"No one could say she was undeserving of the advancement; she was the bright spark wherever she went, top of her classes, and at the Kore company very dedicated to the company's mission."

"Did she ever have any contact with the technical teams? Did she travel?"

Ellie's host switched on an ancient computer precariously perched on a wobbly end table, and on a tiny monitor she opened a folder of pictures. Several recent ones featured Green Hope posing on drilling platforms.

"She went to Hawaii and some place in Africa."

"Ethiopia," Fiver put in. "Kore's pilot geothermal energy projects are in Hawaii and Ethiopia. Before they went live and started producing gads of energy, everyone thought Kore was bonkers, but now the stock's worth more than all the oil companies in the world put together. She even told me to buy stock. Why didn't I listen to her? All I have now is bloody crypto!" His voice trailed off in a rueful, sobbing, self-pitying whine.

Ellie recalled Lord Tempest saying much the same thing about Kore Energy, and remembered the doctor himself at White's Club throwing out fantastically large sums as though he were playing with Monopoly money.

"So Kore's geothermal energy innovations could put other companies out of business?"

Fiver nodded vigorously. "No one will put a penny into fusion, and Parliament's banned any new wind projects until they see how much the first English geothermal project produces."

Then, Ellie thought, why would Kore offer to buy Ran's nuclear project? Speaking of nuclear, the topic of the other dismembered victim could not be put off any longer.

"You mentioned your other friend, Oppie."

Fiver gripped the doilies covering the cushion upon which he was seated and seemed as though he was about to curl over bodily and mash his face onto it. "Two of my best friends! Gone! Just like that, in one month, just at Christmas! Why do these things happen to me?"

He calmed down as Mrs. Goldsmid refreshed his tea and continued to rub and pat him on the back of his enormous bunny sweater.

"He, Oppie, quit his last job, then went off, dunno where. I think he was interested in working for Kore. Oppie was plenty smart, y'know, physics and math and stuff. I saw him talking to Green Hope more'n a few times."

"Do you think there was anything between them?"

"Those two? Like romance? Naw. Also, when he came back from wherever, he was not lookin' too well. Green around the gills, tired, not eating. When he wouldn't see a doctor, Green Hope became very anxious and brought one of her friends from Imperial College by the squat. He diagnosed para-something, paratyphoid. Just needed some antibiotics, though he never looked altogether well, even after he finished with the pills. Musta picked up a bug from some foreign place."

Or was Oppie starting to feel the effects of a lethal dose of radiation? Ellie wondered.

"He was also bummed out. His previous boss wouldn't give him a recommend, probably because of the whizz bang way he done his work leaving."

"Really? Where was he working before his trip?"

"Lemme think. Oh yee-ah it was BritEnergy, run by that all-star jocko fash bastard, Ranulph Oliphant."

Chapter 19

"Hello, Ran."

"Now who's stalking whom?" As soon as he answered, Ellie realized she hadn't a clue what to say. One of Ran's own former employees was a Hereford Five victim. Why had he not mentioned it? Was he keeping such close contact with her not to protect her but to keep her from digging too deeply? The awkward silence carried on until Ran finally broke it.

"I think I have a notion why you've called. We shouldn't speak over the phone."

"My thoughts exactly."

"I'm just shuttling back from France," he said and suggested a time and place to meet in town around seven that very evening.

"Sounds great," she replied with growing trepidation that felt like nausea.

"Are you feeling altogether well?"

How could he tell anything just by her voice?

After stuttering for a moment, she managed to say, "Though it's barely six, I've had quite the insightful and challenging day."

"Same here. Ellie, you're not still pursuing the same series of events you were doing the last time we met?"

"I've taken… a hands-off approach."

"Really? How does that pull together with a visit to a certain City political office as well as popping in to see our mutual friend at the special care hospital?"

"Ran!" He *was* still actively spying on her! It was too much.

"We agreed you were to drop it," he said curtly.

"I agreed— No-nothing, not even the slightest…" Once she had collected herself, she added, "I said no such thing. See you at seven." She rang off and felt her ears get hot with frustration. As she walked toward the *Juggernaut* office, she felt her ears must positively be giving off steam in the biting cold air. As though an atmospheric zephyr had ventured an attempt to dampen her quietly seething hot head, a blast of ice crystals hit her in the face. The wind was whipping up through the streets, and the sky looked dark and not at all calm. Neither was the newsroom—Ed and John were having a go at each other.

"This is exactly why we've all got to do our part," John said, pointing to a TV screen on the wall. It showed the satellite image of a massive pinwheel shape animation tracking from Iceland toward the North Sea. "These huge killer cyclones are only supposed to happen once a century, now they're every bloody year: a constant stream of atmospheric rivers drowning the human race. It's… it's biblical, and it's all our fault for ruining the climate!" The screeching sound that punctuated his diatribe would have done justice to an enraged baboon.

"Go on, mun, epoxy yourself to something," Ed spat back, waving his handset at him. "Look here, the Burns Day Storm, January 1990; the North Sea Flood of February 1953. First you wankers were talkin' new Ice Age in the 1970s, then it was 'we're all drownin',' then when that didn't happen you ranted about global boilin'. Extinction my ass. It's called weather, deal with it."

John, as though thwacked by the horrendous blow of Climate Change Denialism coming at him from the other side of the narrow newsroom, rocked backward in his executive tilter chair and hit his head against the wall with an audible bonk, but he was in a climate-righteous frenzy and did not seem to feel the self-inflicted assault. "Of course, you make my point for me! Climate genocide has been going on since the eighteen hundreds, the Industrial Revulsion! *We* started it. England is guilty of killing the entire planet!"

"Ed! Ed! You realize to believe that, you have to believe by measuring cow burps and farts, scientists can control the temperature of the entire *planet* to a fraction of a degree as though it had a digital thermostat and a tiny minority of the global population can fine-tune the settings thirty years into the future? D'you not comprehend how utterly deranged that sounds?"

Before the *Juggernaut's* climate crusader could launch another salvo of righteous indignation, Ellie opened the front door, which she had just gently closed, and this time slammed it shut with a pistol-shot *crack*.

"Gentlemen, go for dinner." They looked at her as though she were a charity mugger who'd haphazardly wandered in, perhaps thinking the establishment was still a pub. They did not move. "Out! Join Smitty wherever he's gone; it's likely to be warmer there than it is in here. Boss lady says: depart!"

As her only two staff hustled out, grumbling something about "expense reimbursements" and "toxic work environment," Ellie settled into her editor's orthopedic chair. It was located nearest to the fading radiant heat source; she put her feet up on it and checked her email.

Esmunda reported in. She was cleared to leave the hospital, no one had tried to assassinate her since the last time, and she asked Ellie to remind her to get some treats for her guardian pets, Chestnut and Magellan. It was just as well Esmunda had decided to stay at her uncle's house instead of returning to Mayfair. Ellie was in dire need of good counsel, and Esmunda's core knowledge base spanned the narrow range between amateur theatrics, soft drugs, gadgets, and government income assistance programs. Weightier matters normally sent Ellie almost exclusively in Ran's direction, which was certainly awkward in this instance, seeing as she had not quite been able to eliminate him as being somehow involved in the gruesome Hereford Five murders.

It was beyond the pale to consider that he'd personally carved up the corpses and planted the heads in the roadway. On the other hand, Ran had nerves of steel, had received elite cold-blooded killer training in the Royal Marines, and she'd seen him do pretty violent things in the past, but only to people who richly deserved it.

And what was his relationship to Dr. Kore? Could it just be coincidence that Ran's former employee Oppie was a victim, along with Dr. Kore's personal assistant Green Hope? She stared at the ceiling of the former pub and wondered at the strange objects left embedded there. Some were recognizable as steel-tip darts that had gone exceptionally astray on their way to the corkboard; other additions had been painted over by many layers of interior matte acrylic paint and were mere shapeless blobs. Directly above her there hung something that alternatively looked like discarded chewing gum or someone's front teeth, depending upon how she angled her head.

Sitting up, she blew out a breath, which fogged up and formed a vague translucent cone that reached up toward the lumpy ceiling.

"Can they have cut off our heat? Again?" More likely one of her staff had shifted their ration of electricity to their computer so they could download dirty movies or mine crypto. She really hadn't the energy to discover which and just bundled herself more closely in her coat, then she opened the ghastly file folder she had received from Lord Tempest. If she were writing a serious news piece—which was antithetical to the mission of the modern British press, but supposing she were so inclined—what facts would stand out as "leads"? The premier one would have to be the information about Oppie, as one did not come across a dangerously radioactive head every day.

She flicked over to the confidential lab report. Anna had highlighted these in the sort of large capital letters a primary school teacher would mark up students' homework: *CESIUM AND STRONTIUM.*

A few minutes of fishing around on the internet proved that Oppie was almost certainly poisoned at a nuclear reactor. The investigation notes revealed Oppie had been let go from his last employment at Ran Oliphant's BritEnergy for "breaching security and attempting to access unauthorized areas." Why hadn't Ran mentioned Oppie?

In considering the matter, something else nagged her, something that was known to nearly no one else: that weird illness he'd had, which Fiver thought was causing Oppie's ill health after he had come back from a trip to the continent. She typed in "paratyphoid," a range of dates, and "Europe." Among a list of travel advisories, there had been two outbreaks: one in Sicily and one in eastern Poland. The disease was relatively rare: all Britain recorded only two hundred cases each year among a population of sixty million.

"All right, we have the vague recollection of a Polish phrase book and an unusual disease, which must have been confirmed by lab test results. Odds are Oppie's last trip abroad after Ran fired him was to eastern Poland," Ellie said to no one in particular. What had he been looking for? Work? Perhaps he'd applied for a teaching or research position. Given the man's background, no evidence he spoke any language but English, and with his long-standing commitment to eco-fanaticism, was that likely? Poland had no operating nuclear reactors and got eighty percent of its electricity from burning coal and gas. Was he there for a protest? Oppie's file revealed many arrests for public mischief and obstruction, so if he had indeed visited Poland, he was lucky to get in at all, and a work permit would likely be out of the question since they required foreigners to pass a criminal records check. Any arrest by the generally humorless Polish Internal Security Agency would have been noted in his police file under Interpol notices. There were none.

Ellie's frustration only grew as she turned over contradictory facts and dead-end speculations. Almost of their own accord, her hands went digging through her purse for Green Hope's unique earring and the data hidden on it. The smooth metal felt cool in her fingers. She was just about to plug it into her computer's data port when it occurred to her that the last time she'd done so, Esmunda had been attacked and their house ransacked. Could the data on the fob be rigged with a virus or some sneaky stealthy computer booby trap thingy? Had opening its files at Mayfair sent out a secret message to villains who had killed Green Hope and the others?

She thrust the secret data cache back in her purse. What did she know about financial data and geological reports? The only people she knew who were experts and might help her all worked for the hunky-nerdly mysterious, possibly sinister, and certainly not telling all he knew, Mr. Oliphant.

Her phone chimed an incoming text.

"Bugger, how does he do that?"

It was from Ran. He was putting her off.

Something pressing just came up, have to reschedule, stay inside out of the storm.

She was about to angry-text a reply when a massive, jumbled text came in. This one was from the mayor, Lord Tempest, who was either in a great flurry or had HRH-style fat fingers not at all suited to a tiny handset keypad.

Glad I was able to catch/ you Can't say much over the airwaves, rather porous what? Bad going loose ships. If you know what I imply. But the short and long of it is, any chance you could come to Stoke Bramwell, my home on the coast, tonight by…900 nine 10at the latest.? I know short notice but I've just got the last pieces of the puzzle, if you will recall, without putting too fine a point onnit, the one of which we spoke earlier_say no more, profoundly important, not just for justice but the national I,'p enough said, what?? You're the only impartial party who knows most all the details and whom I trust implicitly. You---must---come.

Bloody right I'll go, Ellie thought, then affirmed in a more ladylike fashion, repeating herself more than once to make certain the eccentric old fellow noticed the incoming text on his phone. She thought a moment, then went back to her unfinished text to Ran.

What a coincidence, I've also had 'something pressing' come up. See you at Stoke Bramwell no later than 10PM. 🙂 😊

The silence that ensued from Ran's side of the conversation confirmed that, for once, Ellie had hit the nail bang on, getting the better of him without giga-billions of spying technology.

Chapter 20

"Would the la-day per-raps have a ray-shun card?" The elderly gas station attendant had to fairly yell over the gusting wind even though he was inches from her half-rolled-down window. Ellie dug around in the center console compartment, pulling rather viciously at the polished cherry-wood veneer glove box hatch. What would they do if she'd exceeded her petrol ration allotment? Would the gas station geezer be obliged to impound her car and sequester her in the rear of the convenience store until the fossil fuel coppers came?

"Here you go." She handed him a laminated bar code card. "It's corporate, unlimited fills." *At least until January 1*, she thought bitterly. She didn't mind having no money as long as she could enjoy the perquisites of the ultra rich. "And add yourself fat tip. It's Christmas, you know."

"Couldn't do that, ma'am. I won't profit from people who're bent on killing the ozone," the man said with an eco-smug tone of superiority.

Ellie gave him the finger as his snow-swept figure waddled back to the pump, the bloody humbugger. He was dressed in an odd compound of snow and rain gear, his wide boots sheathed in a layer of frozen snow, barely keeping their purchase on the slippery concrete as the wind howled a higher note.

At the risk of murdering the entire planet, Ellie had decided her journey to Stoke Bramwell, Lord Tempest's country seat, required her to drive the Bentley SUV. As she had fiddled with the controls, which had to rival those in a space shuttle in complexity and number, she'd discovered something called "ice drive." While she had no idea what that was and no intention of researching the topic in the manual, its mere existence was comforting as she passed the bounds of the great city and traffic became sparser and the weather utterly foul.

Stoke Bramwell was situated on a promontory just above Clacton-on-Sea. Normally it lay a two-hour leisurely drive from London. She'd allowed for three to arrive on time at her destination near the coast, but she was still behind schedule. Tonight, of all nights, why had the mayor chosen that location? When she'd been in his office, Ellie had received the impression of an erudite man under immense strain, using all his powers of self-control not to show it. Was this sudden summons something like a dam bursting? Perhaps he only felt safe on his home turf. Was he afraid of Ran Oliphant? Who else had been invited?

"'Ere yee bee!" The petrol station man's voice briefly triumphed in a most unmatched battle with the wind.

Ellie took the receipt. "Thank you very much. Stay warm, and please know I'm doing my very best for the ozone layer."

The man's face creased as he blinked away a clump of blown snowflakes and glared back. As she drove away, she last sighted her thoroughly indoctrinated attendant waving his arm up at the storm, shouting what seemed like: "Look what ye've done!"

While her petrol tank got filled, Ellie had plugged in her fully charged phone. The charging light blinked reassuringly beside a screen devoid of new texts or missed calls. She was half expecting the mayor to call off the meeting, or at least disinvite her. What could this mysterious gathering really be about? Lord Tempest seemed most concerned about the stability of the country's financial markets. Perhaps he feared a scandal involving Ran's company BritEnergy, if the Hereford Five slayings were even distantly linked to the construction of his mega project nuclear plant. Had Oppie received a fatal dose of radiation while working there? Had he gone to Eastern Europe seeking treatment? If so, how had his partial remains ended up in the grotesque display outside Dr. Kore's company headquarters?

A sharp *whap!* against her windscreen dashed these speculative thoughts from her mind.

"Gwarrr!" *Was that a bloody seagull that just hit me?* The impact caused her to swerve so violently she'd certainly have caused a head-on collision had the highway not been nearly deserted. She slowed and stopped. Looking more closely at the object plastered on the glass right in front of her nose, no matter what angle she held her head, she failed to see what she half expected: the blood, guts, and broken beak of a kamikaze seabird. It was more an undifferentiated green-gray mass. Luckily it wasn't hard enough to have broken the glass.

She ducked outside into the roaring wind, closing her eyes against flying ice particles that stung like tiny BB pellets, and discovered… a mass of frozen seaweed. Was she that close to the coast already, or were sea things flying astonishingly far distances inland? She peeled off the flattened glob, and the wind grabbed it and continued it on its merry way down the highway. She shivered a moment, pressing herself into the heated seat, checked her silent phone, then drove on.

Stoke Bramwell was a listed historical manor belonging to the Tempest clan. A website offered paid tours, bookings for weddings, and wine bottles of dubious vintage featuring madcap images of the first historical marquess. Somehow the thirty-acre estate had survived wars, family feuds, and Marxist governments. While it was unclear to whom the estate was entailed, she suspected the financially savvy mayor kept the estate afloat on today's treacherous economic tides.

When the dashboard clock digits flipped to 9:30 p.m., she'd been driving nearly an hour in pitch dark. The heavy SUV hurtled through the deluge of water streaming down from an unseen and nigh-inexhaustible celestial firehose. Gusts of wind buffeted her this way and that, threatening to push her conveyance into the ditch running along the narrow country road.

Rounding a turn, she saw the reflection of something flash. If it was a sign, she mustn't miss it; getting lost or stuck, or both, would make her the butt of Ran's amusement for ages. Hitting the brakes hard caused the SUV to skid to a halt, headlight beams revealing an unprepossessing sign: *Stoke Bramwell, Private Property.*

Ellie leaned forward, saw the way ahead was clear of fallen branches, and proceeded down the nearly hidden side path, vigilantly peering ahead into the blue-white cone that her headlights bored through the turgid firmament of the surrounding darkness. She could not see a thing except the road strewn with twigs and evergreen needles a few yards in front, but had the impression she was passing between a row of evergreen trees grown thickly together. She eased off the gas, was conscious of compacting icy snow under the heavy vehicle's wheels, and anticipated at any moment encountering a gate or sharp turn.

The road, however, remained straight and, after a time, widened, joined now on one side by a path for hikers or horses. Slowly a shape revealed itself. Through hurtling icy snow she could see a large stony pillar, then another of the same dimensions, and between them an archway. Was that a gate? Could she fit through or should she stop—

Out jumped a hooded figure, their appearance so sudden she nearly twisted the steering wheel the wrong way. A flashlight flared right in her eyes, and it was a miracle she didn't mow the reckless figure down.

She blinked and could see mostly spots in front of her as she passed. The fellow had a substantial build and held a hand torch, which he used to wave her through the narrow archway. By the light reflecting from the Bentley's windshield, she saw a flash of other, rather disjointed details. The man had on ski goggles and was otherwise muffled up against the rising storm; he wore a reflective vest with the word SECURITY blazoned across the front. The hand holding the torch was clad in a Gore-Tex glove, on its back was a styled *P*, which she recognized as belonging to the Prada label.

Lord Tempest must be paying his people well if they can afford 800-pound gloves, she thought. As well he should if he expected them to stand under trees, directing traffic during cyclones and electric storms.

Glimpses of grand old Stoke Bramwell caught in her headlights as she drove slowly down the driveway, revealing a more refined sort of greenery—topiary and manicured hedges being tormented by the wind and beads of icy snow in equal measure as was being doled out to their wild cousins dwelling in the surrounding hills. Catching sight of the warm, steady glow from a small lantern that hovered a few feet above the ground, she aimed at it. Though she could see nearly no details of the façade or towers, she had gleaned from the tourist pictures online that the place was one of those rambling structures that had been built and rebuilt over the centuries.

The main drive led up to the most modern structures and toward a small but upright figure, who held the lantern as steadily as though it were attached to the arm of a statue. Though cloaked in a billowing rain slicker, this second member of the staff standing under the porte-cochère was every inch the quintessential figure of a country butler.

"Miss Sato, I presume?" Being the ultimate respectable manservant, he was able to project his voice over the howling wind without appearing to shout. "His Lordship's other guests are all present. I've put their conveyances in the garage, but given how the storm's progressing, I'd recommend leaving her here under this very solid coach gateway, if you please, miss."

As he spoke, he pointed a cautionary and disapproving hand in the direction of a wooden structure of recent construction standing on the other side of the driveway. It was flanked by floodlights on poles bent over at alarming angles. The metal siding covering the garage wavered and waffled in the wind. It would certainly please her not to be electrocuted or have a garage wall collapse on her Bentley, so she cut the motor. Instantly, the timbre of the storm's fury notched up. She hadn't noticed how reassuring the constant purr of the big car's growling combustion engine had been. Despite the thoughtful and respectable reception, she suddenly felt very alone and isolated.

"She won't be staying, Jorkins!" The much less respectable, and anything but welcoming, shouting came from the open doorway.

Oh yes, she will! Ellie thought with some warmth. She stepped down from the SUV and slammed the door, which sent a rain of dirty road ice onto her stylish but impractical half boots.

"Thank you, Jorkins." Ellie put her hand up to her face as much to shield it from the wind as to aid her being heard. "I shall take your kind advice and leave the car here. Oh, and please tell Mr. Oliphant that my comings and goings are entirely at the discretion of myself and your master, Lord Tempest. At some point, someone who is still speaking to that gentleman—and I use that term rather loosely—someone must disabuse him of the notion that he owns the entire world and everyone on it."

With that, she made as dignified an entrance as she could manage while shaking little sticky ice blobs out from her hair. Heavy, iron-studded doors shut behind her, and she was enveloped by the agreeable heat coming from a blazing fireplace in the reception area and the less agreeable but utterly impotent seething energy coming from her angry oligarch chum.

Fortunately, the other guests were assembled nearby, so Ran couldn't continue making a scene, though she'd rarely seen such a grim scowl marring his rough-hewn features. To her surprise, she knew everyone present. To further annoy Ran, she ignored him and walked up to the others, greeting them using her cheeriest "well-met fellow sojourner" voice.

"Dr. Kore, Mr. Riffi! An interesting spot of weather we have all decided to venture out in, wouldn't you agree? How do you do? Ellie Sato, *Citizen Juggernaut.*"

The elderly scientist juggled a whiskey tumbler from his left hand to his right hand then back again when he remembered which one he wanted to extend to her. He'd clearly been getting a head start enjoying Lord Tempest's hospitality. The former prime minister, who had his back to the fire, fixed her with a stern gaze before his forehead tilted forward and the lower half of his face slid into a standard politician's smile.

"Quite so," Riffi said. "We've been waiting for you. Our host mentioned our little gathering might benefit from a dash of beauty and wit otherwise severely lacking, Miss Sato of the *Citizen Juggernaut.*"

Ellie shook Dr. Kore's damp and rather squishy hand. "Speaking of whom, I should like to thank His Lordship for the invite." She glanced through several doorways radiating outward to each corner of the manor but saw no one else.

Ran stepped forward, and through clenched teeth, said, "Right, right. Where is the mayor? I haven't seen him."

"I think Jorkins said he was finishing up some correspondence and would shortly be down," Riffi said, finally pulling his eyes off her, glancing superciliously at Ran, and straightaway heading for the nicest chair near the hearthstone. "Shall we sit round the fire? It seems, as at Number 10, historic preservation has taken precedence over central heating here at Stoke Bramwell."

"You gents go ahead make yourselves comfortable," Ran said. "The inside staff have all been sent home early on, I imagine on account of the weather. Miss Sato and I will gather some refreshments."

Ellie's note of protest turned into a silent giggle as Ran grabbed her elbow and pulled her toward the hallway.

"What do you think you're playing at?" Ran hissed at her when they were out of earshot.

"Same as you, but with a dash more style, I'd say," Ellie said, shaking herself free of his manly and not entirely unwelcome grip, then letting the momentum carry her on into the deserted and quite spacious main floor kitchen. It had multiple freezers and ovens and was certainly the one used for catering large social events. She looked him up and down and gave her best fashionista scowl of disapproval. "Green trousers and a tatty leather jacket? You must have a stern word with your valet or whoever puts your clothes out. What are you thinking, visiting a marquess's seat dressed like a game warden?"

"I'm serious. This thing goes deeper and is more dangerous than you know," Ran added in his most growly voice.

"Really? Dangerous? Geez, I hadn't quite got that through my thick journalistic head, even when persons unknown suffocated me, or who they thought was me, and ransacked my place looking for this." Ellie swung Green Hope's Gaia-shaped earring in front of Ran's delightfully startled eyes.

"What's that?"

"I'm pretty sure something Dr. Kore would like to have kept hidden."

"You'd better give it to me for—"

Ellie slipped it out of his reach, quietly cursing herself for revealing the secret data stash, but Ran was a fellow who could annoy you to distraction. In any event, things would be sorted out soon—all her instincts and every penny dreadful mystery novel she'd read informed her the end game was nigh.

"Not a chance. Mine!" She moved the Gaia pendant away from greedy grasping Oliphant hands. "It's safest right where it is. Let's wait and see what the mayor has to say, then I shall decide when to play this hand." Ellie only then noticed they were in the midst of culinary bounty. Before leaving, the staff had prepared enough food for a dozen guests. Some of it was under shrink wrap and foil on the counters, and there was even more in the nearest of the refrigerators, which had very modern translucent doors. "At least we won't be left hungry if we're stuck here all night."

A rumble of thunder, muted by the heavy stone walls all about, confirmed that was a distinct possibility.

Ellie thrust a canape into her mouth, then looked for the best beverage to go with it. "Oh, look, Italian Pinot Gris. Lord Tempest may not have your money, but he's certainly got aces of style. By the way," she said as she uncorked the chilled bottle, "where is the dear old fuddy-duddy? It's terribly rude to invite us and be so long doing whatever he's doing."

The cork popped out with less-than-expected resistance, which sent Ellie's forearm against a wall panel, whacking a big green button. The big green button activated a large dumbwaiter, which had been installed to serve food to the upper floors. The device *clackity clanked*, and its hatch-style door made a scraping sound as it slowly slid open.

"Oh oh... Ran..." Ellie said, pointing the dripping wine bottle cork at the object that had slid out from the dumbwaiter. It was a man's monocle dangling from a polished silver chain, and the polished silver lanyard was clutched in fingers which lay unmoving, rigid, and horribly pale.

Just then, there was a thunderous crack, and all the lights went out.

Chapter 21

The bottle of wine Ellie had been holding slipped and crashed onto the floor in the pitch dark. She let out a yelp and nearly choked on the remainder of her canape when she felt a sinister bony hand on her shoulder.

"Gah! Get off me!"

"Shh, it's only the lights," said the blandly superior voice of her clueless friend.

"Didn't you see?" she demanded in a harsh whisper, temporarily forgetting the proper name for the food service elevator, "in the... hole in the wall, the things... it fell out."

"Stop ranting or I will bundle you back into your car."

Bloody fat chance of that, she thought. The Bentley had the latest biometric keys and ignition, so only she could open its doors and drive it. "Let go of me or I'll stick you with this corkscrew." She used it to poke his hand away, and it vanished in the black interior of the mansion's kitchen. Where was the door? How did the room get so big all of a sudden? She dare not move. What if she went the wrong way and bumped into... into...

"He's got to have backup power," insisted Mr. Know-It-All oligarch. "I hear something."

Ellie remembered an app she had. She pulled out her phone and tapped the big pink anime boobs icon of the Flash Her in the Dark Torch Light utility app. The camera's LED lit up and cast a steady and startlingly bright white beam.

"There, that's how one sheds light on our situa—Ack!"

In the dark, they had moved a few feet forward without being aware of it and now stood directly opposite the wide-open dumbwaiter, the monocle still hanging loosely from between the open sliding doors, only now she could see the hideously distorted face of the owner of the monocle and the hand which gripped it. He was obviously dead.

"Gad!" Ran exclaimed. "You've really done it this time."

"Me?"

"What possessed you to stick your... Every single time! You're a... a disaster magnet."

"What goes on there?" It was Dr. Kore's slightly slurring voice, which spoke as two shadowy figures approached from the reception hall. They were silhouetted in the diffused warm yellow-orange glow coming from the large fireplace.

Ellie's hands instinctively reached out toward the contorted body. Perhaps she had some idea of pulling him out of the confining square metal box.

"No, don't." Ran pulled her away with one hand and grasped the pallid-colored wrist with his other hand, feeling for a pulse. "It's Tempest, he's dead. And cold."

"Have you a coroner's qualifications, do you now, Oliphant?" Former Prime Minister Riffi's sharp voice split the darkness behind them with a tone of icy irony that was, somehow, even more chilling to her than the grotesquely twisted body of the deceased.

"Tempest! What are you playing at?" Dr. Kore fairly shouted, not having heard Ran's diagnosis. "We've got to get him out of there! Is he all got drunk and passed out? What a rum way to come down from your office. I told you to install an escalator, oh no, elevator, that's it."

From above them came a crackling, strobing sound as the lighting circuits flickered on one by one. The former warmth of the recessed incandescents was sluggishly replaced by the harsh glare of emergency fluorescents, which illuminated their little group from above. Motionless for a moment, to Ellie their figures seemed like a tableau of villains caught red-handed in some despicable act.

"Help me pull him," Kore said but made no motion to pull anyone or anything as it slowly dawned on him that Lord Tempest was far worse off than dead drunk.

"Touch nothing!" Riffi grabbed a device that looked like a stapler, which shot out a red laser dot and aimed it at several parts of Lord Tempest's exposed skin. "He's almost freezing. He must have been dead for hours."

Dr. Kore's face assumed a pallor that closely resembled that of the unfortunate deceased man. For a moment, she thought he was going to faint.

"Th-that's really the mayor, then, is it?" Dr. Kore said in a quavering voice. "Could it have been accidental?"

"Kore," Ran snapped, "you've said some dumb things in your life, but—"

"Gentlemen, this is clearly a police matter. Let me… oh." Ellie's phone had no reception. "A place this size must have a landline."

The telephone on the wall didn't work.

"Where did Jorkins disappear to?" Dr. Kore asked meekly.

Still stunned by the sudden demise of their eccentric but kindly host, Ellie caught Ran's eye and knew he was thinking the same thing as she: If Lord Tempest had been dead most of the day, how could his butler have overlooked this conspicuous fact? Had Lord Tempest been the one who had texted her, or was the message sent by his killer?

"I think I heard the side door open," Mr. Riffi said. "It's over this way."

Perhaps the former prime minister had been here previously and was familiar with the large mansion's layout. He seemed quite sure of his directions while she had only a vague idea of where the front door she had entered was located. Just as they were all about to rush in the direction Riffi indicated, Ran advised, "Hold on, I don't see any surveillance cameras here. A witness must stay with the body, preferably two, until the authorities arrive."

"Quite right," Mr. Riffi said smoothly. "I'll go for Jorkins."

"I'll come with," Ellie said quickly before Dr. Kore volunteered; likely he was more eager to get away from the scene of the apparent homicide than search for the missing butler. As for her, winter cyclone or not, given these shocking events, some fresh air was urgently needed.

But not quite as much as she got. Ellie felt her lungs fairly fill to bursting when she opened the outer door and a gust like an icy bellows aimed straight down her windpipe. No wonder the power had vanished from the remote estate—the rambunctious winter cyclone had matured into a cliff-shaking monster threatening to separate their little patch of England from the rest of the island. Even sheltered by the solid stones of the mansion, she could feel the air currents coursing round, threatening to pull her away as surely as if she had been tossed into the sea and found herself in the vicious grip of a riptide.

She would have slammed shut the door and retreated but for a flash of light from the other side of the circular drive. Sparks blew out from shattered floodlights tottering over what had been the garage building.

"Gentlemen! Look there." Perhaps the men thought nothing could compound their troubles; if so, they were wrong.

"What's happened?" Dr. Kore said, grabbing her shoulder to steady himself and forcing her to grab hold of the doorframe to keep from being pitched out onto the gravel. "Where's that building? Where is my car?" Kore demanded, gesticulating with his other hand at a severely flattened pile of timbers and flapping sheaths of siding.

The mostly wooden structure had collapsed from the front inward, and the top edge of the roof was now flush with the frozen snow covering the driveway.

"Worry about the cars later," Ellie yelled over the storm. "I'll wager anything Jorkins went in there."

As she spoke, a tree bent under enormous strain, and with a tremendous *crack*, gave up one of its bigger branches. It blew sideways at them like a missile, hit the masonry just beside the door, and disappeared round the corner.

"There's no going out *there*," Dr. Kore whimpered, possibly close to old-codger hysterics.

"Jorkins… if he's in there, he could be injured," Ellie snapped back at the dithering scientist. "Or worse."

"If it's that, not much to be done," Riffi, who had slunk up behind them, observed coolly. "Of course, no way to know much of anything from here, and that structure's too unstable to go poking around in. We should wait until first responders can come."

179

"That could be days," said Ran, thankfully seeming to take her side.

The distance was less than one hundred yards, but with all the debris being thrashed about, the safest way to search for the missing butler would have been inside a tank.

"We haven't a tank," Ellie muttered, half to herself. "But we do have a Bentley."

"What?" Dr. Kore blurted. "Your little journalist friend isn't off her head, is she, Oliphant?"

Ran ignored the rudeness and said, "Right. Your car's been left in front. I'll drive. Keys, please."

"Are you kidding? With a million unsolved major thefts each year in London, you think it only starts with a key?"

She led the men, including the sulking Riffi, out to the main entrance, where she wrapped her coat tightly around herself and opened the biometric lock on the imposing SUV. Dr. Kore, who had not looked very robust even before being shocked out of his wits by the sight of Lord Tempest's dead body, did not venture out. Riffi stayed with him.

"Just us, then," Ran said jauntily from the passenger seat.

"Just like old times," Ellie said, peering ahead into the swirling gloom illuminated by her full-beam headlights. "Except unlike in Paris and Jerusalem, here we drive on the correct side of the road."

They crossed a hundred yards to the collapsed garage without incident. Something moved among the fallen debris blocking the garage doorway.

"What's that?"

"Dunno," Ran said, pointing to another spot farther on. "Is that a fire?"

Spouts of thick white, fog-like emanations were spewing above the portion of the flat roof that remained standing. The puffs hovered for an instant, then were snatched away by the howling wind.

"In this storm? Maybe a furnace unit got knocked over by the collapsed wall. Let's go see what that was by the front."

Leaving the headlights on to illuminate the dozen yards of open ground, they exited. Ellie braced herself against the chilled, slush-covered side of the vehicle and crept forward using her other hand to shield her face.

"Hulloooo!"

"There!" Ellie thrust out a gloved hand and lurched forward; a black leather shoe was just visible around the corner. It had come off a foot clad in properly gartered black mid-calf socks. "Jorkins!"

Lord Tempest's butler was soaked to the skin, and he looked in quite a bad way, yet he was struggling to get to his feet and had just managed to rise to his knees. However, just as they were about to seize hold of him and raise him the rest of the way, Ran and Ellie stopped cold in their tracks. Ellie gaped speechlessly, and this uncharacteristically vapid facial expression allowed freezing cold water to stream into her mouth.

What she gaped speechlessly at was the figure that had appeared out from the shadows and now stood looming over Mr. Jorkins— a middle-aged woman in fuzzy slippers. She was wearing a soaking-wet puffer jacket, sporting a severely deranged expression, and holding a shotgun by its stock and breech, the muzzles of the weapon's twin barrels pointed directly at her and Ran.

Chapter 22

"Bloody hell!" Ran yelled and shoved Ellie sideways with such force she narrowly missed being knocked out by a collision with the broken doorframe leading into the ruin of the garage.

"Stop it," Ellie said, rebounding off bent siding. "You're scaring Mrs. Jorkins, and she's liable to thump you with that shotgun."

"How can you tell that's the butler's wife?"

"Who else would be out here dressed in slippers and a housecoat? And look at the way she's holding that gun, like it's a club. I doubt it's loaded."

"You willing to stake your life on that?"

"I'm willing to stake yours," Ellie snapped back with her now quite-numb hand held beside her equally frozen cheek to shout over the gale. "Go in there and talk to her in your manly yet soothing manner, Mr. Royal Ex-Marine Commando." It was her turn to shove Ran, which she did—farther into the tottering remains of the garage. All the poor billionaire could do was raise his hands and employ his aforementioned manly charm.

"Mrs. Jorkins, I presume?"

"Stay back, villains!"

"We're definitely not villains. We're guests of Lord Tempest. We came out to see how Jorkins was getting on. Heh-heh, quite the robust bout of inclement weather, wouldn't you agree? Umnn, you mind lowering the long gun? You've given my girl a bit of a fright."

A fright? Ellie thought hotly, but politely waved her hands as she poked her head around the corner into the interior of the building, which was strewn with timber, bits of roofing material, and crushed vehicles.

"We really are your guests. Your husband's seen us. Tell her, Jorkins."

Mrs. Jorkins looked a little confused but remained wary. "You just hold on there where you be. I found poor Harold like this, knocked half senseless."

"Well that's not surprising, most of the roof has come down," Ellie observed.

"Oh no!" Mrs. Jorkins said with some heat. "Last thing he said was: 'They got me from behind.' Then he fainted. Let His Lordship come out, then I'll put more credence in what stories yer tellin'."

Ellie and Ran looked at each other.

"Well, about His Lordship," Ran began delicately. He was saved from delivering the rather awkward news by a sputtering moan from the prone Jorkins.

"Oh dear," Mrs. Jorkins said, and leaned the shotgun against the wall, muzzle down, as though it were a broomstick. All three of them converged on the downed butler. The headlights streaming in through the sundered doorframe illuminated a nasty gash just over the older man's ear. Scarlet turned to pink as the diluted blood dribbled down the man's formerly impeccably clean starched collar.

"We'd better tie that up." Ran produced a handkerchief.

They helped the injured man to his feet. With her free arm, she motioned to the Bentley, and they stepped into the wild wind. She took a last look back into the wrecked building—by the illumination of the butler's flashlight, she could see there were at least half a dozen vehicles covered in debris. The rear of the building looked completely flattened, and even the brickworks had collapsed outward into the lane on the far side.

As they stumbled over fallen pipes and roofing material, she again wondered at the odd swirl of cloying foggy air. Was that part of the storm? The only thing she'd ever seen to match it was the effect of a fog machine at a fashion show she'd once reported on.

"Oh, that's fine, I can manage," Jorkins muttered, regaining his senses and his manly pride, which balked at being fussed over.

Ellie breathed in the warmer air inside the vehicle and shuddered. "Any longer out there and we'd be hypothermic."

Ran looked at the couple in the back seat. "Jorkins, what happened?"

"I... I had looked out and saw one of the floodlights go down. I thought to myself, I must go and mind about the cars. His Lordship has some valuable antiques stashed here. But there weren't no opportunity... the roof and side wall was come down. The master will be very heart sore."

"Harold," Mrs. Jorkins said, "you told me someone struck you. Were you just dazed? There was no one about until these two youngsters appeared. And sorry for the fright with the gun; it's all rusted and no cartridges for it anyhow."

"Not a worry," Ran said. "We've had less kind receptions. Shall we go back to the house?"

"I should have moved those cars when the storm really began a-howlin'. How will I tell the master?"

Ellie glanced at Ran. "Before we do anything else, let's turn up a spot of brandy. How does that sound?"

Chapter 23

"Hours ago?" Jorkins said in a weak, quavering voice. "His Lordship's been... all this time?"

The normally imperturbable butler's face looked even more ghastly, if that was possible, as when he'd risen up from the wreckage scattered on the floor of the garage, mixed wet and dirt and blood streaming down one side of his face. Ellie feared all their efforts to restore vigor to the senior servant, which included placing him nearest the roaring fireplace and fortifying him with a generous glass of brandy, had been for naught as Jorkins slumped, hanging on to a shelf to keep himself upright.

"Is His Lordship, er, in there?" Mrs. Jorkins thrust a shawl-covered forearm toward the, thankfully, closed doors of the large dumbwaiter. "Shouldn't we open it? And make certain, in a complete way, that there's no...?"

"I really don't think that's necessary," Ran said. "I have to agree with Mr. Riffi. Lord Tempest must have died midmorning at the latest."

"How would you know that? Are you doctors?" Mrs. Jorkins's jowly face wobbled with skepticism, a state of mind likely enhanced by the presence of so many interlopers appearing all at once who had, to say the least, shattered the normal respectable quiet of the coastal retreat. Compared to the consequences following upon their arrival, the cyclone battering the coastline was trivial.

Mr. Riffi stepped forward with that casual imperiousness natural to high-ranking politicians. "I checked personally in the presence of witnesses. There was no pulse, no respiration, and body temperature determined at multiple points with that infrared thermometer was quite conclusive. Shall we retire to the drawing room?"

"That's what that is?" Mrs. Jorkins mumbled, eyeing the plastic thermometer device on the counter. "Don't recall such a thing about 'afore."

Ellie noticed Mr. Riffi's lips compress, so she took Mrs. Jorkins's arm to lead her out. "Probably your cook uses it. I have one myself. They're so useful in getting tea and cocoa temperatures just spot on."

"What I don't understand," Dr. Kore said as he flopped limply into the seat near a humongous bear rug, "is who sent us messages inviting us to Stoke Bramwell? Mine certainly came after twelve noon."

"Mine as well," Ran said.

"Perhaps His Lordship's secretary sent them. That's quite common," Riffi said. "Jorkins, when did you last see Lord Tempest?"

The butler scratched his head gingerly around his recent injury. The gash, though it had spouted copious amounts of blood, was not deep and was now well-bandaged. "His Lordship had ordered all staff to have the day off and be away. All except me and the missus. Said he had some very private and weighty matters to consider, then took to his offices on the second floor about nine in the morning, mebbe half past. What a thing to happen. Cold-blooded murder at Stoke Bramwell. It'll kill the marquess, mark my word. What a blow," Jorkins muttered and looked dejectedly at the ancient hearthstone, above which loomed a portrait of a former Milord wearing an immense curly wig which any Shetland sheep might have envied and which hung down nearly to his brightly patterned breeches; the former Milord scowled down at them with consummate disapproval.

Ran, being the dear man of action he was, was first to break the chilly silence that followed the servant's lament. "Our situation, in short, is this. We have one car that's serviceable. I'll go fetch the authorities."

Mr. Riffi's reply came instantaneously and smoothly. "I see your point, Oliphant, I see it entirely. However, consider this: the storm still rages all about us, making the roadways through the trees doubly perilous. It's more likely cellular service will be restored either to our handsets or via the house Wi-Fi before you get to a local constabulary post which, given the remote locale, may not even be manned."

Had Riffi prepared this little sound bite, as he might have for an anticipated question during a BBC interview? Ellie wondered and glanced at the faces around her. Grim and stoic Mrs. Jorkins, her battered and distraught husband. Ran Oliphant with his bristly hair shining as melting snow ran down toward his hardset jawline. Dr. Kore, who was trying to conceal a nervous facial tic by nursing a glass of brandy and smacking his lips with every sip, and finally the former Prime Minister Sanjay Riffi, his mahogany Indian skin looking even more polished than the wooden banisters of the staircase behind him. But come to think of it, was there someone she'd missed?

"Jorkins, are you sure there are none of the staff left? I thought I saw someone by the gates from the main road." As soon as she uttered the question, she regretted it, but nothing untoward happened. Why did she feel such a fool mentioning it?

Mrs. Jorkins replied, "Tha'd be the tenant farmer's son, Eddie Freeland. He puts in some hours to make some coin at the gate when there's visitors expected. T'otherwise there woulda been some mighty irate posh folks lost among these roads, often as not."

The wind outside had, for the moment, settled into a low dull roar, which was suddenly capped by a snap. Everyone gave a small start when a fresh log in the fireplace gave off a sudden crackle, even the self-consciously manly Ran. In the time it took for the sparks to fly out, up nearly to the head-height lintel, and settle on the somber dull hearthstone, a dozen images raced through Ellie's fevered brain: the strange fog in the destroyed garage, the murdered girl's lips starkly blue and frozen solid, the pinkish-hued faces of her equally icy fellow victims, the dark masked figure who startled her as she passed through the gates of Stoke Bramwell. It all gave her a sinking feeling down in the pit of her stomach, a dreadful feeling of impending danger and doom, which meant only one thing.

"Gentlemen, I believe, at this juncture, there's only one thing for it," she said in as commanding a voice as she could manage, given that she was addressing the former prime minister and a pair of preposterously rich gents. "It's time for some tea. Ran, be a darling and assist."

He glanced toward the main kitchen. "Are you certain you want to—"

"Please use the scullery," Mrs. Jorkins chimed in, pointing to the corpse-free area of the rambling old mansion.

Ellie let the swinging scullery door close and looked out at their companions through the diamond-shaped glass window. "Ran," she whispered through smiling clenched teeth. "Have you got one of your many pistols with you?"

"What? Of course not. One doesn't visit Lord Mayor Tempest armed." Then he admitted, "I did bring one, but it's in my Range Rover, behind the spare tire."

"Fat lot of good that does us, since we don't have a crane to lift the garage off the Rover. You didn't bring any of your commando buddies as security?"

"Tempest told us all to come alone. He was very strict."

"Well, then," she said mostly to herself, "plan E, then." The small room was quite fashionable for a scullery and had a fantastic kettle that brought water to boil within seconds. As they returned to the drawing room, she added, "If things work out, just remember: I apologized to you in advance."

"And, er," he whispered back, completely bewildered, "what if they don't work out?"

"Then I'm really, *really* sorry, but according to every fictional detective story I've been studying, it's the only way."

"Right, right," he said, looking at her with an expression that said *Bloody hell, here we go again.* "And, if you don't mind, what precisely have you apologized so profusely in advance for?" His face held that state of charming confusion, which she suddenly realized was one of his most attractive dispositions. "The stress hasn't made you mental, has it?"

"Shh, quit blathering, or you'll make me forget crucial nuisances and bugger the whole thing." Just then, Ellie remembered a crucial nuance: she had to write something down on a napkin. She did that and slid the folded cloth under the lip of one of the cups on the tea tray. The big antique silver thing weighed a ton, but she waved Ran away, ignored his reworked question as to what "thing" he wasn't supposed to bugger up with his blather, and she carried it in by herself.

"Here we are," Ellie announced, then realized her nervousness had made her tone much too ebullient, and sent it veering toward cackling shrillness. "I mean, er, we must make the best of things, right? Until the authorities arrive, it's best we all stay together. Not that there's much chance of anything untoward happening."

Only half of the lights in the large room were hooked up to the emergency generator. Not surprising since completely powering up the rambling old pile would likely require the output of an entire wind farm. Moving carefully in the dim, somewhat creepy illumination, she carefully lowered the tray, making certain the designated cup was nearest Dr. Kore.

"Jorkins," Riffi said without preamble, "did Lord Tempest have any other communication lines set up? Ones which might still be working?"

"My word," Mrs. Jorkins said, sitting straight up as though jerked by an invisible string. "I just remembered. His Lordship had ordered a satellite internet kit. The Home Office sent one around just in case those horrid Russians or Chinese or Iranians or those other Chinamen in North Korea interfered with the general internet. Do you think it would work in a storm like this?"

Her husband was still in shock but managed to add, "I never even took it out from its packing case... so much to do. Y'don't think if we could have called for help it would have..."

"Don't blame yourself, Mr. Jorkins," Ran said.

"I think I stashed it somewhere, somewhere close by. Oh, just there, the lumber room," said Mrs. Jorkins, half getting up. "Right through the scullery. Shall we have a look?"

As though responding to a silent stage prompt, everyone who was seated rose in unison and pressed through the narrow swinging door. Like bloodhounds on the scent, they were drawn to the prospect of connecting with someone, anyone, outside the gloomy gothic mansion.

Moments later, the butler pulled out a cardboard box marked "FarLink," which had a few wires dangling out from the bottom.

"Microwave," Ran said. "The dish antennae would have to be put outside or at least out a window on one of the upper floors."

Riffi shook his head. "I wouldn't bother. I have the same system, and they're still working out bugs. It took hours setting up, and I got nothing but error messages as a result on mine. Waste of time."

Why hadn't the politician said that before? Since the crisis began with the discovery of their host's body, Riffi had seemed a step ahead at every turn, starting with the way he employed the very conveniently placed infrared thermometer on the corpse. Ellie fumed at the interruption to her well-laid plans and led the way back into the drawing room; she made sure to slide Dr Kore's napkin toward him. Doing so, she realized everything depended on his reaction to the three seemingly innocuous letters she had written on the underside: *ALP?*

The famous scientist reached out with an unsteady hand and took his cup and saucer. What if the bleary-eyed codger took no notice of her handiwork? The tension around the short-legged table opposing the hearth was palpable, especially between Ran and Mr. Riffi. Outside, the storm let them know it was not through with England's coastline. The wind's howl pitched up, sounding an even higher note of frenzy.

"Well," Ellie said, seeing everyone was served. "Isn't that better? A good piping-hot Yorkshire blend will pass the time until our gadgets begin working."

Ellie caught Dr. Kore's eye as he gulped his piping-hot portion all at once, likely regretting it, judging by the face he made. She gave him a slight nod, along with a covert glance down at his napkin. In the half-light generated by Stoke Bramwell's emergency generators, the man's features seemed both puffy and sunken, like a deflated soccer ball. His shadow-hooded eyes looked down at the napkin and then quizzically at her, then slowly down again.

Ellie's plan anticipated that he return either a blank stare, which would make him innocent or an astonishingly talented actor, or in the much more likely alternative, given the diabolical cleverness of her scheme of ensnaring him, Dr. Kore would give some quietly abject sign of accession, confirming she was a genius and he was guilty as sin of killing his personal assistant Green Hope and likely the other Hereford Five victims as well. In the mystery tales she had studied, such traps nearly always worked in favor of the brilliant detective's plan.

In this particular and all-too-real-life instance, things turned out differently. Instead of either option she had prepared for, the eminent scientist chose to violently clap his hand to his mouth, arch backward in his chair with a hoarse scream, and convulse as though he were being electrocuted. His other hand whipped sideways with such force the handle of his teacup snapped, and the bowl flew at the fireplace, landing just short with a tinkle and a hiss as the contents bubbled under the grate and turned to steam.

Mrs. Jorkins revealed a set of lungs worthy of the opera stage and let loose a clamoring yell, which briefly overwhelmed the howl of the cyclone outside. Dr. Kore slid to the floor and rolled onto his side, one hand clutching his mouth, from which frothy saliva was dribbling, the other stretched toward Ellie. His eyes bulged and stared at her, unblinking. Then a devastating crash of thunder shook Stoke Bramwell down to its foundation stones, and all the lights went out.

By reflex, Ellie shot her hands out and grasped... nothing. After a moment of vertigo passed, she found she was still standing upright and tried to picture what was around her in the dark—the overturned chair, and beside it the possibly dying man writhing in agony. She was about to say something when another of Mrs. Jorkins's ear-piercing screams rang out.

Ran and Riffi tried to calm the housekeeper by, respectively, telling her that everything would be fine and to "Stop up the caterwauling this instant!"

Ellie's eyes adjusted to the only light in the cavernous room: the flickering flames dancing in the great hearth.

"Dr. Kore!" She kneeled down and held the older man's head. His skin was hot, as though he were burning with fever, and clammy sweat was gushing from his every pore. Even by the flickering light coming from the blazing logs, she could see...

"My God!" His eyes were hemorrhaging so badly they looked like black holes drilled into his skull; he certainly could no longer see. But still he could feel. Convulsing, he grasped her arm with both his hands.

"I... I'm sorry," he gasped. "Sorry for... only she, only shh..." After those words hissed out with the man's last breath, it was clear he was beyond her help, or anyone else's.

What had just happened? Her plan, which had seemed so ingenious moments ago, had blown up in her face. Instead of snaring the guilty parties, Ellie felt she had succeeded only in trapping herself miles from any assistance in an unfamiliar house with a cold-blooded killer and the bodies of more of his victims.

Could she arm herself? The Jorkinses' shotgun was a rusted old clunker; even if she could find shells for it, it would be as likely to kill the shooter as anyone it was pointed at. Ran said he had brought a pistol, but could she find it in the wreck of the garage?

As these thoughts were whirling through her head, she thought she heard Ran call out for her in the near darkness. Suddenly the heavy outer door slammed open, and the wind sent a cold gust of air whooshing through the room and up the chimney of the large central fireplace. The flames were momentarily reduced to embers as the fire struggled to retain hold of the logs they had been so eagerly consuming only seconds before.

"No one move!" said a voice belonging to none of Lord Tempest's guests, a voice which Ellie recognized and which sent a chill of fear, dismay, and also hardening resolve through her. Resolve to improvise and beat the villains at their own game. All the elements were in place, all but one.

On the far side of the cavernous drawing room, the door was forced shut against the gusts of wind that were insisting it stay open, the door's hinges squealing their resistance until the last fissure was sealed and the latch caught with a metallic *click*. On the opposite side of the room, the fire recovered and shed enough light that when the stranger moved toward them, her eyes quickly confirmed what her ears had told her. The face illuminated by the flickering yellow light belonged to Inspector Harrigan.

"My word! Who are you, and how have you come here?" Mr. Riffi was first to speak, his eyes sparkling in the gloom as they darted from the unexpected visitor to each of them in turn.

"Sirs and ma'am," Harrigan said, shaking a scant bit of snow from a nearly dry and neatly pressed winter overcoat. "I'm Inspector Harrigan, London Police. Lord Tempest asked me here as a precaution. I've been waiting alone in the garden shed for some hours. I hadn't heard from the mayor but became concerned when all the lights went down, for the, uh, second time."

"But certainly you should have been alarmed when your phone failed," Riffi said somewhat indignantly. "How else were you to communicate?"

Ran Oliphant, for his part, merely gazed noncommittally at the interloper.

Harrigan reached into a small kit bag, which he then lay on the floor, and produced a radio. "His Lordship also had one. By the way, where is he?"

Ran, Ellie, and Riffi exchanged glances, but before anyone could speak, Harrigan noticed the body on the floor. The inspector employed a small hand torch, which proved inadequate in the large room festooned with heavy antique furniture. Delving into a bureau on the far side of the room, Mrs. Jorkins found some candles and lit them. The newcomer walked over to the prone form lying in the shadows.

Ellie hung back, took a candlestick, and stationed it on an end table, one close to Harrigan's dropped kit bag. While everyone was gaping at the latest dead body, she quietly rifled through Harrigan's bag. There was no gun there, only some water, energy bars, and handcuffs.

"I'm sorry, this man's dead," Inspector Harrigan said authoritatively. "Who is he?"

"Do you not know?" Ran said curtly. "Lord Tempest assigned you with guard duty. Fine job you've done of it."

"Let's get something straight," Harrigan shot back, sweeping a gloved finger over everyone in the room, "there's evidence this man died by homicide. All of you here are under my charge. No one may leave until crime scene investigators get here. Now I ask you again, where is His Lordship?"

For a moment, no one spoke.

"It would, I gather," Riffi said finally, "be easier if we showed you."

Moments later, with the others, Ellie was back in the main kitchen near the dumbwaiter, averting her eyes as Harrigan shined a stark white LED light onto the grotesquely positioned remains of Lord Tempest.

"This is clearly a matter of national security," the London policeman said. "Home Office has to be informed. Damned thing is, it'll be hours before the area can be cordoned off. But we'll get them, wherever they are."

"W-what about the other chap? The one who struck me," Mr. Jorkins said, pointing to the other room. "Could there be, I don't know, could there be some sort of connection to the possibly toxic vapors in the carport? Should we stay here or go to the gatehouse until help arrives?"

"Before our coroner arrives," Harrigan said quickly, "we can't say that Dr. Kore's death wasn't from natural causes. I didn't see any wounds."

So, Ellie thought, Harrigan had quickly identified Dr. Kore. The drawing room light was very poor, and the scientist's face was half covered in frothy saliva and grossly distorted. Would the man's own wife have recognized him so easily? Ellie's mind feverishly counterbalanced all the poor and rather dangerous options from which she now was forced to choose.

"Gentlemen," she said, loudly enough to make Jorkins jump to attention and everyone else turn about. "Dr. Kore was murdered."

"I knew it!" whispered Mrs. Jorkins.

"Not only that, but the same person who did for him also assassinated Lord Tempest. And furthermore, they are with us right now, and I assure you he is a most dangerous and depraved criminal."

She pointed at the figure closest to her. "The killer is— Ranulph Oliphant!"

Chapter 24

"Quickly! Grab him!" she yelled, mostly to Harrigan as she backed away from the utterly stunned Ran. "Don't let him get away. Seize the villain!"

Even though Ellie was in the midst of a precarious and distinctly dangerous gamble, with more lives at stake than just her own, she felt a thrill, as this was the first time she'd ordered a villain to be seized.

Unfortunately, for quite a few seconds, no one did any seizing. No one did anything other than gawk at her as the roaring fire in the enormous hearth issued a faintly mocking crackle and hiss.

"Really, Eleanor!" Ran burst out with an adorably confused expression on his chiseled features.

"Inspector Harrigan," Ellie said, ignoring Ran and stepping behind the policeman, "it is no accident that we are all here tonight. The mayor was about to reveal a hideous scandal involving Dr. Kore and this wretched fellow. Perhaps Lord Tempest thought he could get Oliphant to turn himself in, or perhaps he didn't know the true depths to which this murderous oligarch had sunk, but upon your honor as a London police officer, I insist you restrain this fellow and prevent him from making a break for it while I explain myself."

No one else was looking for it, so no one but she noticed the slight nod made by Riffi in Harrigan's direction. The strapping but ultimately subservient man dove his hands into his kit bag, then turned the whole thing upside down, and still did not find what he was looking for.

"I know I brought them," Harrigan said, sending the beam of his flashlight left and right over the floor. "Where the fuck are my handcuffs?"

Ellie quietly ducked into the scullery and came back with a roll of duct tape. "Maybe they were lost in the storm, but we can't lose time. Here, let me bind his hands, and we'll sit him down in this chair farthest from the door so he doesn't get any shifty ideas."

With another thrill of guilty pleasure, she grabbed Ran's wrist, taped it round, and then stuck the other one to it, leaning over her work with her back to everyone else. In a show of thoroughness, she wound off the whole roll, then slapped her hand over her prisoner's bound fists.

"There! This ought to handle the murderous swine," she said, shaking his bound hands again as though greeting him. "He's right in the palm of our hands."

Ran's face was a mask of anger, surprise, and confusion, which was the best Ellie could have expected. She pushed him backward into a red leather wingback chair.

"Shall we bind his feet as well?" asked Mrs. Jorkins, with surprising enthusiasm for hobbling a guest.

"Not unless he tries to run," Ellie said, then went over to Harrigan, gave him a thankful half hug, and squeezed his bulging bicep, a move which incidentally shifted his coat far enough to reveal a pistol in a shoulder holster. "You'll tackle him if he does, won't you, Inspector?"

Mrs. Jorkins seized a stout-looking fireplace poker and shook it under Ran's nose. "Move an inch, an' I'll make short work of yeh."

Her husband opportunely revealed a more contemplative disposition. "Before any more violence, please, oh please, will someone tell me what's going on!"

The eyes of all fell on Ellie. Ran's gaze was all smoldering fluster and frustration. Riffi's was piercing and unyielding. Harrigan looked at her with cautious suspicion.

"Perhaps we should, um…" Ellie nodded at the unfortunate corpse in the room.

"Right," Mr. Jorkins said. "Nearly slipped my mind in all the excitement." He retrieved a canvas drop cloth and covered the remains of Dr. Kore.

"Where to begin?" Ellie said, making herself comfortable in a chair opposite their prisoner, who was sitting bolt upright, his whole solid frame vibrating with annoyance. She only hoped he wouldn't do anything rash, at least not yet.

The flames in the fireplace whipped back against the firebox bricks as a sudden inhalation of wind poured through the mansion's cracks and crevices. As though in sympathy for their larger brethren, tinier flames danced above the candles on the three-cornered table.

"Since the net has finally closed on this fetid villain and we'd all much rather have him out of our sight and in jail where he belongs, I will stick to the essential facts." She took a deep breath, which she hoped was inaudible, as she realized the delivery of essential facts would require some measure. More precisely, a large measure of agile improvisation. She began.

"Most people in Britain, all Europe, I would venture, have been shocked by the horrific, occult-like slaying of the Hereford Five. As fate would have it, my very own parents were the first to discover the gruesome scene, where they were so fortunate to receive the kind attentions of the gallant Inspector Harrigan, whom I shall always especially remember for his role in this dreadful affair."

Ellie gave him a nod and a chaste smile, which she felt was appropriate, seeing as there was more than one dead body in their midst. What, if any, change of expression crossed Harrigan's face, she could not tell, for his features were too deeply mired in the shadows cast by the hearth, shadows which caused his strong brow to give his eyes a dusky and hooded aspect.

"That alone would have prompted my keen interest in seeing justice was carried out. However, I was also approached by the mother of one of the victims, and equally consequentially, the mayor personally invited me to investigate the crime. Lord Tempest gave me a copy of the police evidence file, but blind chance alone threw in my way two crucial pieces of the puzzle, which have heretofore been known only to me."

With due dramatic ceremony, Ellie produced the micro hard drive disguised as an earring. "This belonged to the murdered girl Green Hope, who worked closely with Dr. Kore and his executives. The final clue came as a result of my past association with the repugnant Mr. Ran Oliphant." She grimaced in his general direction. "In disguise at White's Gentlemen's Club, I was privy to a most interesting meeting between the late Dr. Kore and the mastermind of the entire tragedy."

"Now you're just blithering," Ran said, rising a few inches from his chair. He was instantly menaced by Mrs. Jorkins and her poker on one side and on the other swatted down on the shoulder by Inspector Harrigan.

Mr. Riffi had not taken his eyes off her since she began speaking. Hardly moving his lips, he said quietly, "Ah, yes, that was obviously you dressed like a man and falsely bearded that night. At the time, I thought it someone's peculiar idea of a practical joke."

"Who knows what fiendish twists are at play inside a freakish mind like the one belonging to Ranulph Oliphant. He took great pains to sneak me into White's to witness his apparently rehearsed meeting with Dr. Kore. This event was designed to avert my suspicion because he realized I was looking into the killings. By so doing, he unwittingly sealed his fate."

"But who killed our dear Lord Tempest?" Mr. Jorkins asked.

"The same person who killed four of the five environmental protestors, the same man who poisoned Dr. Kore right in front of us."

Everyone gazed with dread, hatred, fear, or anger at the tightly bound man near the fire.

"Once I had Green Hope's data cache, it became obvious Dr. Kore's company is a fraud, a trillion-pound fake. Yes, they have pilot projects in Africa and Hawaii, but their geothermal energy technology only works in areas of active volcanism. What use is that in London or Paris?

"Miss Green Hope worked closely with Dr. Kore, and she was smart, unfortunately too smart for her own good. By the month previous, she had gathered enough evidence to prove the money Dr. Kore was being paid to drill his geothermal wells was being diverted to a secret slush fund."

"But how could he imagine he'd get away with it?" Mrs. Jorkins asked, glaring at the scientist's covered body. "The company was always in the newspapers. I even recall His Lordship attending their annual shareholder meeting."

"Word on me!" her husband said. "Is that why Lord Tempest was killed? Because he found them out?"

"In an indirect way, yes," Ellie continued. "Of course, if the mayor had known the full depths of the subterfuge, he'd never have invited the parties here to settle the matter quietly, so as not to ruin the country's financial markets.

"We may never know if Dr. Kore was a charlatan from the beginning or if he really believed in his technology. The maniacal pressure on Western governments to 'go green' is so intense that he was able to write his own ticket and gather nearly unlimited funds for his projects worldwide. That could turn anyone's head around, much less an egotistical head belonging to a lifelong academic who had been toiling on his theories in obscurity for decades. What Green Hope's files do tell us is he had an exit strategy that he hoped would keep him out of prison.

"He gathered data, all as fake as his energy production numbers, data which proved that they had just discovered drilling deep into the earth's mantle in Europe would cause devastating earthquakes. Of course, that would ruin his business, but it was ruined already, so he would use this excuse to delay new geothermal projects, pending studies which could go on for decades. It was that or jail for fraud.

"Which brings us to the meeting I attended between Dr. Kore and the real villain here. In order to claim Kore Energy was still in possession of a viable backup project, Kore offered humongous sums to buy Oliphant's nuclear energy company."

"Wait a moment," Riffi said. "Why would anyone invite a journalist, of all people, to a supposedly secret meeting? He could have stopped your investigation by suing you or having his Whitehall friends place you under the Secrets Act."

"This surly villain"—Ellie nudged Ran's chair with her foot to emphasize how beneath contempt its occupant was—"thought he'd beguiled me with his wealth and testosterone-steeped bravado during stories I covered, which involved some of his international shenanigans. I was to be the tame journalist, and since no one writes their own stories anymore, all the other outlets, *Daily Mail*, Bloomberg, and all, would just cut and paste my scoop. But then came the series of fatal flaws and poor Lord Tempest's partial uncovering of the scheme, which necessitated his hasty murder. And would you not agree, Ranulph, haste makes waste?"

Ran's look of seething hatred toward her was just what she wanted.

"I sort'er follow you, miss," Mr. Jorkins said. "But how you suppose... How does it all...?"

A fortuitous thundering rumble shook the ancient stones of the manor to its foundations. "The storm!" Ellie said with a note of high drama. "It revealed the villainy to anyone who was trained in the arts of observation and deduction. You all witnessed the strange fog swirling around the ruins of the garage building, did you not?"

"Aye, uncommon strange. Never seen the like," Mrs. Jorkins said.

"Only one type of substance could cause those misty clouds: ultra-cold gas, most likely liquid nitrogen. The moment I saw it, it all came together. Me and my, er, special forensic science team." She couldn't exactly say "madhouse-confined serial killer friend," could she? "My team had identified poor Green Hope as the one victim who was not killed by carbon monoxide asphyxiation. Instead, there was every likelihood she was done in by poisoning, her killer having employed the widely available chemical aluminium phosphide, known by the chemist's abbreviation A-L-P."

"You deduced all that from the files the mayor gave you? When the entire Met's Specialist Operations is still in the dark?" Inspector Harrigan said with a note of skepticism. "Last I heard, the autopsy's cause of death results were inconclusive because of, well, to be frank, the lack of remains below the victims' necks."

Mrs. Jorkins looked a bit queasy, and her husband wavered and grabbed the banister as though he was the one more likely to faint.

"Carbon dioxide poisoning often leaves distinctive pinkish-red color on the victim's skin. All the victims except for Green Hope had it. She, on the other hand, had blue-tinged lips, common in aluminium phosphide poisoning. Therefore, it was likely two sets of victims were killed at different times, perhaps for entirely different reasons, then their body parts arranged to seem as though they were all part of one massacre."

She picked up the tea service napkin from the floor. "Tonight I wrote 'ALP' on this and quietly presented it to Dr. Kore. The guilt in his soul leaped to his face, and I knew the truth. He had killed Green Hope in order to keep out of prison."

"But… then this doctor fellow, did he kill himself? Did he take poison right here… in our best drawing room?" Mrs. Jorkins asked with equal parts horror and outrage that someone would be so unmannered as to off himself while a guest at Stoke Bramwell.

"No. Kore was a man who would kill an innocent girl rather than face financial ruin. He was brought to his doom by the very fiendish mastermind lurking in our midst all evening: Ran Oliphant."

Mrs. Jorkins made a soft clucking sound, which to Ellie's trained Anglophone ears signaled quiet skepticism. "Mebbe he worked his villainy on the master. We should have stayed closer by after all the other servants left, but that poor fellow on the hearth rug… I mean how? We were all standin' round. You're tellin' us he did the deed right in front of us all?"

"You think I'm giving him too much credit?" She leaned toward her captive ex-friend. "Well, believe it or not, beneath this brutish exterior and behind that thick Neanderthal brow lies a highly intelligent mastermind who will flinch at nothing. Oliphant saw what I'd written on the napkin and guessed Dr. Kore would crack like a weak-shelled egg and implicate him, so he slipped poison into his teacup, using our search for the satellite dish as a distraction. Likely this was the very same poison he used to assassinate Lord Tempest. No doubt he arrived an hour or two earlier and had a friendly drink with his unsuspecting host in the upstairs office. I'll prove it."

Ellie advanced on the accused man. "Let's search him, but be careful. Mrs. Jorkins, fetch us some rubber gloves. He's likely used prussic acid or a similar compound, judging by how quickly it killed Kore."

Rather ungainly gardening gloves were procured and a search conducted of Ran's several pockets and the lining of his jacket, without result.

"Nothing…" Mr. Jorkins said meekly. "Are you sure—"

"There," Ellie said, pointing to the fireplace. "Those blackened glass shards. He must have thrown the bottle in."

"He was closest to the hearth," Mrs. Jorkins said, seconding Ellie's rather speculative accusation. The fragments could have been from the dead man's shattered china cup, but just as she hoped, everyone in the room was convinced this evidence sealed up the guilty verdict against Ran.

"You horrid man!" Mrs. Jorkins said with vehemence. "And to think the master had you as a guest, even makin' up the guest rooms fer stayin' the night. What a viper we nursed!" Thankfully she did not lay the iron rod she carried across Ran's rugged, but not impervious, skull. She did, however, let it fall on his toes.

Ran let out a strangled cry.

"Serves you right," Ellie said.

"Well, Miss Sato," Mr. Jorkins said, "seems you've got your man an' the inspector here to take him into custody. But how did you know he'd killed Lord Tempest, and how could he have done it in the mornin'? Oliphant might have snuck in an hour early, but not since eleven in the morn. Everyone seems ter agree His Lordship was killed long before that."

"As Inspector Harrigan can confirm, determining time of death without eyewitness evidence is always a matter of informed conjecture. In the case of this brutish man's heinous killing of his unsuspecting friend, Oliphant used the same technique of obfuscation Kore employed when he had finished off Green Hope and had to buy time while he and Oliphant completed the other four cover-up murders. Inside a specially built van..." She turned toward their prisoner and extended an immaculately manicured finger. "He cooled the body."

"He did not!" protested a horrified Mrs. Jorkins, who looked around for an even heavier object with which to punish the villain.

"He did! A man of his resources calculated that if he could confuse the local coroner just long enough, he could frame someone else for the killing of Lord Tempest, perhaps pinning the crime on Dr. Kore after his convenient suicide."

"The monster!" Mr. Jorkins gasped.

"In Green Hope's case, after the scientist had killed her, Dr. Kore panicked. He hastily improvised a cooling chamber and froze her solid. Somehow Oliphant learned of the deed and saw how Scotland Yard would penetrate the amateurish subterfuge if he merely threw the poor girl's remains in the Thames River. If Kore were caught, Oliphant would be implicated, and so to cover up the first murder, he devised an even more heinous act."

Ellie stood up and paced around Ran's chair. His face was, on the side facing the fire, becoming comically flushed. "You tricked the other four Hereford Five victims into the death van, asphyxiated them with carbon monoxide exhaust fumes, dismembered them, and froze their heads. Then you arranged them along with Green Hope's already-frozen head where my poor parents came upon them. The significance of the first murder was intentionally obscured by the apparently bizarre mass killing."

"It's too much." Mr. Jorkins pulled himself over to a wall beside a well-polished suit of armor and slumped down in a state of emotional and physical collapse.

Ellie leaned over the silently seething seated prisoner. "The exact details on how you accomplished your crimes will be revealed in time. What we do know is the activist known as 'Oppie' certainly had a grudge against BritEnergy; he even traveled to Chernobyl and dosed himself with radiation, intending to claim a workplace accident and sue BritEnergy.

"Let us put the case, then, Mr. Oliphant, that you had a seemingly sympathetic security guard tell Oppie how he could burgle or sabotage the nuclear plant construction site which he so vehemently hated. Let us put the case that thusly it would be easy to trick him and three other confederates to go out in the middle of the night and willingly step into the fatal death van. Once locked inside, the four radical eco-activists would have been suffocated by the regurgitated carbon monoxide exhaust in a minute or two.

"So, have I left anything out?" She saw Ran was about to foolishly open his mouth. "No! Say nothing. It's time for you to go, and to finally face justice. Inspector Harrigan, take the prisoner away." While Ellie was under enormous strain and trying very hard to appear in command of the situation, using that punchy little phrase gave her quite the little thrill.

As expected, Harrigan decided he and Riffi should escort Oliphant back to the City in the only serviceable vehicle, the Bentley SUV, which Ellie started up for them. Mr. Jorkins, Stoke Bramwell's conscientious stalwart to the last, despite his injuries and perhaps in defiance of them, insisted on holding an umbrella over her head as she watched the Bentley's taillights grow dim and finally disappear among the wind-whipped bushes along the drive.

In her agitation, she thrust her hands in her pockets, the left one clashing against the pair of handcuffs she had secreted there. They made a small metallic *clink*. No one else heard it. Cold and soaked through, she went back inside, with Mr. Jorkins trailing behind, thrashing left and right, trying to control what remained of the shredded umbrella.

"Well, that's certainly an irrevocable cast of the die."

"I'm sorry, Miss Sato, I didn't quite catch that."

"Jorkins, listen, did you follow everything I said just now?"

"I think so," he said, concluding his futile struggle with the soaking-wet umbrella canopy, which had completely separated from the bent metallic ribs; they rattled and splayed in every direction as he forced them into a stand in the hallway. "Most impressive how you managed to work everything out."

"Regrettably I have to confide to you and your wife it was utter nonsense, every word. There's only one person who can save us from the real villains."

Both Jorkinses gaped at her, open mouthed as Ellie silently seethed, castigating herself for not having a better idea than binding the hands of their one faint hope and sending him off at the mercy of the real killers. The howling wind thrashed the trees along the empty driveway. Nothing for it now, but she had to do her best to protect the elderly servants who must feel their sedate world had utterly shattered.

"Now, there's a good chance one or more of the people who just drove off will be returning shortly, and if it's the wrong ones, we'll need a place to hide, possibly for more than a day. I assume a venerable old landmark estate like this one has some hidden passages?"

She gazed back at the expressions of shock, skepticism, and terror animating the faces of the poor beleaguered elderly couple and added, in a forthright manner which she hoped would engender confidence: "Or even better, does Stoke Bramwell have a dungeon we could hide in?"

Chapter 25

10 Downing Street
London

S anjay Riffi was trapped in a horrible dream. He was prime minister again, but somehow he had fallen in front of his limousine. He could only just raise himself up off the pavement a few inches, and the headlamps of the car were another few inches from his face, and they were all he could see.

All around him, an angry mob howled; he thought they must be trapped on the other side of the thick iron gates, black metal gates, the ones which kept the citizen scum away from his door front at Number 10. They were howling, over and over again, that terrible chant:

"Iffy Riffi

Always squiffy

Off a cliffy!"

No one had ever proved he'd been behind the wheel when his car went off the road and crippled a pathetic bicycling nobody. His cousin testified under oath that it was he, not Riffi, who had been driving. It didn't matter. The filthy press wouldn't let it go, especially that fascist, racist, climate-denying rag the Juggernaut! After all he'd done for the country, his party gave him the sack. The dirty old farts and dried-up harridans on the 1922 committee were afraid of losing seats in the election and asked him, then ordered him, to step aside.

Well, that was going to come back to them, come back to them in spades. He was a million times smarter than Boris Johnson, who had been ousted because he ate a birthday cake during lockdown. If ever there was an obvious trap! How could that fat blond bastard Johnson resist gobbling down sponge cake covered in heaps of frosting topping? But later, those same jealous plebes had conspired against Riffi himself and forced him out of the top job. For that, he vowed he'd show them up, and he had, all the way up, higher than any of them could imagine. Now, if he could only get up…

The limousine headlamps became more distinct, and they hung above him. They were… in a ceiling?

"Lllllmmmmnph." Something was wrong with his mouth. It was dry. More than that, his jaw had fallen asleep.

He tried to think. The last thing he remembered he was driving someone else's car, a big expensive SUV. Rain beat on the roof; wind whipped low branches across the side windows. It wasn't his car. It belonged to that fantastically annoying bitch with the Jap name. His man was in the back seat, watching Oliphant.

Right, right, it came back to him. And he was driving. It was slow going through the narrow country road, watching for downed trees and branches knocked about by the gale. There was some commotion in the back seats. He turned around, about to tell someone not to do anything yet, and above all not to get blood all over the place. Then he felt—ouch! A sting on the left side of his neck, that was all.

"Iffy Riffi

Always squiffy

Off a cliffy!"

Slowly, the crowd's chanting faded. An auditory hallucination? It must be. But the lights above were there. Those lights. They, at least, were real. The ceiling shook, the lights wobbled; he felt pressure on his shoulder and realized it was not an earthquake. The room was not moving, it was he who was being shaken.

"Um, sir? Can you hear me?" Whoever was shaking him was speaking. The voice, he recognized it now. It was one of his men, loyal fellow, would do anything; his main motivation was money and the fine luxuries it could buy, next, and secondary to that: fear. Fear of exposure as a dirty cop, a rapist. Who, while he had been investigating the Rotherham pimps and groomers, had discovered some subterranean kinks in his own twisted psyche. That CID man had fought with and hacked one of the pimps to death, and then he himself started fucking the dead man's underage sluts. My special division at Home Office caught him, we turned him to much better uses. That's the man, trusted bloke, right, right, right... now what was his name...

"Harri-gan?" he slurred. He knew he was hissing unintelligibly through lips which were numb as though they were made of rubber and stuck onto his face, but at least he could hear himself now. "That's uuu? Whrrr we?"

"Shu tang ba," said a new voice; that voice spoke a foreign language, foreign and oddly familiar. Through bleary, watery eyes, he saw a black-haired fellow lean over him. Riffi tried to rise up, but the man pressed him down gently but firmly. The man had some kind of stethoscope apparatus and was pressing it down on skin between his open shirt front.

"Aye, boss, just lie still, let the medic check you out," Harrigan said. "You've been under for a long time."

His head cleared, things came back, a bit jumbled, but he remembered the plan, the make-do scheme they'd improvised during their hasty departure from Stoke Bramwell: get a few kilometers into the countryside, kill Oliphant, hide the body, then head for the Chinese embassy in London and hide out there until the financial markets' Witching Day was over and the financial ruin of Britain irreversibly accomplished.

As Riffi recovered his senses, he also recovered his natural instinct for hostile suspicion. He pretended to be groggier and more disorientated than he was. "Oh, my head," he groaned and glanced around. The man over him was definitely Asian. There were two men standing at attention by an ornate doorway, which had a red-and-gold embossed design of the Forbidden City and the Five Stars of the Communist Republic. The guards were taciturn-looking Chinese gentlemen in blue suits who made no effort to hide the pistols under their jackets.

Still rubbing his brow, massaging out the vise grip of a smashing headache, he snatched a look between his fingers at the window and breathed a silent sigh of relief. Out through a thick, undoubtedly mirrored window, he could see the base of the London skyscraper called the Shard. There was no mistaking it; he was on the other side of the Thames River, where the new embassy of the People's Republic of China stood. Had he done it? Was he home free? He squinted and looked once more. It was day, near noon according to his own watch, but which day? Had the disaster he'd spent more than a year planning struck? Had his plan succeeded while he was incapacitated?

"Time? When is it?" Riffi continued in a helpless, exhausted tone, even as he felt vigor return to his limbs. Would he have to attempt an escape? How far would his Chinese partners go in helping him once they had what they wanted: the ruin of their old colonial adversary, revenge for the Opium Wars and the Middle Kingdom's Century of Humiliation? Then he saw two things that made him start and sit upright.

"Shau xin, sir, please quiet yourself," the Chinese medic urged. Riffi waved him off and swung his feet to the floor. On the far wall was a huge plasma screen; it was tuned to an Asian business channel, but they were speaking a dialect in which he was fluent: the international language of money.

Behind the announcer were the ticker tapes of the London Exchange, Frankfurt, and Euronext. All gloriously red. A flashing alert signaling the disaster for which he had worked so long and arduously, £-GBP had fallen an astonishing 37% against the ¥-RMB, the Chinese currency. That was his doing; he had indeed done it! He'd be welcomed in Beijing as a hero, likely have a private audience with the president. They'd toast the downfall of the stuck-up white limey bastards who forced him out of office and the whole cheesy-smelling, beer-swilling, chavvy scummy lot of them.

The second thing he saw, just in front of the big-screen monitor, was personally gratifying and assured him that while there would today be a quiet murder inside this embassy, he was not going to be the victim. Handcuffed, bound arms and legs, and with her mouth stuffed perversely—and, to be honest, erotically—full with a saliva-coated red rubber ball gag, sat the troublesome woman who had nearly upset everything: Ellie Sato.

Riffi drank the water he was offered and chuckled; his throat was dried out and sore; he drank more. "Put up a fight, did she?"

One of the woman's eyes was swollen shut, dried blood trickling along the side of her mouth, staining her previously immaculate white blouse.

Harrigan grunted.

"How did you manage to get her?"

"It was after the prisoner attacked you with some sort of auto-injector," Harrigan said in his habitual calm and flat tone. "I took care of him right quick, then hid the body closer to the house than we planned, but it's well done. While you were unconscious, the car stalled out, and I had to go back and fetch her to activate the biometric ignition."

The City policeman explained that after he snatched Ellie and dragged her half a mile back to the car, he couldn't very well let her go or do away with her, as the Bentley was their only means of transport. As for the Jorkins couple, they appeared to have fled the scene or had hidden themselves somewhere in the great mansion.

"Once we got into the city, nowhere to hide a body decently; so we brought you both into the embassy here, in laundry bins."

"I see," Riffi said, quietly rankled that he'd been transported in such an undignified manner. "What did he hit me with?" His feet and legs felt like they were encased in lead, so heavy, but he was determined not to appear weak as he stepped slowly over to a table with an ugly sculpture on top, which happened to have a polished silver surface; it served as a crude mirror. His somewhat distorted image revealed a partly healed puncture wound and blue-yellow bruise just above his collarbone.

Harrigan started to speak, but the medic, who seemed to understand more English than he let on, spoke first. "We still working on that, Mr. Riffi, but you be fine. We use anti-opioid to flush your system. You fine now. Sit, recover, drink more water."

Riffi had no intention of sitting, not in his moment of triumph. He dashed over to the flat-screen TV which took up most of one wall, knocking the medic aside and tipping half the water he held onto the polished marble floor. He'd won! He'd shown up those dirty old white English turds who'd sacked him, whose flatulent impoverished sons had looked down on him at Eton when his family in India could buy the lot of the tossers for pennies on the pound. Even the damned king was prejudiced against him. When they were forced to meet due to constitutional conventions, the monarch always seemed to wish he was wearing gloves on his disgusting sausage-fingered, rubbery hands when they shook.

"There!" he shouted. Lunging forward and nearly losing his balance in his excitement, Riffi seized the reporter's shoulders and swung her around on the wheeled office chair to which she was bound. He grabbed her hair and pointed her bruised face toward proof of his triumph. "Look at your precious country now. It's only downhill from here. In a word: you're ruined, ruined a hundred times more than when the Jew Soros broke the bank of England in 1991. This will be worse than the Great Depression. First, the small banks will fail, then the larger ones, then cash machines will refuse to spit out bills, then government pension checks will bounce. Oh, but they'll howl in Westminster and Whitehall, how they'll clamor and screech, all for nothing. They'll print money, but what will it be worth? And the best of it is, no one's coming to bail the country out—quite the opposite, in fact. America is in tatters, and everyone hates you racist colonial bastards. India, which you raped body and soul for centuries; China, where you fought a war to defend the white man's right to sell drugs to its youth; and especially Russia, which England's been trying to break up, enslave, and loot since Catherine the Great. All your enemies will start kicking you while you're on your knees. Kicking you straight in your pea-sized bollocks!"

"Ahem."

Riffi could have gone on at length, and in the process of delivering his impassioned and wide-ranging rant, coated Miss Sato's hair with more atomized bits of his spittle, but a small bespectacled Chinese man he hadn't noticed before was seated in a chair in a corner of the room. This man made the throat-clearing sound which derailed the train of Riffi's well-lubricated rage.

He stopped and gaped at the wizened fellow. The Chinese man sat very still and wore a neatly pressed suit and spoke nearly accent-free English. "We are pleased to have you back with us, Mr. Riffi."

"Oh? Uh, right." Riffi released the shortish-cut rear locks belonging to the disheveled and bleeding journalist and shot a look at his confederate Harrigan as he addressed their host. "I take it, sir, we have you to thank for our current hospitable reception on what is, legally speaking, Chinese territory?"

The small bespectacled Chinese man replied, "As matters have gone, shall we say, in a more involved direction than originally planned, on behalf of the People's Republic, I shall be guiding you through the process of your defection."

Riffi winced at the word. Of course, there was no choice now, he had to activate his last-ditch escape. If only that meddling eco-bitch Green Hope hadn't... Well, it was no use now. The bodies were lying all over, and the false trails and frame-ups would only fool investigators for so long. Still, he had to be cautious. Besides Harrigan, there wasn't a single person present in the room whom he trusted.

"You're not my confidential contact in the CCP. Where is he?"

The side of the small bespectacled man's wrinkled face twitched while the rest of him remained still as a statue. After a short pause, he said, "Of course, you refer to the individual we shall only, even here, refer to as Feng Feng. She is elsewhere dealing with other complications caused by recent events."

The senior Chinese diplomat motioned to a desk facing a wall; on top was a sophisticated-looking portable computer. "If you would be so kind as to log in to your darknet server and confirm all of your transactions have been executed. They are quite large in number and complex in nature. Some stock exchange 'circuit breakers' may have prevented immediate execution, but we still have a few trading hours left in the day to force them through on secondary markets to create maximum damage and panic. Please."

Riffi took a second to consider his position. All his hidden offshore money was on those same darknet servers, stored in cryptocurrency and electronic key-numbered accounts, and logging in using the embassy system was risky. On the other hand, the Chinese didn't need him anymore. It would be as easy to disappear one sad excuse for a journalist as it would be to do the same to him and Harrigan, making the whole affair a clean, completely deniable sweep-up. They didn't want his money, he concluded, they just wanted to see he wasn't holding anything back during the culmination of the state-backed financial sabotage he and the CCP agents had spent many months planning.

Riffi smiled. It had actually been on his mind to make certain all his toxic derivative trades had been executed "at market on the open" as they say in the business. He sat down and logged in.

The stark black background of the shadow web browser was familiar cyber territory to arms dealers, drug wholesalers, and hitmen. The anonymous Tor network's minimalism contrasted sharply with the garish, advertising-festooned civilian internet. First, he checked his money and breathed a quiet sigh of relief. All his funds were still there, and he'd taken the precaution of putting passwords on each little stash. None of the sneaky Asians working at the embassy would be able to rob him. Then he scrolled down to where all his confidential emails were listed, expecting a long list of executed orders.

He scrolled down. "Hmph." He clicked refresh more than once, as sometimes data got hung up in buffering servers. He opened his messages folder and noticed the date of the last received spam email.

12:10PM Sunday, December 17

He checked the clock on the flat screen on the wall: Monday, December 18. The bright numbers and letters swam in front of his eyes. His face got red hot; his forehead blazed and the plastic keys under his fingers became slippery with a sudden coating of sweat.

"If it's… not Monday…"

As former Prime Minister Riffi mumbled these words in a hissing tone, which was barely audible to Ellie Sato, she tugged against the bonds pinioning her arms and legs to the chair. She'd been obliged to remain in this extraordinarily uncomfortable position for nearly an hour, as it was uncertain how long Riffi would take to awaken once given the blue needle containing the second half of Annunciata's Injucunda Somnia potion, the one which was formulated to revive him out of his chemically induced coma.

221

Suddenly the double doors burst open and slammed against the walls with a crack. They missed the two Asian gentlemen posing as embassy guards by an inch. As stage actors, they knew how to keep to their marks. Through the opening burst a pair of uniformed English police brandishing submachine guns, followed closely by Inspector Grantham, the Scotland Yard man who had arrested her parents, who was then followed closely by a rather haggard-looking but certainly alive Ran Oliphant.

One of the policemen covered the triple turncoat and, Ellie thought, extremely pretentious dresser: Arnold Harrigan. Behind him, Riffi leaped up from the computer desk, uttered an incoherent shriek, and made a comical dash for the sealed window with a look of such incredibly addled befuddlement on his face, Ellie would have burst out laughing except for the very realistic and functional drool-inducing gag tied around her head, which jammed her tongue quite far back in her throat.

After bouncing off the tempered glass in a rather limp suicidal gesture, Riffi burst out whining something about "foreign soil" and demanding asylum.

Inspector Grantham stepped forward and formally arrested the quivering politician by proceeding to read him the standard caution. Ran stepped forward.

"Oh, please, Grantham, let me be the one to explain. Who better than one of this man's murder victims to properly embarrass this bungler. Riffi, if you'll look out the window sharply sideways, you'll just see the outline of the real Chinese embassy—you're in the building next over. It's got nearly the same view out the window, and like much of the city's high-end office space during this darned recession, this whole floor was vacant. I'm so glad the constables didn't have to shoot you, as I've only rented the place for the day, and I'd hate to lose my cleaning deposit because of your brains and guts being spattered all over."

Ellie could tell Ran was enjoying the moment and wished she could share in it, which she would have done but for her being bound up like a bondage fetish model. Can you please untie me now came out: "Hmuu flmss neetie eeno."

Revealing himself to be a wholly ungentlemanly wag, Ran downright obstructed the more chivalrous Inspector Grantham just as he was about to come to her rescue. "Hold a moment, sir. I thought I heard something," Ran said, looking straight past her. "But, no, I was mistaken; just the wind. Must be the aftereffects of that terrible storm."

Inspector Grantham, more sensitive to Ellie's plight than that selfish oaf who was formerly her partner, and decidedly junior partner at that, in her previous adventures, attempted to move toward her to extricate her from her bindings. But Ran blocked his way, distracting the possibly none-too-bright fellow by saying, "And this is something that really should headline your report. You know, the one I can arrange for you personally to deliver to the Home Secretary, and possibly the PM, because of its national security implications. Thanks to this brilliantly successful little charade, which I will personally attest was primarily your idea, we know precisely how Riffi got the hundreds of billions of credit swaps he needed to pull off the attempt at crashing the Western economies. Riffi's people are rich, but no one's liquid enough for that kind of money. Most countries are not, but China certainly has the liquidity, having run trade surpluses in the trillions for many years."

Ellie's eye, the one not caked with theatrical blood and prosthetic swelling makeup, glared at the cruelly mischievous oligarch and definitely former friend. The fake scars and scabs felt as though they were fast becoming real permanent features of her face.

"Hmmenit, thmssurtz." I mean it, this hurts.

Somehow Ran understood her; his darkly etched eyebrows arched over his merrily sparkling gray eyes, and he unfastened the rubber gag, which was sopping wet with her saliva. "Serves you right for not giving me any warning before framing me for Lord Tempest's murder, tying me up, and leaving me at the mercy of the real villains."

Ellie flexed her jaw muscles, and when her hands were freed, delicately dabbed at her nose with a hanky. Of course, it was hardly worth the bother until she found the special isopropyl something-or-other in a bottle labeled Remove All that Esmunda's makeup artist had supplied her with.

She looked at the nearest reflective surface, which revealed her normally selfie-ready head to be a dead ringer for one belonging to a wax museum torture victim. Just as she was rubbing feeling back into her wrists, Riffi broke away from the pudgy Inspector Grantham and made a mad dash for the computer terminal.

Ellie kicked out a foot, catching one of his big black Oxfords on her instep, which caused the former prime minister to fall heavily onto the floor. When the armed police had recaptured and escorted Riffi away, Grantham and Ran spent some time consulting the monitor, which showed the inner machinations of the darknet server site.

"Well?" the Scotland Yard man said staring hesitantly at the glowing flat screen. "Wait for the chap from Treasury?"

"I wouldn't," Ran said. "His login could time out at any minute, and while we've keylogged the password, there might be additional challenge questions if we try to relog, and at this point I don't think anything except thumbscrews and a well-oiled rack could get the correct responses out of Riffi."

"If it comes to that, I wouldn't mind having a turn or two," Ellie said. "For Lord Tempest and his other victims."

Ran moved the mouse and clicked a series of boxes. "All set. Miss Sato, would you like to do the honors?"

"Certainly. Uh, what am I doing again?"

"Saving the Empire, at least what's left of it, and the financial future of tens of millions of ordinary Britons. Hit 'Enter,' and you'll cancel all the toxic trades before they hit the market tomorrow."

"Pfft," she scoffed. "This is precisely why I don't invest in stocks. It's all rigged for the people who are already rich, isn't it?" Ellie hit "Enter" and felt only the slightest tingle in her fingertip as something like a quadrillion dollars disappeared into the financial ether.

She stared at the screen for a moment. "You know, while we're on this app, or whatever it is, of Riffi's, you think we could do the same thing to my overdraft at the bank? It wouldn't really be stealing if we just brought the balance to naught, would it?"

Inspector Grantham's big drooping moustache quivered with serious indignation as he plucked the keyboard off the desk and out of her reach.

Chapter 26

Some weeks later
Postman's Park, London

The gray clouds, which had been boiling over the city all day, swaddling the tops of the highest buildings and pouring copious amounts of slushy rain on the city, were, little by little, pulling on darker hues as the diffused light from the horizon quivered between twilight and dusk. At the edge of the wall in Postman's Park, a humble public square dedicated to local heroes who lost their lives in service to others, stood a small scaffolding and a brand-new section of the memorial, which was protected from the weather by an orange tarp.

Ellie angled her umbrella to slide off the accumulating slush. She had contracted a photographer for the Juggernaut to cover the unveiling of this latest addition to the heroes' memorial. The brief but dignified accompanying article would form part of the paper's ongoing series on the shocking resolution to the notorious murders of the Hereford Five. She'd also arranged for the mayor's office to send an invite to the unveiling ceremony and a replica of the stone dedication to Mrs. Goldsmid.

Ellie wondered whether the poor woman could bear it, to attend the formal ceremony the next day. Then, by the dimming light, she saw the outline of another umbrella, held so still it practically merged with the urban landscape. Under it sat, alone on a bench, a middle-aged woman in a light-brown coat. After a moment's reflection, Ellie decided not to disturb her and walked slowly out the park gates onto King Edward Street and over to Saint Bartholomew's Hospital.

As she was diligently rotating and angling down her umbrella in order to keep liquid icy wet from sliding down the back of her coat, she peered through the now well-settled gloom, trying to recall where the entrance to Barts Psychiatric facility was. She took little notice of where she was walking, and as a result, a limousine gliding silently up behind her nearly knocked her down.

"Oy! Watch 'ow you go, girly, an' take yer business indoors, night like 'is!"

Ellie quickly leaped onto the curb and informed the leering chauffeur she was anything but a prostitute.

From the compartment behind the driver's leer, a girlish voice chirped, "Eleanor! Get in!"

The back window rolled down to reveal Esmunda in a madcap evening dress with more feathers than were worn by the average ostrich.

"Hello, Ezzie, I was looking for the entrance. We've got to collect Anna, right?" Ellie shook off the mound of melting snow, which the car, in stopping, had generously deposited on her evening shoes.

Esmunda informed her that the Barts Psych Ward Impromptu Therapeutic Theatrical Players had preceded them to the theatre, on account of two of them needing close guarding due to demonstrated penchants for escaping and committing spates of random violence, while others needed medicines administered hourly to ward off psychotic episodes.

"Sooo, it's just you and me!" her friend squealed as Ellie found herself a not-unwelcome spot on the heated back seat of the executive conveyance. She'd barely worked some sensation back into her numb toes by the time they crossed Southwark Bridge, and by the time they pulled up to the Globe Theatre, was thoroughly sanguine about failing to dry her stylish-but-not-ostentatious shoes by having held them in front of the air vents.

"This isn't like a double date, is it?" Esmunda sniffed—quite haughtily, Ellie thought—as they walked up to the entrance. "That's too bourgeois. You better go in without me."

"No way, Ezzie." She grabbed her companion's feathered sleeve. "No backing out now. And what kind of a lame excuse is that? They gave you a hundred thousand pounds for helping solve Lord Tempest's murder," Ellie said, once again reduced to shivering in her evening dress, even under her dramatically-chic-but-not-very-functional Rinaldi winter coat, one of the few fashion items she had not put into storage when she was forced to leave Mayfair and repair to an ultra-compact bedsitter in the small house Esmunda had leased. "Therefore, through very little effort on your part, you are bourgeois, until you squander the money buying makeup at Tilbury's and bailing out your protestor friends at the Old Bailey."

"That won't take long. You still won't have any of it?"

"Oh no, I'm done with all that publicity, ever since the Daily Snail twats called me a 'social-climbing, attention-seeking spinster adventuress' in my obituary. Besides, it was you that horrid turncoat Harrigan nearly killed when he and his fake medic friend broke into Mayfair House and went looking for Green Hope's data cache. All he did to me was toy with my affections, and worse, viciously kick my Labradoodle."

Come to think of it, that was possibly why Chestnut briefly growled in her direction after she'd been in Harrigan's car—because she had a smidge of his scent on her. Disgusting.

"But you got him back in spades, you did! The dirty, bent copper."

After cooperating fully with the deception to stop Riffi's dastardly financial scheme, Harrigan had been hustled away by MI5's anti-terror unit to assist them with their inquiries, which would likely fully occupy his calendar for a decade or two.

Ellie had been offered a reward but instead spent the goodwill she had with the City getting them to expedite the dedication of Green Hope's memorial tablet at Postman's Park. She also prepared for her upcoming godmother role by dispensing much-needed financial advice. "And don't forget to put by some of your windfall—you'll need it when your little blessing comes."

"How can I forget?" Esmunda said, grasping her baby bump as though it were a ripening melon under her sequined dress. "I have to pee every five minutes."

"Try to hold it tonight. This Fiver fellow is… a bit skittish, nervous fellow. I mean, he's…" Ellie stammered, trying to come up with points of attraction when the only mental picture she could conjure at that moment was of the overgrown man-toddler clad in his oversized bunny sweater and attacking her with a golf club. "He has good points, which offset his natural nervousness. Just treat him as you would a huge psychotic bunny, and you'll have him eating out of your hand." As long as there's carrots and cabbage in it, she thought wickedly.

Two doormen in top hats and tails held the theatre entrance doors for them.

"Won't they feel daft performing just for us?" Esmunda asked as they walked past the silent empty galleries, down to the floor area where there sat two tables, each illuminated by flickering candles.

"Most of them are committed to Barts Hospital for indefinite terms. They're sure to welcome any change of scene. Annunciata said the warden promised that if none of them ran off or mutilated anyone tonight, he'll consider letting them perform at other venues."

A page in a tasseled cap handed them playbills.

The Barts Psych Ward Impromptu Therapeutic Theatrical Players
Present
Philip Marlowe's
Massacre at Paris – The Musical

Their definitely-not-dates for the evening stood up in unison as they approached. Ellie breathed an inward sigh of relief that the gift parcel she'd sent over had gotten to Fiver, and he'd changed out of his usual rough-sleeper attire and into an almost formal-looking sweater. The Playboy-branded pants and top were the only things she could find in the Harrods catalogue featuring a bunny logo to ensure the highest chance of the obsessive-compulsive nerd actually wearing her gifts.

"Ran," Ellie said, allowing him to seat her and watching him limp back to his own chair. "You've healed up quite nicely."

"Nothing a few more sessions of arthroscopic surgery and a knee replacement won't fix," he retorted without any hint of recrimination. "But let's make a pact: next time it's your turn to take on two lunatics and get thrown from a moving SUV, and instead I'll put on the makeup and pretend to be a torture victim."

"As uncomfortable as that was, it was brilliant, wasn't it? Did you see the look on Riffi's face when he saw me? Pure sadistic satisfaction. And the thing is, that was Esmunda's idea. When she's not baking her brain with cannabis, she's really quite clever. Without her friends from The King and I cast, there was no chance we could have rounded up so many Chinese actors to play the parts of the embassy guards and staff."

Ran looked fetchingly uncomfortable in black tie. He gave a resigned shrug as the sommelier approached with the wine. "I'm going to need something stronger than that to get through this performance."

Ellie assertively sipped her wine and felt more relaxed than she had in weeks, and it wasn't just the wine or even being through and finally past the terrible sequence of ordeals that began the night her parents' car broke down at the horrendous crime scene. She suddenly realized she was in the close, comfortable company of her two most dear and stalwart friends: flighty Esmunda and the introverted, overachieving oligarch. The addition of a grown man who thought he was a Watership Down bunny and the criminally insane musical players assembling themselves on the stage only made the moment more mercurial and precious.

"There's a top quality end to it, eh?" She raised her glass to Ran, who smiled and did likewise. "Here's to getting justice for Mrs. Goldsmid's daughter, Lord Tempest, and the others."

"Here," Ran agreed heartily, and gulped the toast wine as vigorously as politeness allowed. After all they'd been through over the years, she could not recall ever seeing him drink alcohol. He was also squirming in his shoes under the table, which was odd. Surely he could afford custom-made shoes that fit.

She decided to put him at ease by recapping past violence and mayhem. "It's been such a whirlwind these past weeks. I've barely texted with you. I never got the whole story of what happened after you drove away from Stoke Bramwell in the storm."

"You mean those events which happened after you framed me for a mass killing, duct-taped my hands together, and thrust me into a car with the real mass killers?"

"Precisely those events, subsequent to the ones I witnessed, of course. I assume you realized what was in the self-injecting syringe was when I slipped it to you?"

"Thanks to the digital traces I had on your every move, I knew you'd been to see our friend and top mistress of lethal chemistry, Annunciata at St. Barts, so I had a pretty good idea it wasn't this year's flu jab," the unashamed remote stalker said. "I was placed in the back seat of your Bentley with that turncoat thug Harrigan. Being a thorough sort of villain henchman, he holstered his gun and pulled out a knife in case he had to kill me quietly.

"Fortunately for me, and the expensive interior of your Bentley, he forewent the opportunity of opening my throat then and there, and was busy cutting out pieces of seatbelt in order to tie up my legs when I leaned forward and jabbed Riffi, who was driving. Wham!" Ran brought his hands together in a way that startled the waiters. "Riffi loses consciousness and control of the steering, and we go knocking into an enormous fir tree. When the scramble was done, I had Harrigan at gunpoint, and Riffi was safely comatose until we'd prepared the Chinese embassy deception and roused him with the anti-toxin."

"Then you came limping back to Stoke Bramwell just as the Jorkinses and I were bickering about the best hiding spots to crawl into. Seeing the game was up, Harrigan cooperated with the whole charade, gave us all the passcodes he knew, as well as details about Riffi's plan to defect and his dealings with the Chinese intelligence agents. In getting him to flip on his boss, did you have to torture him mercilessly?" Ellie said hopefully.

"The naughty former policeman revealed himself very squeamish about violence when it was applied to his own person. I'd no sooner clicked the safety off his service weapon than he started jabbering all he knew about Riffi's escape plan and swearing he'd do anything to cooperate, even help us fool his boss into giving up access to his secret dark-web server, which Harrigan knew existed but for which he didn't have the logins."

"That neatly wraps up the case of the Hereford Five, wouldn't you say?"

Ran considered that for a moment, a moment which was prolonged by his gulping down another bulbous glass of wine and motioning for the waiter to let flow the grape. "Nearly, nearly. Except, of course, for the greatest mystery of all: how you managed to figure it all out."

She looked archly across the daintily flickering candle flames. "You mean figure it out before you did?"

Ran made a noncommittal sound into his napkin.

Ellie briefly related how her thirst for new literary horizons and fear of homeless poverty had led to her studying the mystery genre with a view to penning her first work of fiction. "The more I read, the more it seemed as though all the great detectives just kept making wild guesses that fit all the facts as they gathered them, until they had enough facts to be certain that their best guess was the truth. When Dr. Kore dropped dead, there were really only two suspects left, and only one could have had any connection to Harrigan, who I spotted at the entrance while I was driving up to Stoke Bramwell."

"But this wasn't fiction. I mean, you were gambling with your life, not to mention, to a rather more pointed degree, mine."

Ellie retraced her thinking that night. After ascertaining the truth about Riffi and Harrigan, the only loose element, or volatile inconnu, as Edgar Allan Poe's detective Auguste Dupin would say, was whether Harrigan had any accomplices in the woods. As it turned out, one accessory villain had indeed been minding the vehicle carrying the liquid nitrogen used to chill Lord Tempest's body, but that fellow had frozen solid when the garage roof crashed in and the tank burst. Harrigan, lurking around the grounds, had to knock out the butler Jorkins before he discovered the mess.

"Of course, Ran, I had every confidence in your ability to handle a pair of overconfident criminals. The main thing was to get that dear old Jorkins couple clear of danger. We were unarmed with possibly several trained and desperate killers on the estate grounds. Our best chance of Riffi not killing the lot of us after he poisoned Dr. Kore was giving him the opportunity to sow more confusion to cover whatever escape plan he had. If he disappeared you, and then had us all swearing to the authorities when they arrived that you were the killer, that was clearly his optimal choice, much to be preferred to killing four more people and trying to hide our bodies when he had no vehicle and was down one henchman."

It really reminded her, she went on, of a combination of the plots in Hammet's Glass Key and Sayers's Five Red Herrings, with historical allowances, of course.

Ran nodded, more emphatically than really was necessary. Was the wine he'd fairly guzzled down going to his head? "That's so like you, just... admirable. I'm admiring you, have done, for a long time, I truly am, truly."

The light around the upper gallery dimmed, and up came the stage footlights. The musical play was about to commence; the imminence of the performance seemed to press her definitely-not-date into urgent and decisive action.

"Look, uh, see here," said the fidgety-looking master of the financial and technological universes. "It was really awful, what they said, you know. In the press, the spinster thing." He produced a square black box and pushed it forward across the crisp white tablecloth. "Would you, could you, consider being my not-spinster?"

At this rather sudden turn of events, all Ellie could think to do was first grasp the little black box, which, judging by its weight, contained either a lump of lead or a ring crowned with an obscenely large diamond, and next be struck silent by the nervous schoolboy smile impressed on Ran's face as he awaited his fate: her answer.

Just then, the opening piece of Massacre in Paris – The Musical began. It was an aria, and performing it was the St. Barts patient Lucy, whom Ellie had last seen pulling out and eating her own hair strand by strand. Tonight, Lucy wore a large wig styled in a French pouf and heavy makeup, which made her look quite presentable as she stood in a single spotlight. She carried forth in an achingly beautiful singing voice.

Ellie raised her finger to her lips and shushed her suitor quiet for the duration of the opera. This was such a delectable moment, holding her good friend—no, her best friend—in agonized suspense, that she was determined to draw it out as far as respectability would allow, and then a little beyond.

-Fin-

Your honest reviews help:
Amazon.com
Goodreads.com

...

Social Media

X

R.K. Syrus
@RK_Syrus_author

Business enquiries: ykpebooks@gmail.com

OTHER BOOKS FEATURING THE INTREPID ELLIE SATO:

Start reading today:

https://amzn.to/3eWJrTX

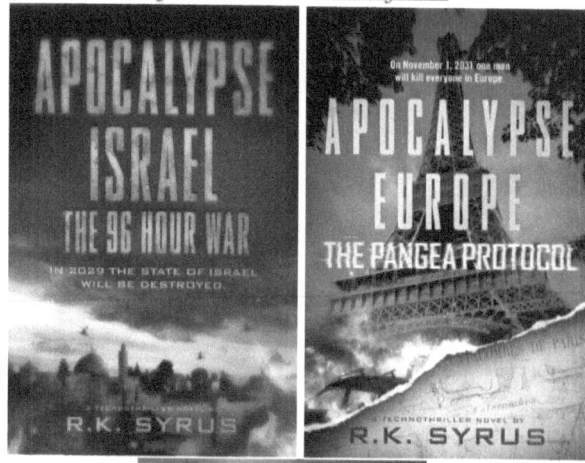

Praise for the books in the series:

"…an intriguing world of futuristic technology, made more familiar by contemporary references."

"Radiant descriptions also enhance the story."

—Kirkus Reviews